St. James Road

St. James Road

A Post World War II English Family Saga

The Second Book in the 'Somerville Trilogy'

MARY CHRISTIAN PAYNE

Sign up for the newsletter to get news, updates and new release info from Mary Christian Payne:
http://bit.ly/MaryChristianPayne

Published by TCK Publishing
www.TCKPublishing.com

ISBN: 1631619837
ISBN 13: 9781631619830

Dedication

To Tom Corson-Knowles for making my dreams come true.

Table of Contents

Chapter One

SEPTEMBER, 1945
A NEW BEGINNING

Sometimes I dreamed that the war wasn't over. Night after night, I dreamed that I was sitting with my little girl, Isabella, crammed into an Anderson shelter, while German bombers made every attempt to obliterate London. Sometimes I dreamed that I was running down glass-littered sidewalks, with Isabella in my arms, breathing the fumes from broken gas pipes and detonated bombs, trying to escape a German soldier, my cheeks and lips pale and the loose hair under my hat clinging to my forehead in damp ringlets. And, sometimes I dreamed that I'd received a Western Union wire telling me that Spence was dead. I would awaken in a cold sweat, the sheets wringing wet, my hair stuck to my head in soggy whorls, my heart galloping mile a minute, and it would take several moments for me to calm down, and realize that Spence was safe, right there beside me. I would reach out and touch him gently, and he would be warm. He would pull me close to him, and throw his arm over me in his sleep. Then, I would come round, and realize that everything was well and that the ghastly war was truly behind us.

However, even though the six years of fear and horrendous worry were in the past, there was still so much to be anxious about. I should have known that there was no way England could easily transition from brutality of war to a resumption of the tranquility we had known before that dreadful time. Certainly English history was littered with brutality, and World War II had not been the first war in our land. If one were to cast a look back at our history, it only required going back to the second decade of the twentieth century, when the Great War raged, to remember what war could do. But, I had not lived through those times, and my recollections began after the Treaty of Versailles, which was meant to end wars forever.

Oh my beautiful, beautiful England! Memories of warm summer afternoons on the green expanses of lawn at *Willow Grove Abbey*; soft laughter from the garden workers in the meadow below the terrace, the sound of hoofs cantering gracefully across the rolling hills. Was it all to be forgotten? Would it never be the same? It seemed doubtful. A way of life had come to an end. Not abruptly. It would continue for another decade, or even two, but in my heart, I knew that nothing would ever be quite as it had been before the Nazi's caused us to lose the lovely way we had lived. We'd survived the Great War, and when *it* ended in 1918, we'd resumed the pleasant Eden-like existence we had known before. Not exactly the same, but close to it. This time it was different. To begin with, even though the beastly war had finally ended in 1945, England was still in dire straits. We may have been victorious against the vile Third Reich, but we were also flat broke. If we'd lost the beauty of the life we'd known, had we really won after all? Winston Churchill had warned that when the war was over Great Britain would be bankrupt, and he was not far off. I would often lie awake for hours, wondering where life would take us next, and whether I would ever see the England of my memories again.

There were problems with transport, factories out of fuel, and people with no electricity with which to cook. Rationing was still in force, especially with bread. Petrol was hard to come by. Britain went through enormous social upheaval, as well. Money was in short supply, and while we may have thought that life would return to normal, that was a foolish belief. While it certainly wasn't the concern of most Englishmen, after the war many upper class families did not have enough money to keep their servants and old mansions. Our family was part of that landed gentry. It was the beginning of the end of our exceptionally privileged lifestyle. The nobility may not have fully realized the changes that were about to overtake us, but it was clear that changes were indeed coming. The economy was in shambles. Even at *Willow Grove Abbey*, my ancestral home, where my parents still resided, and where Spence, Isabella and I were living until we could establish our own home, circumstances were transformed greatly. Papa was concerned about finances for the first time I could remember. For very high earners, the top rate of tax became 82.5%, plus 15% surcharge on investment income. It was astonishing. People were told to be very brave and just 'take it on the chin'. Papa had to cut back on staff. *Any* modification in our elegant lifestyle was shocking. Mummy was stunned when Papa made the decision that she could get by without the help of a Lady's Maid, and also without Perkins, our Butler, who had served our family for so long. Perkins wished to retire, and Papa did nothing to try to dissuade him. Nan, our long time housekeeper would take over his duties, as well as continuing with her own. There was no talk of finding someone new to replace Perkins, and even if there had been, there were few people willing to work as servants anymore. After World War I, which we'd all referred to as the *Great War*, (even though the last one, was every bit as *Great)*, England had already begun to change from primarily an agricultural economy to one based upon manufacturing. The introductions of the car, electricity, running water and other mechanized developments had a vast impact upon society. We in the upper classes rarely paid attention to the gradual shifting of our country's economic base, but after the Second World War, the impact was actually startling. People no longer wanted to work as servants, and didn't have to. There were many more jobs in the manufacturing arena. Also, women could now work in offices, especially with the advance of the typewriter, and they no longer found themselves at the mercy of titled gentry who expected them to work seventeen hours a day for fifty pounds a year. Papa also cut the number of parlor maids, and basically Nan had only two people to help her with our enormous mansion. He also gave up his personal valet, in order not to have Mummy feel as though she were the only one sacrificing something. Because our estate had such a vast quantity of land, Papa decided to sell off some five hundred acres. It frightened me to think of our five thousand acre estate, *Willow Grove Abbey,* reduced in size by even a miniscule amount. Thank goodness the war had not affected the house itself, so there was no need for extensive repairs, as there were at some of the old, palatial manor houses.

During the war, almost every person in Britain was compliant with the rationing of food and luxury goods, and there were few complaints, as people seemed glad to be able to join in sacrificing something for the sake of freedom. But when the end came, in 1945, we assumed that we would go back to the life we had known before, where food was plentiful, and we could once again go shopping when we wanted a new frock, or a replacement for a place setting of china. Sadly, that was very far from reality. Even Wedgwood, the makers of one of England's finest porcelain china's, had to export more than ninety percent of their product, because Britain needed the dollars from America. Britain was unable to produce enough goods that anyone would want because of war damage and because its industry was entirely tooled for war production, and would require time to convert. No country but the United States had an economy after the war that could produce any consumer goods. Everyone wanted dollars. To quote Charles Dickens about a different era in British history, "*It was the best of times and the worst of times.*" It certainly *was* the best of times, in terms of the war being over, and the end of such death, destruction, and tumult. But, it was the worst of times for the very reasons I have cited above. In addition, I had foolishly believed that my adored husband, Spencer Stanton, and I would simply be able to pick up where our life had been interrupted in 1939, and continue our lives as we'd always dreamed, with our precious daughter, Isabella. I also should have known that there was no way that we could return to a placid, stress-free existence, after Spence had endured the ghastly experience of four years as a German Prisoner of War. Thus, while it was heaven to have him home again, I quickly came to the realization that we would not return to a cozy, comfortable existence for a long time.

In October of 1945, the first of what became known as the Nuremberg Trials began. There were actually two sets of trials. The first, and probably most well-known, were the trials of the leaders of Nazi Germany. Although we had a lot on our minds, everyone I knew listened intently to those legal proceedings. They were organized by the International Military Tribunal. Judges and prosecutors were from the four wartime Allies, France, the U.S.S.R., the United Kingdom and the United States. Charges were brought against twenty-four major war criminals and twelve of them were sentenced to death. Some were imprisoned, some committed suicide, and three were acquitted. We finally learned that Rudolph Hess had signed orders authorizing the persecution of European Jews and the ransacking of churches. The trials became controversial, even among those who wanted the major criminals punished. However, most observers, including Spence and me, considered the trials a major step forward in the establishment of military war. We were appalled at some of the things we learned. Of course, there had been rumors during the war, but from listening to the trials we learned with certainty about the horrific things that were done to people who were sent to the internment camps. For the first time we learned that an estimated six million Jews, and 11 million people in total were killed. I often cried as I sat and listened to the wireless, as I'm certain many in my country did.

Aside from listening to the trials, I was so consumed with thoughts of Spence's homecoming, and the end of the war, that I really didn't give a lot of thought to the transformation that would take place in our country, and in our home. And I am ashamed now to admit that I gave little thought to the very real, muddled feelings that so many of our returning heroes, including Spence, were dealing with. Of course he was thrilled to be back home, with his wife and daughter. And to be alive. But, he had an almost childish homesickness and a longing for the men with whom he had spent those years. There was a bonding that nobody, even a wife and daughter who worshipped him, could begin to understand. I would find him in the library, writing letters to his RAF friends, or simply staring out of the window. He was deeply depressed, and it confused me. He would go for days without bathing, or shaving, and his lovely hair was unkempt. We made love very infrequently, and even then he seemed disengaged and distant. This distressing behavior went on for nearly two months, and I finally decided that it was time for us to have a serious chat. I found him in the library, his usual refuge. Sitting down across the desk from him, I asked him to go to our bedroom, and clean up. I then suggested that we go on a nice walk and have a good chat. I am certain he had an inkling of what we would be chatting about, but he didn't argue. He just sort of sighed, and moved toward the staircase. I too went upstairs to my own bath, and changed into a fresh outfit. I dressed in jodhpurs, high boots, and a riding jacket, even though we had no intention of going horseback riding. The weather was cool, and it seemed good attire for a crisp, fall day. I was keenly aware that Spence had spoken very little of the ordeal he'd been through during the war, and I knew that if we were to move beyond this current period, he needed to speak to me, and share his deepest feelings. He had to know that he *could* do that, and that I would listen, empathize, and try very hard to understand. He came down the stairway, looking fresh and immaculate; like the Spence I'd always known. He looked at me, smiled, took my hand and said, "I like your idea of a walk. I haven't been getting enough fresh air lately."

"Nor have I, Sophia. It's a lovely day, and I think it will be good for both of us." We left the house, and leisurely strolled across the flat, rolled grounds at *Willow Grove Abbey*. It truly was a splendid day. The sky was as blue as the sea, and leaves were still on the trees, in their autumn colors of russet, gold, and red. The last of the summer roses were blooming, and I stopped and picked one, placing it behind my ear. Spence leaned over and kissed me, and said I looked like a Spanish señorita. We wandered out to the Summer House, where we sat on the benches encircling the inside of the structure. Spence lighted a cigarette.

"Spence, I began, "we need to talk. I'm concerned about you. You've been so withdrawn since your return, and certainly I understand why you would be, but we need to chat about what can be done to move you beyond this phase of your life."

"Sometimes I wonder whatever is the matter with me. I have a nagging feeling of guilt."

"Guilt?" I echoed. "What sort of guilt? Guilt over what?"

"Guilt that I'm alive and in one piece, when so many of the other chaps didn't make it, or made it, but lost limbs and suffered such bloody awful injuries. Many are totally destroyed mentally." He put his head in his hands.

"Oh my poor Spence," I answered. "You must see that this is the sort of mystery that none of us is meant to understand. Why one person dies and another lives? Don't you think you have to try to find a reason in your heart? Your faith has always been so strong, Spence. It's always carried you through. Isn't it any help now?" He sat with his head bowed, looking utterly defeated, and I so wanted to help him through such a dreadful time. Birds sang in the trees, and I could hear squirrels scurrying about underneath the Summer House.

He raised his head, and looked at me. "My faith has been shaken, Sophia. I don't believe a human being can go through the brutality of war, witnessing the atrocities that men commit upon one another, without wondering how there can be a benevolent God."

"Spence, this isn't a perfect world. You taught me that yourself. God made us creatures of choice. We have free will. Some men choose evil ways."

"Sophia, it's not that simple. I keep asking why I was spared. What purpose does God have for me in this world? Why would my life be worth more than the fellow who dropped dead in the snow on the forced march to Maskau?" He stretched his arms out toward me, trying to make me understand.

"It's not for us to know, darling. I believe you need to find a way to take what has happened to you, and make something positive and good out of it. In a manner of speaking, you *have* done that. If it hadn't been for your skills as a physician, there would have been many more boys who didn't return." I stroked him on the arm.

"That's true, I suppose. Nevertheless, I'm finding it difficult to contemplate a life of country doctoring. Where once that was all I wanted, I feel that I need to do more."

"More in what way?" I asked. I could certainly understand those feelings, for I actually shared them. I believed that there were undoubtedly many people who had come through all of the horror of war feeling that they owed everything to those who had not. Suddenly, it seemed that those of us who had survived needed to search for a higher purpose than before.

"I don't know, Sophia. I don't know. That's my struggle. This war has changed everything. None of us is the same. People can't go through such an incredible rupture in their lives, and not have it turn their heads upside down." He ran his fingers through his hair.

"I understand that, Spence. In addition, I so desperately want you to be happy. We have a lifetime ahead of us now, and I want you to know that when I committed to you through our marriage vows, that included supporting you in any decision that you made about the future. Whatever you decide, Isabella and I will be at your side." I put my arms out and said, "Come here to me, sweetheart."

He moved over closer to me, and then into my arms, placing his head upon my breast, like a small boy. I ran my fingers through his hair, and murmured comforting words. Then he began to shed tears; copious tears, weeping convulsively in great gulps and heart wrenching sobs. I held him closely, wishing I could stop the pain, but knowing I couldn't. He wept for the friends he'd lost, for the men he couldn't save, and for the stupidity and waste of war. He pounded his fists in rage, and disgorged helpless feelings he'd stuffed deeply inside for four, beastly years as a Prisoner of War. "The most difficult part of it wasn't the deprivation and lack of creature comforts," he exclaimed, "but the inability to fight back against the evil and wickedness that was destroying our country and her people." Spence had anger mixed with grief, as well as guilt and heartache. He needed to expel all of those emotions. It was a cathartic process, and when it ended, he seemed drained, but also freer of demons. Of course, I knew that one such show of emotion would not cleanse him of the anguish and emotional distress that he'd likely carry with him for the rest of his life. However, it was a beginning. It seemed that I had always been the needy one in our marriage, until that moment. Spence had always been my refuge, my port in a storm. The tables had suddenly turned. I realized for the first time that as much as he was my strength, I was also his. It was another of those watershed moments in life, and I felt that I'd taken a giant leap forward in my own long journey toward adulthood. After that purging of emotional tension, we found ourselves holding one another and kissing, and we made slow, languorous love, in a way we hadn't since his return.

Therefore, we entered what became a new, normal existence, which included a re-examination of exactly what we both intended to do with the rest of our lives. For the first days and weeks after that moment, we merely luxuriated in the joy of his being home. My parents went to London, and left Spence and me alone to readjust to one another in private. They took Isabella with them, so we had all of *Willow Grove Abbey* to ourselves, except of course, for the servants. In essence, it was the honeymoon we'd never had, since our marriage had taken place when Spence had only a short furlough during Christmas of 1940. We slept late, ate when we felt like it, and made love often and well. We finally had time to discuss the sad realization that we would not have more children, due to the hysterectomy

I'd been forced to undergo back in 1941. However, we were so happy to be together now, that it no longer mattered. I remembered Doctor Hardwick's words when I miscarried, and now understood them far better. He had comforted me and said that such things had a way of working themselves out, and while I didn't believe it at the time, he was correct. I would always wish that we could have had the large family we'd originally planned, but in time, I grew to realize that there were other things we might not have experienced in our lives if our dreams had become reality. God knew best. Spence now seemed more ready to discuss what the next step should be on our future journey. The first question of monumental importance was where we were going to live. I wanted our own home so badly, and so did he. It was amazing to think that we had been married five years, yet hadn't lived together as a family. It was past time for that to happen. Yet, before we could make such a decision, Spence needed to know what he wanted to do, in terms of a career. Finally, after many, many long talks, lying in bed cuddled in each other's arms, Spence reached a decision about the direction he wanted to take.

"Sophia, how would you feel about my pursuing additional medical training?" He asked. The look on his face clearly showed that my answer meant the world to him.

"More training? Gosh, Spence, what sort of training are you lacking?" I chuckled. "It seems to me you've been trained very thoroughly indeed."

"Yes, darling, but what I'd really like to concentrate upon is a relatively new field of medicine. One that will be coming into its own, what with all of the men, and women too, who've been severely affected by the war."

"What branch of medicine is that?" I asked, snuggling into the crook of his arm.

"Psychiatry," he answered. "Of course it's been round for hundreds of years, and grew enormously during the Great War, but psychological treatment has expanded through the unique experience of treating wounded soldiers. Sir Aubrey Lewis, at Maudsley Hospital in London, is a pioneer in the field. There were so many times when I was in Germany that I wished I had been able to do more, in terms of the ghastly mental problems men faced. They can range all of the way from mild depression to severe psychosis. A mind can only take a certain level of stress. I'd give anything to work with Sir Aubrey."

"How incredible," I answered. "Here I've been studying Psychology all of these years, and am so near to earning my postgraduate degree, and now you show the same fascination with the subject. Do you remember that we spoke of our shared interest in psychology that night we first met, at my debut Ball at *Willow Grove Abbey?* Spence, if you made such a change, in terms of specialty, perhaps someday we could even work together, in some capacity. Is it possible that you might be able to study under Sir Aubrey Lewis at Maudsley?" I asked.

"Yes, of course. I vividly remember that conversation darling. It was one of the things that first attracted me to you. Not only were you beautiful, but you had such intelligence and curiosity." He leaned down and kissed me on the nose. "I've made some inquiries, and yes, it seems a very real possibility that I could train under Sir Aubrey Lewis. Maudsley Hospital is in South London. It would mean that I'd be moving you and Isabella twice darling, since after I trained, probably for three years, I'd have to find myself a permanent staff position. I don't have the foggiest notion where I might land."

"Darling," I smiled, "'Whither Thou Goest, I Shall Go'."

"Do you mean it, Sophia? You wouldn't object to a bit of gypsy-ing about?"

"I won't object to anything, as long as we're together," I smiled.

"But, you do realize that money won't be plentiful. I'd probably be employed at a training rate of pay, and we couldn't purchase a home, since we'd only be leaving it after a time? Are you certain this is a life you'd want?"

"Yes, Spence, I'm sure. I want you to be happy. I think your idea is a brilliant one, and I can see why it would appeal to you. It appeals to me too. I think it's a marvelous concept; using your skills and talents to help those poor boys who have suffered so because of the war. I've no doubt that you would be excellent at such a thing."

He held me closer and said "Mrs. Stanton, I love you very, very much, you know. Thank you for being so wonderful."

"Spence, darling, I think it will be a great adventure. I'm excited to think of the change. But, there's one thing we need to discuss."

"What is that?" He asked.

"The comment you made about money. Spence, I think you're being silly about that. I know you have your masculine pride, but you know that I'm a very pragmatic sort of person, and it seems terribly silly for us not to make use of the funds I have from my Winnsborough settlement. There's no need to struggle, and I can't think of a better way to use that money than to make it easier for you to get the training you need to help others."

My first husband, Lord Owen Winnsborough, had left me a great deal of money, as well as the lovely flat I'd lived in before the war, on Sumner Street in London. Owen had committed suicide, after I'd learned that he was a homosexual, and my confession that the baby I was carrying, Isabella, was not his child, but Spence's. The money had been invested since his death in 1936.

"Sophia, you should have been the Irish one in the family, with your gift for making things sound so charmingly simple. However, the fact is, I don't intend to live on Owen Winnsborough's money. Of course, you may do whatever you wish with that money, and ideally, I think it should be put aside for Isabella. Even though she isn't Owens's child, he left it to you with the idea that she'd carry the Winnsborough name. Although, I want to make it clear that I intend to adopt her, as quickly as possible now, so that she'll carry her rightful name."

"I want that more than anything, and so does Isabella. And, I have no doubt that Owen would be happy about it. But, I feel you're being foolish about the money, Spence. Owen had no intention that I only use the money for Isabella's welfare. He clearly stated in the suicide note he left, that his fondest hope was that I would be able to spend my life with the man I loved, meaning you. Won't you please reconsider?"

"No, Sophia. Absolutely not. I'm sorry if I seem stubborn. Perhaps I am in this instance. But, I insist that I be the one to support you and my daughter."

"All right, Spence. I won't argue about it. The money will continue to draw interest. What do you feel should be done about the flat on *Sumner Street*?" I asked.

"I'd prefer that it be placed for sale. I realize that if our plans work out, it is certainly possible that we'll land permanently in London, but, if we do, I'd really prefer to have our own place. I'd like a fresh start, with no memories of the past. However, I'll defer to you about that."

I completely agreed with Spence on that point. It was time for us to have our own home, with absolutely no ties to before the war. "I'll contact a property agent," I said. "We'll have to go up there anyway, at some point, to make plans for moving our belongings. I pretty much left things as they were, and have only removed things bit by bit while I've been here at *Willow Grove Abbey*. Wherever we're to be, I'd like to have my own things round me again."

"Yes, and I even have some things of sentimental value over in *Twigbury*," he concurred.

"Did you leave things in the cottage there?"

"No, they're in storage. All I need do is let the chaps know where I want everything delivered." *Twigbury* was the tiny Cotswold village where Spence had lived and practiced medicine before the war.

"Shall we mention this to Isabella yet, or wait until we have more definite plans?" I asked.

"More definite plans, I should think. It does mean a new environment, and I want her to be prepared. She's undergoing a lot of changes in her life, in a rather short time."

When we went to bed that night, my heart was much lighter than it had been in weeks. We finally had a direction, and the entire scheme excited me greatly. I couldn't wait for a letter telling us that Spence could follow his dream. I spent that time on pins and needles, watching for the post every day. It was but a bit more than a week later when a letter *did* arrive. It contained the news they we had been hoping for. Sir Aubrey Lewis wrote to say that he would enjoy the honor of meeting with Spence to discuss the possibility of a mutually beneficial working arrangement. Spence immediately began to make preparations for a journey to London, to meet and talk with that distinguished gentleman. Through several telephone conversations, an appropriate date was finally chosen, two weeks hence, on November 30, 1946.

I accompanied Spence to London. We stayed at The Savoy. I needed to take care of matters pertaining to the flat on *Sumner Street*, so while he was interviewing with Sir Aubrey Lewis at Maudsley, my first task involved contacting a moving company, and setting a time for them to come to the flat to give me an estimate. Many items had been shipped to *Willow Grove* at the beginning of the war, for safekeeping, so the quantity of packing was to be minimal. Next, I contacted a property agent, who seemed happy at the prospect of listing the flat. I met her there one morning, and we walked though it together. So many memories came flooding back to me. The time spent there while I was married to Owen Winnsborough held no particularly fond recollections, but the years between 1938 and 1940 were filled with reminiscences. That was the period when Isabella and I, along with Martha, my combination maid and nanny, had shared many happy times. I remembered Spence kissing me goodbye in the parlor at Sumner Street, when he left for Duxford RAF base, just when the war began; and I remembered, like it was yesterday, the night he figured out that Isabella was his child, and how ghastly infuriated he had been with me; then there was the night he returned to me, in September, 1939; the night England declared war on Germany, wanting to see Isabella, and tell her the truth about the fact that he was her father; And, perhaps my worst memory of all; the night Papa brought Edwina to stay at Sumner Street, when she had escaped France. I had tried so terribly hard to pretend that their actions didn't cause me pain, but, in spite of such efforts, I was in agony, and never should have agreed to such folly. I'd wept so many tears in that flat, but also had experienced happy times that helped me to survive those war years, as well as my tremendous loneliness for Spence. *Sumner Street* fostered my growth, and helped me to become a much more honest and clearheaded woman. The independence it afforded was a very healing part of my life. When the real estate agent and I discussed what price she felt should be placed on the flat, I was astonished at the figure she quoted. The war had created such a shortage of housing, that prices were very high, especially for a lovely property, in an exclusive area. I didn't make any firm commitment, since I wanted to discuss the matter with Spence, but felt very optimistic about the prospects of selling the flat easily and quickly. I had completely renovated it in 1938, and it had not been damaged from the Blitz that the Germans rained upon us. Thus, although I wanted to give it a thorough cleaning and some fresh paint, there was little to be done to prepare it for sale.

Upon my return to *The Savoy,* after meeting with the property agent, Spence was already there. He'd visited Maudsley, and was terribly impressed with Sir Aubrey. As soon as I sat down with him in the parlor of our suite, he began to tell me of their meeting. "Sophia, this man is so impressive, I'm just overwhelmed. His credentials are superb. Sir Aubrey—that's what he prefers to be called—was born in 1900 in *Adelaide, South Australia.* He's Jewish, but attended a Catholic school, the *Christian Brothers College.* He was something of a child prodigy. Then, he attended the Adelaide Medical School, which wasn't the most advanced, but in the post-World War I period a new era began, and emphasis was placed upon research. Apparently, numbers of new appointments were made. He graduated there in 1923, and was appointed resident medical officer at the Adelaide Hospital, where he later became medical and surgical registrar." He stopped and took a deep breath, and then continued. "Then, later that year, he was awarded a Rockefeller Medical Research Traveling Fellowship, for study in psychological medicine, nervous diseases, and the like. Because of that fellowship, he's studied with some of the greatest scholars around the globe. Sophia, in two years he worked in Boston, with Macfie Campbell, and at Baltimore, with Adolf Meyer. Then, he traveled to London, and worked with Gordon Holmes at *Queen Square,* and in Heidelberg with Karl Beringer, as well as at the *Charite* in Berlin, with Karl Bonhoeffer. I'm just amazed at the breadth and depth of his background. He became totally committed to Psychiatry, and decided to immigrate permanently to London, becoming a member of the Royal College of Physicians of London. He took all four of his language papers in Greek, Latin, French and German, much to the surprise of his examiners, I should think. Then, he joined the staff of the Maudsley Hospital in 1929. He's revolutionized clinical practice, and has contributed greatly to the understanding of depressive illness."

"He sounds like an amazing person. I can certainly understand why working with him would be thrilling," I answered, smiling at his tremendous enthusiasm. Spence looked the happiest that he had since his return from the war.

"Sophia, ever since the war began, the entire population suddenly became a matter for public health concern. The effects of bombing, evacuation and social interference with civilians have been sources of vulnerability.

The depressive aspects contained in military service have been seen as a major problem from the beginning. Lewis saw these things as a challenge and opportunity. The focus of his work shifted from individual, clinical studies to the broader social framework in which Psychiatry has become a branch of what he calls 'social medicine.'" Spence was so excited that he scarcely paused for breath during his recitation. It was wonderful to see him animated and optimistic again. In just the past few weeks I had seen the fatigue and lines of apprehension, which the years in Germany had brought to his face, disappear, and he looked again as he had before the dreadful turmoil; handsome, relaxed, and optimistic, with his marvelous dimpled smile, and the sparkle back in his sapphire blue eyes.

"And, so, did Sir Aubrey look favorably upon your coming to study with him," I asked?

"Yes, Sophia, yes. We talked at length about my training to date, and he seemed impressed. Primarily, I think, he was impressed with the commitment I've made to the field of Psychiatry, and my reasons for wanting to do this. We got on splendidly."

"Right. So, then did you discuss a timetable?"

"Not specifically. He told me that he was in tremendous need of additional help, and the sooner I could make the move, the better for him. So, I plan on looking at the calendar, and then ringing up Dr. Lewis and giving him a specific date."

"Oh Spence, this is such wonderful news. Of course, I never doubted that he would want you, but it's so wonderful to hear your excitement and to know, to really know, what the immediate future will be."

"I know, darling. I haven't been so enthusiastic about something in eons. It's so good to have something challenging to look ahead to, after so many dismal years when mere existence was the goal." I hugged him tightly, and told him that I thought it was only the beginning of a wonderful, bright future. We discussed, at length, exactly where we thought we would like to settle when Spence took up his new duties at Maudsley Hospital. Neither of us was particularly thrilled at the idea of going back to London proper. Thus, we decided to explore small towns within a commuting distance from South London. Finally, we settled on villages in Kent. We discussed the relocation with Isabella, who was not in the least distressed at the prospect of leaving *Willow Grove Abbey*, which was one of the things that had worried both Spence and me. I had been afraid that after four years with her grandparents, not to mention the splendor and grandeur that living at my childhood home had offered, our daughter might be reluctant to leave. However, Isabella was excited, and looked forward to moving where there would be more children, which we vowed to make a priority.

Thus, the next week we embarked upon a motor trip, first to *Maidenstone*, and then to *Tunbridge Wells*. We decided to make the first trip by ourselves, as we did not think that Isabella was quite old enough to undertake a full day of looking at houses. We had studied the area south of London, and those two villages seemed charming and accessible. Neither place was a great distance from the other. As I remembered from my *Ashwick Park School* days, the landscape of Kent was lovely. There were miles of unspoilt countryside, bustling market towns, and picturesque villages. The scenery was truly stunning. The area has always been known as the 'Garden of England', and it lives up to its name. First we visited *Maidenstone,* which is a charming river town, but we weren't so taken with it, because it seemed heavily populated with manufacturing; mostly brewing and paper mills. We didn't rule it completely out, as there *were* other smaller villages within a short drive from the town center, but before we looked at any property, we decided to go on to *Tunbridge Wells*.

When we reached *that* town, which was, after all, just a bit more than a half-hour's drive from London, we were absolutely charmed by what seemed a timeless haven of peace. The town itself was some 400 years old. In Georgian times, it was a well-known and popular spa resort and rival to nearby Brighton. It became a very desirable place for wealthy business and professional people, not just for a holiday, but also in which to live. A great deal of building had been undertaken to the north of the small spa, as large villas and family homes were built. Indications of that grand period of architecture still survived. I was thrilled with the beauty of the homes. Needless to say, the idea of leasing a home there was extremely attractive to both of us. Before we became too excited, however, we explored the rest of the village, and looked into the village school situation. We discussed the possibility of sending Isabella to board at *The*

Ashwick Park School at some future date, but until then she would be attending a local school, so it was important to us that it be of the highest quality. We learned that the local school had an excellent reputation, and the majority of the residents of *Tunbridge Wells* were persons of a professional nature. Thus, we felt that Isabella would feel comfortable in such an environment. We then turned our attention to seeking a house for lease. We contacted a property agent, and she took us to view several listings. I had my heart set upon one of the Victorian homes, but there were none for letting. However, there *was* a five bedroom Victorian townhouse, arranged over four floors, *for sale.* It was situated in the popular *St. James* area, close to the main town center. We decided that we would at least look at it. Of course, it stole both of our hearts. It had a white, clapboard exterior, and as one entered there were stairs rising to the first floor entrance hall, with frosted windows to the side. The ceiling was coved, and contained a center rose medallion. There was a very large living room, with two double glazed windows to the front. Again, the ceiling was coved, and there was a picture rail, a low-level meter cupboard, and an exposed, painted chimney. In addition, there was a well-equipped kitchen, and a breakfast room, with French doors to a patio area, a library, and a cloakroom, with a small half-bath on the first floor. The second floor was taken up with the enormous en suite master bedroom, and with built-in cupboards, a white tiled bath and built-in vanity. On the third floor were two more bedrooms and two baths, each of good size. They would be perfect for Isabella, and a guest room. The fourth floor housed two servant's quarters, as well as a nursery playroom. All in all, we immediately fell in love with the property. The problem was that we had not planned to commit to such a large purchase. Both of us were tempted to make an offer on the property immediately, but restrained ourselves, deciding to lunch and talk it over. We stopped and ate at *The Old Vicarage Pub*, which was as quaint as its name. Once seated, we launched into a discussion about the house on *St. James Road.*

"What do you think, darling?" Spence asked me.

"Well, you know what I think. I adore it, but can we afford it? And, assuming that we can, is it wise for us to purchase a home, since we don't know that we'll be here forever?"

"I don't see that as a major obstacle," he answered. "I'll be at Maudsley for three years. I should think that's reason enough to put down roots in the area. Of course, there's always the possibility that I might wind up being offered a permanent post at the hospital, so we'd be staying much longer than we think now. In any event, this area is so especially lovely, that I don't think there would be any problem with selling it if the need arose. The way real estate prices are rising, I should think that in three years, there would be money to be made on a sale. Or, we might keep it as an investment property, depending upon what my income is at that time."

"Then, what of the money? I know we could afford it in nothing flat if you'd let me contribute from my money, but you've been so dead set against that."

"Yes, I still am".," he smiled gently. I looked down at my plate, chewed my cheek, and tried not to react negatively. I so badly wanted that house.

"But, Sophia, in this case, I might be willing to take a loan from you," he added.

"Oh, Spence,, really?" My heart leaped with joy. "That would be perfectly acceptable to me. I mean, you could pay me back any time you wanted. You wouldn't need to sign a note or anything like that." I didn't give a whit if he ever paid anything back but, if such arrangements made him feel better, I wasn't about to disagree.

"I would let you buy the house, and put it into your name. That way it would be totally yours, should anything happen to me, and Isabella would be assured a home. Would that be all right with you?"

"Well, that would be fine, except I'd really rather your name be on the deed as well. The same argument applies. What if something happened to me? Wouldn't you like the feeling of knowing that Isabella was secure in her home?"

"Yes, I would, Sophia. However, that could be taken care of in a separate legal document like a Will or Trust. We should have a solicitor draw one up anyway, now that I'm home, and we have a child."

"Spence, please let me give you this house as a gift. Please. It is something I really want to do. I shall be receiving money from the sale of the Sumner Street flat, so I'll not even be touching the principle that's invested. Won't you please let me do this?"

He was silent for a few moments, as he stirred a cup of coffee, seemingly in deep thought. Finally, he looked up and met my eyes. "This really means a lot to you, doesn't it?" He asked.

"It truly does. It would be the beginning of our new life, in a lovely home, which is simply perfect for us. It almost seems to have been meant for us."

"Perhaps it's 'Serendipity' again," he grinned. "All right, Sophia. I'll acquiesce to your wishes on this. But, I *do* intend to pay you back, in full. Do we have a deal?"

"It's a deal," I nearly shouted, leaning across the table and giving him a huge kiss. "Oh darling, thank you so much. You won't regret this. We're going to be so happy in this house. I'll make it the most wonderful home. I'm going to learn to cook, and grow roses and…

Oh so many things."

"It's wonderful to see you so happy, darling. I'm happy too. I think this is going to be a sensational new beginning for us."

We took a suite of rooms at the charming, old country house hotel where we had lunched. It was run along the lines of *Twigbury Court*, where I had stayed with Drew and Annie during my incredible, life-altering weekend in 1935, when Isabella was conceived. The *Old Vicarage Inn* was filled with charm, warmth and generous hospitality, with its beautiful gardens, wonderful dining, luxurious bedrooms and Wedgwood style dining room. After depositing the luggage, we rang the agent back, and asked to meet with her about making an offer on the *St. James Road* property. She was available immediately, so we met at her office soon after. The whole procedure went very smoothly. Because we were making a cash offer, there was little question as to whether it would be accepted. She called the owner, who didn't have to think two minutes. He agreed to the sale, and said he'd sign the papers on his way home from his office, that very evening. So, within an hour, Spence and I had committed to purchase that beautiful, old home, and we were in seventh heaven! We left the agent's office, and drove back by the house. That time we got out of the car, and simply walked around the grounds, which weren't large, but were landscaped beautifully. Best of all, I discovered that in back and at the side there were lovely gardens. The real estate agent had provided us with photos of the house taken in the summer months, and we were able to see from them that the gardens were filled with roses, larkspur, lavender, delphinium, peonies, and fox-glove. I suspected many other spring bulbs would appear in about three months. I loved jonquils, paper-whites, hya-cinths and tulips, and if they weren't there, they would soon be planted. I was as excited as a child at the thought of that lovely house becoming our first real home together. We decided upon a date between Christmas and January first so that Isabella would be on break from school term, making the move to a new school easier. Spence informed Dr. Lewis that he could begin working at Maudsley the first Monday in January of 1947. Our new life had begun.

Chapter Two

JANUARY, 1946–AUGUST, 1946
A MOVE

Spence and I were established at Tunbridge Wells by the time he began working. He was studying under Sir Aubrey, as a Resident in Psychiatric Medicine at Maudsley Hospital, in London. He loved his work, and came home at the end of each day filled with new ideas and exciting stories about the wonderful things he was learning. I was thankful that I had some knowledge of psychology from my studies at University, and my work as a co-author on Doctor Hausfater's textbook project. He was an esteemed professor at *The University of London*, and he and I had been collaborating on an Adolescent Psychology textbook since shortly before the war. I had also been completing my own courses in Psychology. That project helped me to understand more of the subject that was consuming my husband. On one day a week I was still traveling into London to meet up with Dr. Hausfater, as we were very close to finishing the book. I had received my Master's degree in June. Next, I'd begun work on my Doctoral Degree. We announced our plans to my parents after they were solidified, and I was surprised that they didn't find fault with what we wanted for our future. Papa was not terribly thrilled at what he believed would be a pittance of an income, and of course, Mummy never would completely accept that I had not married a Duke, and wasn't living the life of a wealthy Duchess. Overall though, I think that they were relieved we would be setting up our own home, and would no longer be living with them at Willow Grove Abbey. There weren't words to describe how gloriously happy I was.

My primary task, besides being a good wife to Spence, and a good mother to Isabella, was creating the first home Spence and I had ever shared. I was adamant that it should reflect both of our personalities. The decor in the house was pre-World War One, and it was quite dilapidated, although the bones of the structure were superb. It needed a good, thorough cleaning and a facelift. We began with a fresh coat of paint on all of the walls, which made a huge difference. We did not want to change the charming look of the old structure. We simply wanted to lighten it, to add appeal. We moved furniture that had been stored at *Willow Grove Abbey,* and had several pieces re-covered in bright chintz fabric, with masses of carnations and greenery on a white background. I also had draperies made to match the upholstery. Bookcases were built on either side of the fireplace in the living room, and those in the library were refinished. We refurnished that room in a chocolate calf's leather. By the time we began the redecorating project, the flat I'd lived in on Sumner Street sold. Spence agreed that we would use the funds from that sale for expenses involved in refurbishing St. James Road.

Isabella's room was rather a repeat of the one she had so loved on Sumner Street, with its pink, white, and taupe décor. Of course that had been a nursery, as had her accommodations at *Willow Grove Abbey* during the war. We purchased a decorative, antique brass canopy bed and it dominated the majority of the space in her room. The floors were hardwood, and I found some lovely, old rugs stored at *Willow Grove Abbey,* which Mummy said that we might take. The colors were perfect, with patterns of rose and crème. Our bedchamber overlooked the charming garden, and we were able to lie in bed, enjoying the scent of honeysuckle, white jasmine and old roses, which emanated their sweet perfume on evenings when summer arrived. I had guessed correctly about spring flowers. The entire front lawn was filled with paper-whites and Jonquils. Hyacinths appeared first in the beds near the house. We often left the window sash drawn up when it was warm. It was a splendid home, and I had never been so happy. I'd never truly *lived* with Spence before, due to the war and our dreadful absence from one another. Although we had been married for some five years, there was a bit of adjustment, becoming accustomed to sharing a home with a husband. We were still learning to share a bed, let alone a loo! Of course,

I had formerly been married to Owen Winnsborough, and we had shared his family's ancestral home, but it was so vast, that we could have spent days without ever seeing one another. In addition, Owen spent less time at *Winnsborough Hall* than he did at *Sumner Street* in London, so we never really shared a traditional married life. With my marriage to Spence, I vowed that I would be the perfect wife to the man I adored, and set about trying very hard to do just that. Having been used to a bevy of servants during my growing up years, and even well into adulthood, I had a great deal to learn. Nevertheless, I wasn't put off, and looked forward to the challenge.

I read all of the women's periodicals of the day, and became quite well versed in the parlance of cooking, as well as the best methods for cleaning, washing, and ironing. Unbelievably, I had never performed any of those chores. Naturally, I had my share of catastrophes in the kitchen, and didn't always manage to get the glasses as sparkling as Nan, our housekeeper at Willow Grove Abbey, or Martha, the lovely girl I'd hired while in London. Martha had moved on to be married shortly after the war. Overall, I was quite pleased with my progress. Spence seemed delighted at having a wife who could cook, entertain, and be an exemplary mother. More importantly, I thoroughly enjoyed it all. Our home became a haven for many of the young Interns and Residents with whom Spence worked. It served as a place to unwind after a grueling day. We made many, many friends, who were never to be forgotten. Spence was somewhat older than the others, as he had completed his medical training before the war, and had already practiced family medicine. But, the age difference wasn't vast, as the war had interrupted many a man's studies, and a large number were only now returning to complete their degrees. In the beginning, several of the people I met were a bit skeptical of me, when they learned that my name was originally Sophia Somerville, and that my father was an Earl, which technically made me a *Lady,* although I had completely stopped any use of my title. But, when they learned that I was not enamored with all of the fuss and frivolity involved with being of the nobility, I was taken under their wing, and, if anything, they all pitched in and helped me to adjust to being a normal, suburban housewife.

I became active in the local Catholic Church, helping to plan jumble sales, and offering to cook potluck dishes for various events. I even took on teaching a Sunday school class at one point, and found that I seemed to have a natural gift for it. Quite simply, I took to my home on *St. James Road* like a duck to water. Instead of an extensive wardrobe of designer gowns, I now had a closet filled with shirtwaist dresses, pleated skirts, cozy, warm jumpers, and smart women's trousers. Before we were completely settled, I'd rounded up several little girls of Isabella's approximate age from the village, and brought them home to meet our daughter. All lived within a few blocks, in one direction or the other, and from then on there was a steady stream of friends into and out of the house. I made friends with the other mothers, and we traded recipes and gossip, helping when one or the other needed assistance. One day a week, at two o'clock in the afternoon, one of the women would entertain at a small tea in her home, and it became a ritual for all of us to meet to discuss the weeks' activities over strawberries and crème, scones, freshly baked bread, jam and lots of fresh, hot tea. It was a wonderful time in my life. We would gossip, laugh, and commiserate about problems, and then would pick up our children at the local school. Spence initiated adoption proceedings immediately after the move to Tunbridge Wells, and Isabella finally legally held the name she should have been born and christened with. She was no longer Isabella Winnsborough, but Isabella Stanton. Owen was deceased, and had known that he was not Isabella's biological father, and I knew that he would be happy to know that I had finally married the man I loved so terribly much, but had been forbidden by my parents to marry. Both Isabella and I were thrilled, and we celebrated with Mummy and Papa, and Drew and Annie, with a special dinner at our favorite restaurant. My brother Blake and his wife, Susan, were not present, although they were invited, which made me feel badly. I'd heard nothing from either of them since the war's end.

A rift had been created between Blake and me that appeared to be permanent. Just as I had suspected, nasty words spoken in Bristol during a confrontation with Blake had caused an irreparable fracture. I wasn't even certain who knew that the scene had taken place. Of course, Susan was present, so she knew, and Papa was there. I'd even had a private chat with Papa afterwards, and he admitted to me that everything I'd said during the kerfuffle was true. I assumed that my brother Drew and his wife Annie also knew, but it had never been discussed. They were as dear to me as they had always been. I strongly suspected that Blake or Susan, or both, had told their children, since I'd not heard from them for ages.

In the meantime, Spence absolutely adored his work. And, Sir Aubrey Lewis, as well as the other staff members at Maudsley Hospital, seemed to hold Spence in equally high esteem. Sir Aubrey was so highly regarded, and Spence was fortunate and delighted to have the opportunity to study under him. Of course, it didn't surprise me that everyone was so keen on Spence, for I knew that anyone who became acquainted with him was always immediately able to see what fine character he possessed. He worked terribly hard that first year, and sometimes I worried about how tired he was when he returned home. But, he reminded me repeatedly of how much he loved what he was doing, and that he'd so terribly much to learn, so I disciplined myself not to be alarmed when he was called to return to Maudsley, sometimes, at 3:00 a.m., when he'd only flopped into bed two hours before. He promised that it would not last forever, and I knew that was the truth. He'd probably not always be working with Sir Aubrey Lewis, and he needed to learn all that he could during the important training period.

Spence had been a successful physician, and a superb RAF Flight Surgeon during the war, and his decision to seek further training in Psychiatry was one I heartily agreed with. If there'd ever been a time when I had wondered if I'd done the proper thing by marrying Spence without knowing him for a longer period, those thoughts vanished. It was uncanny the way our minds worked in tandem. We disagreed on practically nothing, and then never crossly. The years of being apart, during the war, and before we married, when I had been a stupid, little fool and had not told him the truth about Isabella being his daughter, had made us terribly grateful for the blissful time we were sharing with our precious little girl. When I look back, all of these years later, I realize that the time on *St. James Road* was one of the happiest I ever experienced. There were no rows, no rages. Our life was so entirely different from the ghastly nightmare I had lived for so many years with my parents. I was so used to Mummy's rages, and didn't realize what it was like for two people to live together in harmony; just endless periods of intimacy and happiness. There was a lot of laughter between us, and many, many quiet nights, when we sat outside at the ornate, wrought iron table in our lovely garden, speaking of times past, and times to come. Isabella was going on ten years old and the time was fast approaching for us to make a decision about whether we intended to send her away to boarding school. I had extremely mixed emotions about the subject. I had loved *The Ashwick Park School* with all of my heart, and felt that the foundation I'd garnered there was nonpareil. I tried to keep memories of Edwina, my *Ashwick Park* roommate, and what happened later, out of the equation. It was not the fault of the school that some fourteen years after our graduation, Edwina had become embroiled in an affair with my father, and nearly destroyed our family. I still thought of Edwina, at times, but she was far, far away, and I wanted to keep all of that tumult in the past. I didn't expect that I would ever see her again. The Edwina I had grown up with might as well have been dead. Papa and Mummy were reconciled, and limping along in what I firmly believed was a loveless, but somehow mutually dependent, union. Losing Edwina had left a definite blemish. When one has lost a friend as close as Edwina and I were, I don't believe it is possible to fill that hole. Of course, I would meet other women, but no one would ever again experience life with me from the age of fourteen onward. In addition, what had taken place between us had forever harmed my trust. I certainly met and knew others, but I was never as open with any friend again. My friendships became superficial.

Naturally, Isabella wanted to go away to *Ashwick Park*, and was very taken with the idea of attending the same school that I had attended. I had no reservations about her doing so, other than the usual ones that most mothers experience when they let their child go off into the larger world. A part of me wanted to keep her close forever, but I also knew that was not a healthy outlook. We still had at least three years to make the decision, as *Ashwick* did not take girls younger than thirteen, but it is amazing how fast such things approach. Time drifted by in a flurry of activity on *St. James Road*, and as a result I saw little of my parents during that period. They *did* come to visit in March 1946, after Spence and I were settled. Mummy was, of course, horrified to see where we were living, and under what conditions. You would have thought we had put down roots in a third world country. She couldn't believe that I was actually cooking meals and cleaning the house, not to mention washing clothes. Spence and I told her that we were surviving splendidly. Instead of feeling like a slave, which Mummy had predicted, I felt *free* for the first time in my life. It was a marvelous feeling to learn that I was capable of so many things. Spence offered to hire a live-in girl to deal with cleaning, but I preferred not to have anyone.

I *did* have one major row with my parents after Spence and I had settled into our new life. It all came about when I decided that I wanted to do something nice for them on their approaching thirty-fifth wedding anniversary. It seemed a milestone, especially since there'd been the wretched time of the affair with Edwina, and its exposure. I thought it might be nice to have a family get-together and anniversary party for them. I drove to *Willow Grove Abbey* on an unseasonably warm May afternoon. The skies were a brilliant blue, and the temperature was in the high seventies. When I arrived at *Bedminster with Hartcliffe*, the pretty little village that was nearest to my former home, I was in a tranquil, nostalgic mood. I passed the rail station and it brought back so many memories, both happy and sad. At that tiny station so many moments of great consequence in my life had occurred; Leaving home for the first time to attend *The Ashwick Park School*, arriving at *Willow Grove Abbey* to tell my parents of my deep love for Spence, ready to beg for their consent to marry him, leaving *Willow Grove Abbey* on that same day in 1935 and vowing never to return, after a terrible blow up with my parents when they refused to give their blessing to a marriage. I'd returned to this quaint station and to *Willow Grove* to announce my decision to marry Owen Winnsborough, having learned I was pregnant with Spence's child, and needed to find a husband quickly. I'd stood there many, many times waiting for Spence to come home on furlough during the war and again before his completely unexpected proposal and our subsequent marriage, Christmas 1940. We'd said goodbye there again, when he had to return to Duxford and Fowlmere, the bases where he was assigned as an RAF flight surgeon during those difficult years. I slowed my little auto, and peered at the station platform. I could almost see the ghost of Spence, handsome and brave, in his RAF blue dress uniform. My fondest memory of that small depot was of the day I anxiously waited, with Isabella by my side, peering down the tracks to see if Spence's train was in sight, on his return from four years of German captivity.

I continued on to my parents' grand estate, and turned into the grav-eled circular drive. It was the first time I had returned for a visit since leav-ing *Willow Grove Abbey,* and there are not words to describe my feelings. I was delighted to be only visiting, and thrilled that I had a home of my own and a husband and daughter waiting for me back on *St. James Road.* But, I would be lying if I said I didn't also hold nostalgic feelings for the home I had always adored. Climbing out of the car, I briskly walked up to the enormous doorway and pulled the heavy rope that rang the visitors' bell. It seemed odd to do so, since I never had been a visitor before, and moments later Nan responded, welcoming me warmly, with a big hug and kisses on both cheeks. Nan, who had been with our family since my birth, was so very dear to me, and I considered her a second mother. Oft times, I had wished she were my only mother.

It was a month before my proposed date for the anniversary celebra-tion. I found both of my parents in the library, and the moment I entered, I could sense that there was an air of unease in the room. When you grow up as I did, you have what I refer to as a 'built-in radar system' that warns you of impending doom. I should have listened to my internal radar on that spring day. However, I'd rung them and said that I was coming for a day visit, and that I had an idea I wanted to speak with them about. So, the seed had already been sown. There didn't seem any discordance when I made the call. Now, Mummy was not even dressed for the day, although it was well past noon, which was an excellent clue that something was amiss. I suspected that they were either having a row, or that she was building up to one. At the least, her mood seemed malevolent. I entered the room, and kissed each of them on the cheek. Then, I settled myself into a chair by the fire, and without any preliminaries, I broached the idea. I commented that I knew their anniver-sary was approaching, and that I thought we should mark it in a special way.

"What sort of special way?" Mummy asked, with a deep frown.

"A party, I thought. Just family, or perhaps a few close friends, as well. Whatever you'd like," I replied.

"This family cannot get together," Mummy stated, firmly. She slapped her hand down on the leather sofa.

"Why ever not, Mummy? I know there've been problems, but perhaps it would be a nice time to put the past behind, and celebrate a happy new beginning together. There's not been much happiness to celebrate of late. Now, the war has ended, and we've not all been together since then, so why wouldn't it be lovely to use your anniversary as a splendid time for a reunion? Of course all of this is predicated upon the boys wanting to make the trip. I'll even take the lead, and write to Blake and Drew. If I must, I'll apologize to Blake for any troubles we've had."

"I'm not having Blake in this house."

"Mummy, can't you find it in your heart to forgive Blake?" I asked. "I have."

"Don't you tell me who I should and shouldn't forgive. This is that damned Catholicism of yours. It's none of your business how we choose to acknowledge our anniversary," she replied, in a very nasty voice. "You're always poking your nose into things that are none of your business, Sophia."

I felt tears welling in my eyes. "I was only trying to think of something happy," I said. "I didn't mean to start a row."

"Well, you *have* started a row. You're *always* starting rows. Lord, I've been so damned glad that the war finally ended, and that you've moved on to your own home and stopped giving orders here," she lamented. The conversation was ludicrous, since I'd never even attempted to give an order at Willow Grove Abbey, or anywhere else, for that matter.

I pushed my chair back, stood up, and began to weep openly. I was so thoroughly fed up with such scenes. "Mummy, I don't believe you care a whit about your children," I cried. There was a feeling of déjà vu, as I remembered saying those identical words to her before, when I'd asked permission to marry Spence. "All I've done is make a suggestion for a nice family get-together to mark a special date in your lives. Why must that be cause for upset?"

She jumped up too, and ran over to Papa, who was standing by the sideboard, in his usual state…mute. As I continued to cry, Mummy jabbed Papa in the ribs, and pointed a finger at me. "Look at her, Nigel. Look at her. You told me that I simply have a bad temper, but that Sophia is crazy… crazy…. totally crazy."

Her words were horribly painful. Who would say such a thing about their daughter? And if they *really* believed it, then why wouldn't they take her to a physician? Would someone call a person 'crazy' if they had a disease like diabetes or cancer? Such a comment only served to prove their complete lack of understanding about mental health issues. It was beyond ridiculous. "I'm about as far from crazy as a person can be," I replied, with clenched teeth. If there is anyone in this family who's crazy, you should look in the mirror, Mummy." I am surprised I even used that word, for I despised it. People were either suffering from a truly diagnosable mental illness, or they were acting in a manner that the other didn't particularly care for. But they were not crazy. It was a juvenile, uneducated word. I was more of the belief that my mother was truly suffering from some diagnosable mental disorder, but we would never be able to treat it, since she and everyone else in the family shielded her from the realities of life.

Papa knew that my words would cause a furor, and he quickly moved next to me, and pushed me toward the stairway. "Go back to *Tunbridge Wells*, Sophia," he ordered. "Or, if you aren't planning a return trip today, go to your room."

"Go to my room? Papa? I'm a twenty-eight year old, married woman, and the mother of a nine-year old daughter. Don't you think it's time you treated me as such? Can't we ever have a conversation in this family without saying hurtful things to one another?"

"Sophia, I'm on your mother's side," he answered.

I knew that he had little choice but to take such a stance, but my sense of fairness was deeply offended. All I could think about was the myriad things I'd done to help and protect him throughout my lifetime. I had lied for him about his affair with Edwina, I had protected him when he molested me as a child, I had defended him when Mummy went into rages toward him. Couldn't he just once say that he supported me, instead of agreeing with Mummy? Sobbing in huge gulps, I started to climb the staircase. Then, I turned. "I've never seen two people so well suited as the two of you," I shouted. "You are both horribly cruel and unfeeling. What sort of father would tell his wife that he thought his daughter was crazy? Not a very nice one, I can tell you that. And what sort of Mother would repeat such a beastly comment?" I ran to the Great Hall and retrieved my handbag. Leaving by the front door, I quickly made my way to the auto. As I slid behind the steering wheel, I kept going over and over in my mind their scurrilous remarks. Why would Papa say such a thing? He absolutely *knew* that there was no truth to such a statement. I thought and thought, and finally it became totally unambiguous. Papa was afraid. He was afraid that I was going to lose control, as I had at the hotel in Bristol when Blake and Susan were present, and tell Mummy the truth about his affair with Edwina. The true length of time and actual details, which went far beyond the one night Papa had convinced Mummy had been the case. I strongly suspected a well-thought out plan to convince Mummy, and probably the rest of the family, that I was, indeed, *crazy*. He was terrified that again, as in Bristol, I would blow up and tell Mummy about his inappropriate acts towards me when I was a child. It was all perfectly obvious. Without a doubt, if I blurted something like that out, he was ready to say, 'Well, I told you that Sophia is crazy.' I could only feel sorry for him, and his obvious weakness. I wondered if he had carried the guilt ever since the molestation had taken place. I suspected so. The almost comical aspect to the entire situation was that I would never have told Mummy, any more than I had when the actual incidents occurred. I was always certain that each despicable act would have been turned around and made to be my fault. Later in my life, what had been said on that May afternoon at *Willow Grove Abbey* would return to haunt me. Obviously, there was no celebration to mark my parent's anniversary in 1946. Of course, in reality, there was nothing to celebrate.

When I arrived back at *St. James Road*, I was so happy to see Spence, and couldn't wait to enlighten him about how my day had turned out. I knew that he could tell by the look on my face when I walked in the door that it had not gone terribly well. He hadn't been terrifically enthusiastic about my idea to begin with. Spence knew from the whole nightmare of our past difficulties with my parents, that the proposition of a normal, family reunion to mark a special event would spark uproar. More than that Spence was quite upset about Papa's clear intentions to paint me as a mentally ill, conniving, wicked daughter. At first, he debated making a trip to *Willow Grove Abbey* himself, to have a chat with Papa. I probably should have allowed him to do so, but I just wanted to let the matter drop. I knew that if he spoke to my parents, it would only raise the stakes enormously. Spence had a fairly decent relationship with both Mummy and Papa, and I wanted it to stay that way. Finally, he acquiesced to my wishes, but he did tell me that he had reached a point where he was openly convinced that my family was more than simply flawed, as are most families to some degree. He now felt certain that Papa was what he termed a Sociopathic Personality, and that Mummy suffered from a very real mental disorder. I asked him what criteria made him arrive at such a conclusion.

"Sophia. I know your father well enough to be crystal clear about the fact that he is a pathological liar. He will say anything that he feels he needs to say, in order to be successful in accomplishing his goals. Not only is he dishonest, but he also shows no guilt about immoral acts. I fear he would or could ruin anyone who got in his way.. He is narcissistic, with a complete lack of empathy. He is enormously manipulative, especially with your mother, but also with you. He also lies in a braggadocio sort of way; telling stories about events that are very unlikely to have taken place, in order to receive accolades from the family. Basically, Sophia, he has no conscience. I detest sounding so critical and nasty. I don't mean to, really. On the surface, your father can be very charming. That's the difficulty with people with his sort of personality problem. They usually *are* charming."

"But Spence. I was just thinking on the drive back here this afternoon that Papa has probably carried guilt for a long time about what he did to me as a child and fears that he would be found out. Doesn't that show that he has a conscious?"

"No, Sophia. It shows that he has fear. He is frightened of getting caught and will go to any extreme to keep that from happening. Your father has built a sterling reputation, and he has no intention of seeing that ruined. He needs the praise and admiration of others. If people were to know the truth, it would ruin him. He would rather ruin you."

"But what about the fact that he didn't lie and deny that it ever happened when I confronted him in Bristol? And what about what he said to me when he returned to *Willow Grove*, after Mummy let him come back? Remember? He said that perhaps the reason he had chosen to have an affair with Edwina was because it was the closest he could get to me?"

"Sophia, that was probably one of the few times in his life that he has ever been truthful. He had been through a lot of stress. A heart attack, your mother discovering his affair with Edwina, the confrontation with you in

Bristol, the very real possibility that his life was going to be turned on its head regarding a possible divorce, or at least separation, from your mother; and fear of the exposure to the world that he isn't the revered gentleman that everyone has always believed him to be. That is a lot of stress. Facing your own mortality, alone is terribly unsettling. I imagine for one of the few times in his life, he'd done some real analyzing, and begun to ask himself some tough questions. Don't forget that it was only your father and you, alone both times he made any admission of culpability. If necessary, he wouldn't have any problem denying that he'd ever admitted to anything so sordid. Thus, the reason for his comments about your 'craziness.' God, I hate that word. It's so terribly inane. Now that he's feeling stronger, and has made the decision to stay with your mother, I'm sure he's dreadfully sorry that he ever made such an admission."

"And what about Mummy? No one in the family has *ever* been able to figure her out."

"Sophia, there is a syndrome known as 'Borderline Personality Disorder.' I know you've read about it. It was first mentioned in psychiatric journals in 1938. An individual needs to meet three of the nine criteria to be diagnosed as such. I can assure you that your mother meets every one of the nine. I won't go through each, but suffice it to say that the core reason for a person to develop such a problem is fear of abandonment, and lack of ability to cope with everyday stress.

"Oh, Spence, I wish I could have known all of this when I was younger. I would have understood so much better. I'm beginning to feel sorrier for Mummy than for Papa. But, Spence, why is she so horribly cruel to *me*?"

"I suspect it's because you threaten her in some way. Deep down, she knows that you are a good person, and she also feels that she isn't. I'm certain that your intellect also intimidates her. Your mother is a very intelligent woman, but she has never risked *doing* anything that would prove that to herself or to anyone else. I doubt anyone has ever told her that they're proud of her. She really isn't capable of empathy. Of putting herself in your position and understanding how her cruelty hurts you. But, don't misunderstand, Sophia. Neither is your father. In fact, he uses your mother as an instrument to strike out at others. It's called passive-aggression. You know all of this, Sophia.

"Yes. I do. Lord, Spence. What am I to do? How do you fight against something like this?"

"I think, for a start, we should have you begin to see a psychiatrist on a weekly basis. *Not* because I think for one moment that you are anything but completely sane and normal, but because most persons by now, who've had to deal with such manipulation, especially where there are also feelings of love involved, would have broken down. You are so strong and resilient Sophia, but everyone has a limit. I don't want to see you pushed to yours."

"I believe that my family feels that I should just keep silent about any difficulties, for the sake of the Somervilles. That is what I *have* done for so long, but shouldn't I, as an individual, be given consideration too? How is a psychiatrist going to make any difference in any of this?"

"Sophia, a well-trained psychiatrist can help incredibly. Yes, of course your family should be as concerned about your feelings and pain, as they are about keeping the family secrets. There is a strong streak of self-centeredness in your family. This is just another example of how your own identity has been negated. By letting you go back to the very earliest memories, and talk them all through a psychiatrist will help you sort out the entire muddle that your life became as a result of living in such an environment for so long. You will be amazed at how much talking with a trained therapist can help. He can put everything into perspective for you. You must be completely honest about everything, Sophia, even small things that you think may not be important could be enormous. The whole purpose of therapy is to develop deep insight; to peel away the layers of denial that you have built up over the years. It will be like putting the pieces of a puzzle together. The entire picture will be much clearer. Once that is accomplished, it can help you to feel so much stronger.. Your own coping mechanisms will be strengthened. It will help you to understand how your behavior evolved, why you continued to protect your father all of these years, why you were willing to let your mother disallow your forming of an identity, and to live in denial, even when you knew the truth about your father's affair with Edwina. Will you do as I ask?"

"Of course, Spence. You know that I believe a great deal in the practice of psychiatry. My Gosh, I'm married to you, and I'm studying it myself. At some point, in order to earn my advanced degree, I'll have to go through therapy myself anyway. Can you find someone I can see? I'd feel much more comfortable if you can recommend someone."

"You know I can, and will. Let me do some checking. I'm sure I can find a good person right away. Would you prefer a man or a woman?"

"Absolutely, without doubt, a man. You would think it would be just the reverse. Because of what my father did to me. But, women intimidate me terribly. Small wonder, growing up with Mummy." I felt relieved to know that I would be moving forward with some positive action toward resolving my difficulties with my family. I knew that it would be a relief to talk with someone who wasn't emotionally involved. So, in August, I began twice weekly meetings with Dr. Bruce Avery. I liked him immediately, and found that the process of venting my feelings was, indeed, therapeutic. He understood at once why I was so confused and wounded by my father's actions. Just knowing that there was someone, besides Spence, Nan and close friends, who thought that any normal person would feel the same way helped me. He was an objective third party, which was very good for me, as I knew he didn't have an emotional stake in the situation. We also dealt with the childhood sexual abuse I had suffered, and I began to understand how it had affected my life. He made it clear to me that what I had experienced was, indeed, abuse. Slowly, I began to feel myself returning to a more normal state of mind. But it certainly didn't happen overnight, and there was to be a lot more upset before Spence and I resumed anything resembling the life we had shared before. He was in complete accord with Spence's suspicions about my parent's mental health, and there is no question that once I crossed that bridge, my own self esteem leaped forward. For the first time I understood why I'd always felt terribly uncomfortable when there was silence. In the current situation, with my brothers building a wall of silence about me, I sometimes felt panicky. Dr. Avery helped me to understand that it was a holdover from those times when Mummy used silence to punish me. He explained that to use silence in such a way was one of the cruelest forms of hostility. I began to understand why, when Spence and I were first married, I used to feel nervous and ill at ease, if he didn't chatter to me every second, or took significant pauses before answering my questions.

With Dr. Avery's assistance, Mummy and I reconciled. As always, I apologized for something I hadn't done, and wasn't sorry for, and my apology was accepted. The difference was that I was *choosing* to do so, and wasn't caving in to the anxiety caused by her refusal to speak to me. To commemorate the reestablishment of our loving mother-daughter relationship, we met in London for what was supposed to be a delightful day of shopping. Actually, for most of the day, that is exactly what it was. We both chose new frocks, and laughed together as we tried them on. Mummy could be so witty and really quite wonderful at times. We went to the cosmetic counter, and purchased lots of fun skin care products, which had been unavailable throughout the ghastly war. She even bought me a new bottle of fragrance. Toward the end of our shopping spree, we were wandering through the Great Food Hall at Harrods's. Accidently, Mummy brushed against a display of blueberry jam, which, in my opinion, was stacked too near the aisle. A jar fell off the shelf, and smashed, resulting in a huge pool of blueberries oozing across the marble floor. Neither of us was particularly concerned, because when we reached the end of our browsing, we fully intended to pay the sales associate for the smashed jar. However, some fool man whom we had never laid eyes upon, pushed his nose into the matter. He made an exceedingly loud, rude, and unnecessary comment.

"I was always under the impression that when one broke something, one was obligated to pay for it," he arrogantly stated.

He had chosen the wrong woman to shame. Mummy began to shout. "Why just look at you! As though you would know the slightest thing about what is proper etiquette. You look like an American hillbilly. Isn't that what they are called? You have on white socks, with business shoes, for God's sake! Do you think I wouldn't know to pay for the broken jar of jam before we left the Hall? I am a *Countess* my dear fellow. A *Countess*. My husband is an *Earl*. I'm sure he pays more in taxes than you earn in a year." She continued on and on with an embarrassing tirade, and I'm certain the nosy parker wished he'd never opened his mouth. There was a queue of people waiting to complete their purchases, so it wasn't a simple matter of just leaving the area. Others in the queue were turning their heads and looking at Mummy, and at the man she was derisively beating on verbally. I knew better than to open my mouth, so I just stared at the floor. Finally she mentioned something about Papa owning *Somerville, Ltd.* The foolish man in the white socks turned his head and said, "Well, the Vice-President of *Somerville, Ltd.* is my next door neighbor."

"Well, how marvelous," exclaimed Mummy. "Now you can go home and tell him you have met Countess Pamela Somerville. *"* She continued harassing him about his white socks until we were through the line, and she had paid for the broken jar of jam. Then, she marched back to the place where the jam had broken, and was just then being cleaned away. She scooped up a handful of the gooey blueberries, and briskly walked back to the stranger. He was just about to pay for his purchase. She reached round him, and smeared her handful of jam in his face. Then she grabbed a towel, which was lying on the counter, wiped her hands thoroughly, and regally left Harrods. We didn't speak a word all of the way home. Naturally, Mummy was in a splendid frame of mind, but for once, I did not tell her that I agreed with what she had done.

That August everything changed, and like a snowball rolling down hill; it didn't stop until the entire landscape of our lives was significantly altered. It was a Thursday afternoon, on a warmer than usual summer day, and I was in the garden tending to hollyhocks and roses, as well as cutting back some honeysuckle, which had become unruly. Isabella ran down the path through the rose garden, and called for me to come to answer the telephone.

"Who is it?" I asked. "Can't you tell whomever it is that I'm busy in the garden and I'll ring them back?"

"It's Grandfather, Mummy. He sounds upset. I think you'd better speak with him," Isabella replied. I put my trimmer and clippers aside, and made my way inside to the telephone, which hung on the wall in the kitchen. Removing my gardening gloves, I answered.

"Hallo," I said. This is Sophia."

"Sophia, Papa here."

"Yes Papa. Is everything all right? Isabella said you needed to talk to me. That you sounded upset. Is there something wrong?"

"Well, yes, I'm afraid there *is* something wrong, Sophia," he answered, in a rather peculiar tone of voice.

"What is it, Papa? Are you ill? Have you and Mummy had another row?"

"No, No, nothing of that sort," he chuckled. "I'm feeling fit. However, it *is* Pamela. It seems she's some sort of tumor growing in her female parts. I didn't want to alarm you, so I waited until I knew I had something to report."

"What do you mean some kind of tumor? Where exactly is this tumor growing and is it malignant?" I enquired, a bit impatient with his lackadaisical attitude.

"I believe it's in the uterus, or perhaps it's the ovaries. Spence would be able to understand it all better than I."

"Where are you now, and where is Mummy?" I asked.

"We're in London. Pamela had surgery this morning. They simply opened her up and saw a growth the size of a grapefruit, so they've closed her up again, and I expect that her days are numbered."

"My God, Papa are you telling me that Mummy is dying?"

"Well, not in the next few days, but I should think, yes, fairly soon."

"What are the doctors saying?"

"I can't really get a straight answer out of them. Some say she could be gone in a matter of weeks. Others say it could be months. I'd be most grateful if Spence could come up here and talk to these chaps and get some solid answers."

"Yes. Papa, of course, we both shall. We'll leave at once. Where shall we find you?"

"I'm at the hospital with her, so come straight here. We're at St. Bartholomew's Hospital of London, on Turner Street, fifth floor, suite 5006."

"All right. I'll ring Spence at once, and just as quickly as possible, we'll be there. Thank you for calling, Papa."

My hands were shaking as I dialed Spence's number, and I silently thanked God when I heard him answer. I'd feared that he might be making rounds, or consulting with a patient. I quickly explained what had transpired and he said that he'd be home within the hour. True to his word, through the door he came at exactly the appointed time. I'd hastily packed a few items, in case we had to stay overnight, and rang Denise, one of my friends who lived just down the road. She agreed to retrieve Isabella from school, and watch her for however long Spence and I were gone. I told her that I would ring her as soon as we knew anything. Then, Spence and I jumped into our automobile and headed for London. When we arrived at hospital, it took some time to find Mummy's room, as it was a vast conglomeration of wings, which spread in seemingly all directions. Spence assured me during the drive that it was one of the best facilities in London, and one of the oldest. He thought my mother was in very good hands. Finally, we found her room. Papa was there, sitting by her bed. He got up and came over to me, and I embraced him. Then, I went to Mummy's bedside, where she lay with her eyes closed, looking quite pale and thin. Leaning over, I kissed her lightly on the cheek. Mummy opened her eyes, stared at me blankly for a moment, and seemed to take a few seconds to register that I was her daughter.

"How are you feeling, Mummy?" I asked, taking hold of her hand.

"Not terribly well, Sophia. I'm dying." She answered. She wriggled her hand out of mine. Mummy never liked to be touched.

"Now Mummy, has anyone told you that?" I asked, smoothing her bed linen.

"Not in so many words. But, I can tell by the looks in the nurses eyes."

"Let's wait until we get some facts from the doctors before jumping to conclusions." Spence added. "I'm going to go out and see if I can scare up the physician in charge and have a chat with him. So, if you'll excuse me, I'll hope to return with some information."

Papa was pacing up and down, jingling the change in his pocket. He was absolutely the most impatient human being I had ever known. Always had been. "Papa, why don't you see if you can't find us all a nice cup of tea?" I suggested. He jumped at the opportunity to have something to do, and quickly headed for the door. I sat down on one side of the bed. Mummy did not seem particularly thrilled to see me, but that was not necessarily unusual.

"So, what have you been doing in that dreadful little village that Spencer has dragged you off to?" Mummy began.

"I've been doing all of the things I love, Mummy. Taking care of Isabella, cooking, gardening."

"Let me see your hands," she demanded. I held out both of my hands to be inspected, as though I were a five year-old.

"Yes. It's just as I thought. You have not had a manicure in ages, and one can tell that you have been doing actual *labor* with them. They no longer look like the hands of a lady, Sophia."

"Mummy, I couldn't care less. I'm happier than I've ever been, and I'd sacrifice a manicure any day of the week for the wonderful life I share with my family."

"Well, at least I'm glad that you're happy," she replied, smiling a bit. "So, you like your little house, with no servants? Don't you long for all of the special things you had when you lived at *Willow Grove Abbey?*"

"Not really, Mummy, I honestly love to cook and clean. And it's fun to have friends who live just down the road. Our house is no different from theirs. I like that."

"Well, the war certainly changed things, didn't it? I never thought a child of mine would be living in a cottage in Kent."

"It's hardly a cottage, Mummy. There *are* five bedrooms, and four floors. We do love it there, but, of course, it won't be forever. And it wasn't just the war that changed things. I think this is who I really am. I'd never had a chance to discover what I did and didn't like until now. Of course, I also loved living on *Sumner Street*, but I didn't have Spence then. When Spence completes his Residency, he'll decide where he wants to practice, and we'll undoubtedly make one more move, to wherever he wishes to settle permanently," I added.

At that moment, Spence came back into the room, followed by a good-looking doctor, who was wearing a long, white coat. He had a name badge on his lapel, which read Doctor Christopher Ellis*, Obstetrics and Gynecology*. Shortly after his arrival, Papa returned bearing a tray of paper cups filled with tea. Introductions were made and Dr. Ellis pulled up a chair next to Mummy's bed. "Well, let me try to explain what we've found, Countess Somerville," he began. "There appears to be a rather large tumor in your uterine cavity, and unfortunately, it is malignant. It has spread to adjoining organs, most notably the ovaries. I'm afraid there is very little that we can do. Someday there will be treatment for these sorts of diseases, but at the moment we are very limited in our resources. Some of the best hospitals in the world are making use of a new form of treatment, still in experimental stages, called chemotherapy. Unfortunately, the medication has serious side effects, and you are already anemic, so I do not believe you would be a good candidate for such treatment, even if we were to enroll you into an experimental program."

"I don't want to go to an experimental program. I've lived my life. I'm ready to die." Mummy exclaimed.

"Mummy, are you certain you mean that?" I asked.

"Yes, yes. Nigel and I had some good times earlier, when you children were small. The last few years have been beastly. I can't endure anymore."

"Pamela, are you absolutely certain? You know I'd do anything. Take you anywhere to try to get you the best help that is available," Papa added.

"I simply want to go home and end my life with dignity," she responded, emphatically.

"If that is the case, Countess Somerville, then we can arrange for that to happen. Obviously, I'm assuming that you have the resources to avail yourself of round the clock private duty nurses, so that you will have excellent care. The hospital will be able to arrange such things," added Dr. Ellis.

"That would be splendid. When would we be able to make arrangements to take her home?" Papa asked.

"I should think we could discharge her in a week. She's progressing well following the surgery. I'll get on with the arrangements for transferring her immediately. We can transport her by ambulance, which I believe would be easier on her than an automobile ride."

"Yes, I'm in favor of that. All right. Let's work on a week from today as the date, and I'll alert our household staff to prepare for her arrival."

"She'll need some specific items, a hospital bed and so forth. I can arrange for those, as well," Dr. Ellis continued.

I went over to the bed and held Mummy's hand, and she didn't fuss. Generally she would have. She intensely disliked physical contact and "fawning," as she generally referred to it. I was truly in complete shock, and the realization that my mother probably had a very short time left was difficult to grasp. Mummy did not seem unduly alarmed, and that also surprised me, as I'd always felt that she had an intense fear of death. In fact, while Dr. Ellis was speaking of the arrangements that needed to be made, Mummy began to hum! It was then that I realized my mother was in a mentally fragile state. Of course, such a thing shouldn't have surprised me, as Mummy's mental state had *always* been tentative, at best. Naturally, the stress of learning that her life was about to end was overwhelming. Spence and I darted outside to speak privately with the doctor before he left. I needed answers to other questions.

"Dr. Ellis, what are we to expect?" I asked.

"In terms of her decline?"

"Yes. How much time does she have, and what will the end be like?" I was trembling.

"There shouldn't be a tremendous amount of pain, and we'll control what there is, as it intensifies.

She will become more and more fatigued, and will not have an appetite, but I understand from her record that those are the symptoms that brought her to us initially. She'll gradually fall into a coma, and her death should be quite peaceful. As to how long she has, it is difficult to say with any great degree of accuracy. It could be as short as two weeks, or as long as three months. Generally, I'd say that we err on the side of longevity. In other words, I'd expect her to live, at most, another few weeks. The cancer has metastasized to several locales, so that's why I feel more comfortable with the shorter time frame."

I was truly stunned. Mummy was going to die in as little as three weeks! I mentally began a checklist of preparations that needed to be made. I knew that it was out of the question that I'd be able to count on either of my brothers for much assistance, so it was clear that I would be moving back to *Willow Grove Abbey* for the duration of the illness. I needed to arrange for Isabella's care first and foremost. When we re-entered Mummy's room, she was asleep. I kissed her gently, and Papa walked to the elevator with Spence and me, as we prepared to check into a hotel and return to hospital later in the evening.

"Papa, I'll come to *Willow Grove Abbey* to be with Mummy," I stated. "I have quite a good bit of experience from when I volunteered with the Red Cross during the war. I should think I can be of substantial help for her."

"I knew you'd be there for her," he answered. "No matter what pain she has caused in your life, you have never abandoned her when she needed you."

"No, Papa, I haven't and I don't intend to now. I think children should be there for their parents. Have you spoken with Blake or Andrew?" I asked.

"No, not yet. I wanted Spence to speak to the physician. Wanted to get a clearer picture of where we are. Obviously, it's time for us to ring them."

"Do you intend to ring them, or shall I?"

"It might be helpful if you could handle that, Sophia. It's difficult, since I'm staying here with your mother. I'd rather not speak to them from her room."

"Yes. That makes sense. I'll ring them from the hotel. I'd think they'd want to see her, at least."

"Oh, I'm sure they will," he replied.

"Well, I'm not one hundred percent certain about Blake," I said, somewhat sarcastically. I still had not had any communication with him or Susan. Mummy had cut Blake from the family, because he had taken Papa's side when she learned of his affair with Edwina, and had been in favor of a divorce and Papa's marrying Edwina. Forgiveness was not one of Mummy's strong suits.

"Come Sophia, let's get on to the hotel, and we'll return later to see your mother again," Spence interjected. Then, he turned and shook Papa's hand, and patted his shoulder. "It'll be all right, Nigel. We'll cope with this together."

Papa shook his head, looking solemn. "This is hard to comprehend. I didn't think it would end this way. I always thought I'd be the first to go," he murmured.

"One never knows what God has in store for us," Spence answered.

Chapter Three

OCTOBER 13, 1946

GOODBYE

We made our way to the car, and went directly to the *Savoy*, where we were able to reserve a small, one-bedroom suite. Once we'd unpacked our few belongings, I sat down on the bed, and placed a call to Blake, at his home in Scotland. Since I'd not spoken to him since that ghastly scene in Bristol years before, I had no idea what sort of reception I'd receive. A servant answered the telephone, and when I asked for my brother, the maid asked who she could tell him was calling. I wasn't certain he would accept the call, but shortly thereafter his voice came on the line.

"Blake Somerville," he said.

"Blake. It's Sophia. I'm calling to let you know that Mummy is in hospital at St. Bartholomew's, in London. She has cancer and is dying."

"I doubt that, Sophia," he replied.

"What? What do you doubt? Do you think I'm not telling you the truth?" I was stunned.

"Oh no, I'm sure she's in hospital with cancer, but I doubt that she's dying. She's a tough old bird. She'll live to be one hundred. You've always had a propensity to get a bit hysterical over these sorts of things."

"Blake, we've spoken to the physician. Spence has spoken to him at length. I have spoken with him. Mummy is dying." I felt like screaming.

"Yes, but when?" He answered, with a tone of ridicule in his voice.

"In as little as three weeks."

"Really? Well, that does sound rather soon. So, then, what is it you're wanting of me?"

"I thought perhaps you might want to see her again before the end. She'll be here in London for a week yet. Then, she's decided to go home to *Willow Grove Abbey*."

"I suppose I could come to London. It would be easier than making the trip home…less complicated." His narcissism was overwhelming.

"Well, Spence and I shall be here for a couple of more days. Then, we're going back to *Tunbridge Wells*, so that I can make preparations for Isabella, since I'll be going to *Bedminster-with-Hartcliffe* to help care for her."

"Oh, quite. I would expect that you'd be doing that," he replied. There was no offer of help from him or Susan, my sister-in-law.

"Where is Dad?"

"He's staying with her at hospital. Room 5006," I replied. All I wanted was to hang up the telephone, before I lost my temper.

"Right. I'll ring him there, then. Thanks for calling." And there was a dial tone. He didn't even bother to say goodbye. I was livid. Spence could see my rage, as I replaced the telephone receiver.

"What did he say to get you into such a state, darling?" He asked, as he came across the room and sat down next to me on the bed.

"Oh, Spence. He's such an arrogant idiot! I just cannot believe it. I know that Mummy's terribly flawed. No one knows her faults better than I do. However, Blake is so cold, so unfeeling. He just doesn't seem to care a whit. She *is* his mother, after all, and anyone with a brain should know by his age that Mummy has had mental difficulties all of her life. She never chose to act the way she has."

"Sophia, Blake is awfully like your mother. You know that. He has feelings about this, but is completely closed off emotionally. He doesn't know how to deal with feelings."

"Well, that may be, but he certainly knows how to be nasty," I said.

"We can't let these sorts of feelings get in the way at such a time. You will simply have to make a great effort to shrug off his comments. This is the time for you to be an adult, even if *he* can't act like one."

"I agree, but it's truly difficult, Spence. If a family can't be close at a time like this, I guess they never can be," I reflected.

"There's the truth," Spence responded. "So, let's give Drew a try. Perhaps you'll have a better reception there. After all, he *is* a Clergyman," he smiled. So, I placed a call to Drew, and he answered the telephone himself on the first ring. He was much nicer and I felt infinitely better. When I told him what was happening, he said that he and Annie would come as quickly as possible. Then, Annie got on the telephone, and offered her help. I told her that we would discuss it further as events warranted, and thanked her profusely for offering. Thank God for Drew.

With those tasks completed, we made reservations for an early dinner in the hotel dining room, and then took a short lie-down. It was already three o'clock and we intended to dine at six. I also wanted to ring Isabella, as well as Denise. Isabella loved her Grandmother Somerville, but had never been overly close to her, which only meant that Mummy had managed to carry her aloofness through to a second generation. That didn't mean Isabella wouldn't be genuinely distressed, but I knew that my daughter already understood that life ends for everyone at some point, and she would not want her Gran to suffer. She had lived enough years with her Grandmother to know that Pamela had never been a particularly happy person.

Later that night we returned to St. Bartholomew's, and Mummy acted as though it was the first time that she'd seen us that day. Obviously, my earlier observations had been correct. My mother appeared to have blocked from her memory the fact that she was dying, and instead she chatted on about the fact that autumn was approaching, and soon after it would be the Holidays. Of course, I knew that she would probably be gone by then. Spence and I exchanged glances, but let Mummy ramble. It was clear that she wasn't able to endure the terror of impending death. Perhaps when Drew arrived, he'd be able to deal with this phenomenon, since his experience in the religious arena might bring her comfort. I did have doubts about that, however, since Mummy had never espoused any strong faith, and had once told me that she didn't believe in an afterlife. It was painful for me to think how frightening it would be to face death without belief. However, interestingly, she spent the next few days reading *her* mother's Bible, and marking specific passages that she especially wanted to re-read. When Drew and Annie arrived, they were wonderful, and told us to feel free to return to *Tunbridge Wells* and prepare for my stay at *Willow Grove Abbey*. Drew said that both he and Annie would make the trip to our ancestral home on a daily basis, to help with Mummy's care, which meant the world to me. They were living in a small village called *Wraxall*, not a far distance from *Willow Grove*, but it was still extremely thoughtful of them to make such a gesture.

Spence and I returned to *Tunbridge Wells*. Spence needed to go back to his work at Maudsley Hospital, and I needed to get things packed and ready for my move to *Willow Grove Abbey*. I immediately rang Denise, who was caring for Isabella, and explained our plight. At once, she offered to have Isabella stay with their family for the time I would be gone. That greatly relieved me for, although Spence wouldn't be leaving with me, his schedule was so erratic that I didn't want to count on his being able to care for Isabella, even during nights. Isabella was delighted with the arrangement, as the idea of spending time at a friend's home was exciting and different. I packed carefully and simply, knowing that undoubtedly I'd only be at the house, and my wardrobe requirements would be minimal. Mostly I packed trousers, shirts, jumpers and comfortable shoes. I *did* also pack my black *Chanel* suit, with the knowledge that I would need it for funeral services at some point. I was certain that Mummy would be buried in the old churchyard at the Abbey, and that services would be also be held in the Chapel. I was amazed at my calm demeanor throughout that process. Perhaps I, too, had removed myself somewhat from the reality of the situation, or perhaps there'd been so much turmoil in my family over the years that I was worn down emotionally. Whatever the reason, I found my emotions very stable, for such an unstable time. On 30 August 1946, I kissed Spence and Isabella goodbye, and drove my little car to *Bedminster-with-Hartcliffe*. I arrived about half after noon. Nan ran out to the car to greet me. There was no question that she was relieved to have me there.

"How are things progressing, Nan?" I asked, as she hugged me.

"Oh, not so good, Milady. She's in a bad way. Course, she's thin as a rail, and don't want to eat, but she's not in her right 'ead either."

"Yes, I'm not surprised, Nan. She was acting like that in the hospital. Is she still refusing to discuss the fact that she's dying?"

"Yes, Milady. She talks about Miss Edwina. That's about the only thing she talks 'bout."

"Oh no, Nan. I'd hoped that she might let go of that at the end. I guess it's not to be."

"No, I don't think so. Your Papa will be mighty glad to see you."

"Yes, I can imagine that he will," I replied, as I entered the Great Hall. Papa was just inside, and he looked older and tired. I embraced him and kissed his cheek.

"How are you Papa?" I enquired.

"All right, Sophia. Glad you've come. It's been difficult. She's still ambulatory, but agitated. She keeps hiding things from me. I found a bracelet in one of her shoes the other day. And, of course, the never-ceasing topic is Edwina."

"So Nan told me. I suppose it shouldn't surprise us," I answered, while putting my gloves and bag down.

"Well, let me go up and see to her," I murmured as I climbed the staircase. When I entered the room, Mummy was sorting through one of her large jewel boxes, scattering items about on the top of her dressing table. She was dressed in a pink satin robe, and her hair was arranged in a lovely upsweep. Nan must have done it for her, as there was no longer a lady's maid. She really did not look horribly ill, other than the fact that she seemed even thinner than she had in hospital.

"Hello Mummy, it's me, Sophia," I said, walking over to her. I began to put my arms around her, but she backed away.

"Sophia. What are you doing here? I didn't know you were coming for a visit."

"Yes, Mummy, I've come to stay for a bit."

"You haven't brought that beastly friend of yours, Edwina, with you, have you?"

"No, Mummy. I'm just here by myself."

"Where is that husband of yours? Have you come to your senses and left him?"

"Now, Mummy, you know that Spence and I are very happily married. Of course I haven't left him. He's hard at work at home, and I came by myself for a nice visit with you."

"Why are all of my children suddenly paying visits?" She asked, in an accusatory tone.

"Well, you've been ill, Mummy, and we've all been concerned about you. Everyone wants to see that you're all right."

"I'm fine. At least I would be fine if I could stop thinking about that evil, wicked Edwina. You do know that she seduced your father, don't you? Did I tell you that?"

"Yes, Mummy, I know about that. But it was a long time ago, and it's over now. You mustn't let it continue to upset you."

"It's good for me to talk about it. I must keep remembering it. I must stay vigilant. It could happen again, you know."

"Oh, I don't think so, Mummy."

"You must promise me something, Sophia."

"Of course, Mummy, anything."

"If anything ever happens to me, you must promise that you won't ever let Edwina back into your father's life. You don't suppose he would do that, do you? After all, he has promised me that would never happen, but Edwina is a disgusting person, and he might not be able to withstand the onslaught of affection she would try to throw his way. She managed to seduce him once, so why not again? Especially if I weren't here to keep watch over him." *What a beastly thing to promise! I was not at all certain that I could keep such a promise, but I certainly couldn't tell that to Mummy.*

"That would happen over my dead body, Mummy," I answered, not completely certain how to reply. I *did* mean it. There was no doubt in my mind that if anything the likes of that transpired, I would fight tooth and nail. "You mustn't worry about such things. If anything like that happened, I would be here to watch over things." My answer seemed to satisfy Mummy, who went back to sorting jewels. Her mental state was so erratic that it was difficult to hold any sort of conversation with her. At one point, she stopped what she was doing, and pointed to the wall in front of her. "That man's a priest," she said. It was obvious that she was hallucinating. With that, I made the decision to ring Spence. I knew that his knowledge of psychiatry might be able to aide in this current crisis. Later, I was so glad that I'd come to that decision, for it turned out that there *was* a new medication used for dementia. It was experimental in nature, but he thought he could get some of it, as cases such as Mummy's were the sort they were studying. The drug was called Haledon and it was sent by messenger to Dr.

Hardwick just two days later. I asked Papa why in the world he hadn't told me on the telephone just how much Mummy had deteriorated mentally, and asked him if she had been having the visual hallucinations before my arrival. He said that she had been, but that it was an embarrassing thing to discuss! I shook my head in exasperation. This was more evidence of the denial in which my entire family lived.

The effect of the Haledon was magical. As Papa said, it was "as though a page had turned." Mummy suddenly became logical and rational. She understood completely that she had cancer and was terminally ill, but she never did stop her obsession with Edwina. She still spent her days sorting jewels, but now it was with the aim of making certain she left specific items to whomever she felt deserved them. She sorted them into piles, and placed each pile into a little bag, with a slip of paper inside, naming the recipient. Annie and Susan each had bags, as did each of the grandchildren. Of course, there was one for me, but I had no idea what had been ear-marked to be mine. Mummy also had a large collection of furs, and she did the same thing with each of those, placing a slip of paper into each pocket. Then, she turned her attention to plans for her burial.

She chose a peach colored, floor length Schiaparelli gown of silk chif-fon, with a long-sleeved jacket. It was a bit fancy, in my opinion, but it was, after-all, Mummy's funeral. The next choices she made touched me greatly, and made a rather sad statement about what had mattered most in her life. She chose to be buried holding in her hands the lace handkerchief that she'd carried when she married Papa. She also wanted to wear the plain gold band that had been her original wedding ring, which he had given her because they were married so quickly that there wasn't time to have an ostentatious ring made. She replaced it, soon after, with one of platinum and diamonds. Around her neck, she wanted to wear Papa's identification tags from his days in the Army during the Great War! In addition, she would wear the identification bracelet that he had worn during the war; a rather ugly, large linked chain, with a space for his initials to be engraved, made from cheap metal. It was such a departure from her usual opulence, and I could not help but think about the fact that she had clearly loved Papa madly, but for some reason had never been able to show that to him. Perhaps she'd always feared losing him, if he knew the truth? Instead, she'd lost him because he didn't know how much she cared. I remembered that she had told me once that I should never let Spence know how dearly I loved him, because if I did, he would take advantage of it. Seeing the preparations for her burial, I understood just how very serious she must have been when she made such a statement. How truly sad it all was. That was a lesson to be learned. It was easy to comprehend, when I saw the preparations she had made for leaving this world, just how accurately Spence had diagnosed her. He had so clearly described her deep-rooted fear of showing love. That fear had caused her to throw away so much happiness in her life.

Annie and Drew drove over to *Willow Grove Abbey* every afternoon, and Drew was able to have many conversations with Mummy. I was not present, but I was certain that he put emphasis upon an afterlife, and belief in a higher power. He left later in the evening, and Annie stayed, to take the night shift, so that I could get some rest. Papa also sat with Mummy for long hours, holding her hand. We could have had nurses from midnight until seven in the morning, but Annie and I were able to care for her during the daytime hours, and I actually preferred it that way. I liked having the opportunity to attend to her. Mummy had always been so standoffish, and I'd never been able to show affection to her in a normal way. We were definitely closer during that time than ever before. How I wished that we'd been able to avail ourselves of the *Haledon* medication years before.

After I had been there a week, Mummy grew so weak that she had to move to the hospital bed, which we brought into her room. She didn't fight it, and was more complacent than I had ever seen her. There was only one, last vestige of the old Mummy. She made me promise again and again about Edwina. She also made me take possession of the telephone bills, which she had carried with her since her discovery of them, back in 1941. They were unkempt and falling apart from her having handled them so often, and I had to promise that I would make certain they were preserved. She had discovered them after she'd learned about the affair with Edwina. They had been proof that Papa had been obsessed with her. In a three-year period, he had literally placed hundreds of telephone calls to Edwina, when she was in Paris, and after she returned to London when Paris fell to the Germans. Mummy's biting sarcasm never left her though. She still could be vicious in her rhetoric. In fact, the very last words she spoke to me were terribly hurtful. I brought her a drink of water, and put my arm behind her head, in an effort to raise her up for a sip. When Mummy took the water, it came right back up, running down her chin, and onto the covers. I dabbed at it with a tissue and apologized.

"I'm sorry, Mummy," I said, as I helped lower her head back on the pillow.

"You don't know anything, you stupid fool," she replied, through clenched teeth. "You never have." I simply agreed with her, went into the lavatory, put my head down and wept. I didn't know then that those would be the last words spoken to me, or surely I would have wept harder. Nevertheless, I reminded myself that it wasn't a time to feel sorry for myself, and drying my eyes, I returned to my mother's bedside. She had fallen asleep, and that was the last time she opened her eyes. She lay like that for over a week, seemingly lifeless, yet still breathing, sometimes quite regularly, and sometimes, in heavy gasps. However, for the most part, it was a peaceful time. We administered pain reliever to her, in the form of drops under her tongue, which gave me comfort, knowing that she wasn't suffering. Dr. Hardwick came twice daily, and listened to her heart. He told us when he thought the time was very near. The night she passed away, only my father and I were in the room. Annie had a cold, and we felt it wasn't wise for her to be staying up all night. It was about ten fifteen at night on 13, November 1945. We were talking about, of all things, Edwina. He had begun the conversation.

"Sophia, I want you to know that if you've been at all concerned about the possibility of my resuming a relationship with Edwina after your mother is gone, you can put that thought right out of your mind." I was so happy to hear those words. The one thing I *did* believe was that Papa had most often been a man of his word.

"Oh Papa, you don't know what a relief that is to me. I *have* been worried about that, and Mummy has mentioned it to me as well. I'm so glad to hear you say this," I sighed.

"It would never, never happen. I would never want to be married again, and Edwina means nothing to me anymore. It was a foolish thing for me to have done."

"Everyone makes mistakes, Papa. The important thing is that it's over and done with now. I shall always wonder how I could have been so mistaken about Edwina, myself. I don't know how I could have had such a deep friendship with someone whose values were so vastly different from mine."

"You were both young when you met. People change, Sophia," he responded.

"Yes. In our case that is certainly true."

All of a sudden, as we were speaking, I saw Mummy begin to make strange facial expressions. This, after nearly a week of no responsiveness at all. I stood up, and said, "Papa, something is happening." He stood too, and we went to the hospital bed. I took Mummy's hand. Unexpectedly, she threw her head forward, and then, slowly, she fell back against the pillow. Turning her face to the side and closing her eyes, her expression became very calm and still. We both knew that she was gone. Neither of us wept. That did not seem strange to me, but later I realized how very odd it was. Papa immediately galvanized himself into action. He telephoned Dr. Hardwick, who took care of the necessities, including alerting the undertaker. While waiting for his arrival, I put a fresh nightgown on Mummy, and brushed her hair. Then, I took her favorite hyacinth-scented body lotion and smoothed it over her body. I'd never had such intimate contact with Mummy before, and I considered it a privilege. It was the only time in my life that I ever brushed her hair.

Chapter Four

NOVEMBER, 1946-JANUARY, 1947
A LETTER

I felt it was a lovely service, very simple, and what Mummy would have considered Top Drawer'. The entire family gathered, and we all managed to be civil to one another, if not terribly cordial. There was no music, as Mummy had always voiced an intense dislike for church hymns. By contrast, there were many flowers. She had always loved flowers, and would have been pleased by the enormous number of arrangements, bouquets, and nosegays, surrounding her casket.

Each of her children wore a white rose, and the grandchildren held a long stemmed yellow variety, which was placed upon her casket at the end of the service. The family contributed a blanket of Lily of the Valley for the top of the casket, and the yellow roses showed well as they peeked from open spaces in the Lily of the Valley. Drew officiated at the service, which had to be difficult for him. He read several scriptures, and most dealt with Love and what it truly meant according to Christianity, but there seemed a hidden message in his words, for most of what he read and said concentrated upon not putting all of one's faith in earthly goods, and loving one another as you do yourself. Of course, we all knew that those were lessons Mummy had never learned. Individually, we all had our own memories. We had all suffered the ghastly rages, and upsets over trivial matters. Yet, each of us also carried some special memory pertaining only to him or herself. Blake spoke of how much Mummy had always adored Christmas, and told of a time when he had injured his leg badly in a sledding accident, when Mummy had stood my his side during the surgery for hours.

Drew spoke of how kind Mummy had always been kind to Annie, and of Mummy's love of flowers. I spoke the longest, for I suppose being the only daughter, I'd spent the most time with her, and tried the hardest to win her approval. I spoke of being with her in good times and sad, of trips we had taken together, and of her love of literature. I thanked her for filling our home with books, so that I had learned early in my life to adore the written word. I reminisced about her love of animals, particularly dogs, and her kindness towards those who had less than she did. It was not easy to come up with a lot of examples of such kindnesses, for Mummy's behavior in such circumstances was not consistent. Yet, every now and then, she would do something terribly nice for someone in difficult straits.

When the service ended, we held a reception at *Willow Grove Abbey*, and everyone who was present for the religious ceremony made his or her way to the main house for the gathering. Each of us kept our grief deep within.. It was the first time I had seen Blake since the end of the war. I loved him so, and hoped I would have the occasion to speak with him at length in the not too distant future. I wished we could put the past behind us, and carry on with our lives. What he didn't realize, because he hadn't spoken to me, was that I had forgiven him, just as I had Papa. Since I had begun therapy, I was more eager than ever to be able to sit down with each of my brothers and talk about the whys and wherefores of our feelings toward one another, and how they related to our childhood. It was so clear to me that our feelings toward one another could be traced back to our younger years. It was also abundantly clear, perhaps for the first time, that each person in the family was a separate individual, and while we may have grown up in the same household, we each had vastly different memories and perspectives. Blake was so totally stubborn about anything to do with the topic of psychology, and I am not certain he ever would have discussed it with me. No matter. I had to accept things the way they were.

I was surprised at the number of attendees at Mummy's service. Many persons from London, and other areas came. The family did the proper and expected things, and I could not speak for everyone else, but I know that I felt rather numb throughout all of it. Mummy's grandchildren had scarcely known her, so there was no overt grief shown by them, with the exception of Pippin, who had adored her, and was overtaken with grief.

She was thirteen years old, and an adorable girl. She had long, thick blonde hair, and the deepest blue eyes that I have ever seen. She was also a very tiny little thing, and although she was still so young, it was quite obvious that she was going to be petite all of her life. Mummy had loved her with all of her being; the only person I had ever seen her show such affection toward. She seemed to be able to show Pippin all of the love that she was unable to show Blake, Drew and me. I was so sorry for Pippin's grief, but also glad that Mummy had someone present who truly adored her. Pippin, to my knowledge, had never seen Mummy in one of her rages, and had only known her positive side. It was good to know that her memories of Mummy were loving and solicitous. The rest of the family was respectful, but dry-eyed. Blake was his usual avoidant self: perfectly mannered, but aloof and distanced. Spence was my usual brick. He was at my side every moment. Along with being poised, he was also tender and concerned for my feelings throughout the entire ordeal. Naturally he looked so handsome, and I couldn't help but feel immensely proud of him. He had gained back the weight he'd lost while a POW, and his face had filled out. His hair was still very dark, and it was flecked with silver at the temples. It meant so much to have him by my side. I had dressed in my black Chanel suit, and there is no question that Spence and I made a handsome couple. My hair was longer again, behind my ears, and curls at the shoulders. Several people complimented me on it.

About half way through the gathering at *Willow Grove Manor*, after the internment, Papa called all of the ladies into the library, and set about dispersing the envelopes that Mummy had prepared. I felt that his decision to do so, with all of us present, rather than one-on-one, was a bit of poor taste. Perhaps Mummy had requested that it be done in such a manner, but I didn't really think so. Knowing Mummy as I did, I knew that she would never have equally divided the items she wished to leave to the family, and it seemed somewhat ill-mannered to let every person see what every other person had been bequeathed. In any event, the envelopes were doled out, and we each gingerly unsealed them. Mine contained her large, opulent, five carat diamond ring. That was all. I had no desire to own her ring, and knew there was no way I would ever wear it. I could just picture myself counseling a patient who might be struggling with financial difficulties wearing that lavish ring on my finger. There was a small sheet of paper in my envelope, as well, which listed her setting of Wedgewood Queensware China, which I had always loved. In other words, her bequest to me was the ring and the china only. I really do think that Mummy believed I would be thrilled by such gifts. The ring had been the favorite of all of her jewels. But I was so vastly different from her in style that it really would have looked absurd on my hand. I didn't pay a lot of attention to what each of the others inherited. But, it was very hard not to overhear the gasps and oohs and ahh's as each discovered they had been given some long wished for treasure. Even Susan had a sapphire and diamond bracelet on her wrist and was admiring it intensely. There was also a piece of paper in each envelope that listed other items that person was to receive.

Susan read hers aloud. "Havilland Limoges China, white with gold band, with gold initial 'S', 24 place settings; Sapphire and Diamond Bracelet; Sapphire and Diamond earrings; All oil paintings; one white mink, double breasted fur coat, with diamond buttons; and all 14K jewelry, not set with gems." After she finished reading her list, she said "All right, Annie, you're next. Read what you got."

It sounded like a gathering at Christmas, or perhaps a birthday celebration. Annie looked a bit chagrined, but everyone, except me, urged her on, so she took up the paper and began to read; 'one diamond cross pendant; one large diamond starburst pendant; one suite of rubies, including necklace, earrings, bracelet and ring; one set of diamond drop earrings; one full length Lynx coat; one full length Black Mink coat.' Annie looked embarrassed, and I felt sorry for her, having to reveal everything in public. When she reached the end of the list, she didn't say anything else, and didn't spur anyone else on to announce bequests. Most of the grandchildren were too small to be able to read, so we didn't have to hear what they had been given. The only one left was Pippin, and I was certain that Mummy would have been superlatively generous with her.

Pippin held up her papers and began: "one diamond heart pendant; one set emerald earrings; one string of pearls; one set of Francis the First sterling silver flatware, 24 place settings; all silver serving dishes, and sterling silver chargers; one set of sterling silver candelabra, one sterling silver epergne, all baccarat crystal; one Sable full length coat; one Beaver jacket;

one Chinchilla cape; one Ermine cape; one full length Somalian Leopard coat; one Silver Fox jacket; one suite of garnets, including necklace, earrings, bracelet and ring; one diamond and emerald bracelet; one diamond bracelet, one Tiffany diamond watch; one Rolex watch; one set china, 24 servings in Wedgewood Florentine Gold pattern; two antique cut crystal vases; One large Russian cut crystal bowl; all Waterford crystal items; any furniture she wishes to have; all other artwork; all Louis Vuitton luggage; all Hermes scarves; all Chanel handbags; all Beleek china; all other Wedgewood objects, all Capidimonte Italian glassware; all Chanel sweaters; All Havilland Limoges Collector's boxes; Collection of antique dolls; All antique family heirlooms, and any other clothing she wishes to have." There was a deep frown on Susan's face, especially when she saw that her own girls had been left very little of any value. I said nothing. I really didn't care. The only ring I gave a whit about was the one Spence had given me upon our marriage. I had turned it down from him once before, when I told him I wouldn't marry him, simply to save him from threats Mummy had made to ruin him if I married him. It was perfectly obvious that Mummy had paid me back for becoming friends with Edwina, which had introduced her into our family. She had never stopped blaming me for Papa's affair with Edwina. I had expected as much. Actually, I was happy that Mummy had seen her way clear to leave so much to Pippin. Of course, she probably should have left some of those things to Gabrielle, Emma, and Alexandra, and also more to Annie, because she had two boys, who would someday marry, and with luck, there would be Somerville offspring from them. But she was not close to them, so I could understand her reasoning. I really believe that she thought of Pippin more like a sister, than as a granddaughter. Oft times when I heard them chattering away on the telephone, I would think how much Mummy sounded that she was Pippin's age. I'd always been of the belief that bequests upon death are gifts, and a person has a right to give those gifts to whomever they feel the closest with. There were also a few items she left to her grandsons, so that they might give them to future wives someday. Mummy had always been quite concerned that if a girl who married into the family ended up wanting a divorce, which was becoming more and more common, such a girl would not see fit to give back anything that she had inherited. Thus, Drew's boys, or

Blake Jr., were not left nearly as much, although I was certain that she *did* love them, she just didn't trust their anonymous future wives! I was only glad that the whole rather tawdry scene was over.

When everything ended, and it was time to say farewells, everyone in the family acted their assigned roles to perfection. We had been schooled well in such niceties. We said goodbye, and pretended that it would be a short period of time before we saw one another again. In reality, none of us knew when or if that would be. All of the proper things were said. Susan told me to call if I needed her help in writing notes of acknowledgement, and Annie offered to see to it that everything was returned to caterers and others. Annie had already done so many remarkable things, and I appreciated her so. I could see no need for either one of them to help. I returned to *Tunbridge Wells* with Spence and Isabella, fully intending to put everything behind, and to get on with living our own lives. It was past time. I had done all of the things a good daughter should do. And then some. I wished to stop being the 'parent' to my own parents.

However, God did not intend to let me go so easily. I felt as though I was skittering across the burning landscape of life, like a drop of water skidding across a hot pan, when I learned that Papa intended to resume his relationship with Edwina. It was simply unfathomable. Of course, I had been relying upon the promise my father had given the night Mummy died; that I could put out of my head any concern about a resumption of a relationship with Edwina. What a fool I felt. I'd been so glad to return home to *St. James Road*, and to resume my normal life, which was, of course, so vastly different from the stifling atmosphere at *Willow Grove Abbey*. Although I dearly loved my ancestral home, with its Eden-like, pastoral setting, mullioned windows, turrets and stone walls, after beginning my new life with Spence, in our charming Victorian in *Tunbridge Wells*, I'd begun to realize how vastly stuffy and uncomfortable it had been to live at *Willow Grove Abbey*. It wasn't the *home,* of course, but the persons I'd shared it with. I'd had to tiptoe my way through my growing-up years, for fear of a misstep that would result in one of Mummy's horrific rages, and my bedchamber was like a prison after darkness fell, with a chair under the doorknob, and a chest propped against that.

It all began after Papa came to visit Spence and me for Christmas that year, 1946. I was happy to have him in our home, and delighted to cook the traditional Christmas dinner with all of the trimmings. He seemed content, and I felt that a milestone had been met, as it was the first Christmas in over thirty-five years that he'd spent without my mother, and undoubtedly the first Christmas we'd shared without a major row. Papa didn't seem to mind the accommodations, which, of course, were exceedingly less elaborate than those at *Willow Grove Abbey,* and his mood did not seem depressed. He stayed three days, and I enjoyed having him there. In fact, he commented more than once upon how glorious our simple way of life suited him, and he truly seemed to find solace and comfort spending time with us. When I said goodbye, as Joseph collected him, we had plans for Spence and me to return to *Willow Grove Abbey* for Papa's birthday, which would fall in January, 1947. Thus, I knew we were not facing a prolonged absence, and didn't feel unduly sad. If anything, I felt we were facing a new beginning; a time when Papa could finally feel free to be who he was, as the rest of the children could too. There would no longer be a need for subterfuge and playacting. I felt that I had managed to lay his early violation of me to rest, and hoped it would never rear its ugly head again. *Except that it had not truly been dealt with.*

So, in January, Spence and I returned to *Willow Grove Abbey* for Papa's birthday. Blake was there, but he didn't bring Susan, and both Drew and Annie were absent, because Drew had to officiate at a wedding that weekend. We marked Papa's seventy-fifth birthday with a lovely dinner at a rather smart local establishment, followed by after-dinner-drinks and coffee in the Drawing Room. Blake and I spoke in civil terms, but were certainly not warm with one another. Spence took a photo of Drew, Papa, and me, and later, when I saw it, I noticed that Blake's arm was over my shoulder, but not touching it, and his hands were curled into fists. I was struck by the overwhelming changes that had taken place in my family home. Papa had sorted everything in the house into substantial groupings in various rooms. As an example, in the Drawing Room there was a large table stacked with everything from paintings to silver flatware, porcelain figurines and object's d'art. In another room, he'd sorted through the kitchen and pantries, and there were stacks of pots and pans, kettles, spice racks, and every other conceivable accoutrement that one could wish for in the well-appointed kitchen. In a third room, there were linens of the finest thread count, Egyptian cotton sheets, thick bath sheets, table linens of exquisite cutwork designs. In still another room, there was an enormous collection of sterling silver; everything from Francis I sterling flatware, to an intricately carved coffee service, complete with service tray, coffee server, teapot, sugar, creamer and waste, in the same pattern. There were literally piles of silver casseroles and chafing dishes, as well as candlesticks and candelabra. It was clear to me that these were things that had been named in the bequests Mummy had left, and Papa was preparing them for the people who were designated to receive them, so that each individual could come to *Willow Grove Abbey* and gather them up.

Mummy's clothing remained in her closet, but all items were tagged with the names of the designer, the year of purchase and the value. It was clear that Papa intended to sell those items. Most paintings had been removed from the walls, and were stacked in the library, and I assumed that they too, would be going on the auction block, except for those designated to go to Susan and Pippin. It was amazing that he had accomplished so much in such a short period. It seemed as though he was trying to rid himself of any memory of his life with my mother. All of the children's photos were sorted and waiting for each of us to claim. It was a depressing sight, at least for me. Knowing Papa as I did, these actions didn't totally surprise me. He wasn't one to wallow in grief for a prolonged period, and I would have expected such an organized approach to dispensing of Mummy's possessions. I was in agreement with the method he'd used to do this, although concerned that he was letting go of items that he would still need. It seemed most peculiar to me. After all, he was still intending to continue life at *Willow Grove,* so there didn't seem to be a need for disposal of practically *everything,* unless they had been earmarked as bequests. Then, he made an announcement on the last night that I was there, which gave me some insight into his actions regarding clearing out the house. Spence had returned to *Tunbridge Wells,* and Blake had disappeared to his own room, so I was the only one to hear the bombshell that Papa chose to drop. He and I were sitting in the library, and I was admiring the colour scheme of dark green fabric walls and the Kermin rug on the parquet floor, with a pattern of dark reds, greens and blues. There was still a lovely portrait above the fireplace of a young girl with her treasured dog; a pastoral oil that I had always admired. It would be going to Susan. We were sitting across the room from one another, not saying a lot, but quiet and content.

Then, unexpectedly, Papa said, "I've had a letter from Edwina."

My heart plummeted to my toes. *Oh my Lord. How to handle such news?* "I wondered how long that would take," I responded, trying to sound normal, but still showing some sarcasm.

"Now Sophia, Don't take that tone of voice with me. It was a very proper letter. She learned of Pamela's death, and simply did the 'done' thing in writing to express her condolences."

"How on earth did she learn of Mummy's death?" I enquired. "I thought she was in the States."

"She is. In New York City. I imagine one of her brothers or sisters saw the obituary in the *Times*, and wrote to her."

"Well, Papa, that's really lovely, except that the last time I saw her she was espousing nothing but disdain for my mother, so forgive me if I'm a bit skeptical of her motives."

"What are you implying?" Papa asked.

"I'm not implying it. I'm saying it straight out. Edwina has always had some scheme or another. She is not writing to you because it is the proper and 'done thing.' She's writing because you're finally free, and she's looking ahead to fulfilling her dream of becoming Countess Somerville."

"Sophia, I think you're much too cynical. Edwina has been through a lot too. There's no indication that she has any interest in seeing me or in resuming any sort of relationship."

"Papa, I'd wager everything I own that you've not heard the last of Edwina. I only ask you to remember the promise you made to me the night Mummy died. You said you would never, ever become involved with her again. I hope you don't disappointment me."

"Well. I could certainly see her, without getting involved, as you put it."

"I'm not at all certain that's true, Papa. I wish you'd just leave it where it is. If you are lonely, and you feel the need for companionship, I can understand that. However, why does it have *to be Edwina*? There are thousands of women who would find you attractive; women nearer you in age. Why not see what and who is out there?"

"I'm not saying I don't intend to do just that. Nevertheless, I am also saying that I have a perfect right to see Edwina again if I wish. It is very tiring to start all over with a new person."

"I'm sure it is Papa," I sighed. "I just feel that there's so much baggage connected with her, it would be better to let it alone." I suddenly had a sinking feeling that Papa's sorting through all of the items in the house, had a connection to Edwina. *Had she already visited?* Had they already made plans for a future together? Had she told him what she wanted kept, and what should be sold? There was no way to prove it, but I suspected that I was right.

"Pamela was the sticking point. That is no longer an issue. I'd like to see how I feel about Edwina, without that impediment."

"Papa, you're seventy-five years of age. Edwina is thirty-one. That's an enormous age difference. You're of different generations and different worlds. Please, please think carefully about this before you find yourself once again embroiled in a relationship that is easier to get into than it is to get out of. I'm quoting you now."

"I've told you, I've no intention of marrying. I mean to tell her that. If she is willing to settle for that, then all will be fine. If not, there can be nothing for us."

"I hope you mean what you say, Papa. Please promise me one thing."

"What is that, Sophia?"

"That before you make any major decisions, you'll come to me and discuss what you are thinking."

"I promise you I'll do that," he answered.

I believe he meant it. What I did not reckon with was the power that Edwina had over him.

Chapter Five

FEBRUARY, 1947
A RETURN

I did not really believe him, though I desperately wanted to. The only thing I knew to do was keep an open line of communication and pray that a marriage between Edwina and my father would not come to fruition. However, not all of the prayers in the world could possibly have had an impact upon Edwina's strength of purpose. In February, 1947, just a bit over one month after Papa's birthday, and only three months after Mummy's demise, Papa announced that Edwina was going to pay him a visit at *Willow Grove Abbey*. I could have told anyone who asked that Edwina's visit was the beginning of the end. At least for me. It was resumption for Papa and Edwina. I could also have told anyone who asked that I did not believe it was Edwina's first visit to see Papa at *Willow Grove Abbey*.

My father wrote me a long letter, designed to gain my support, and it created a terrible conundrum for me. He said that he so desperately wanted to be happy in the years that he had remaining, and believed Edwina was the person who could best fulfill that dream. He repeated the old twaddle that I'd heard from him before; that two women had loved him unconditionally in his life, that I was one of those, and that Edwina was the other. I certainly knew that *I* was one of them, since I had endured a lot of pain and heartache through the years, resulting from my choices to protect him. That was now my dilemma. I first needed to analyze and understand why I had done so. I quite understood why Papa might want to consider another companion. Even a wife, if he so desired. However, *Edwina?* I had a strong suspicion that her unconditional love was also tied to Papa's title and wealth, and the lifestyle Edwina would attain if she ever became his wife. That sort of motivation didn't meet *my* definition of unconditional love. In fact, it was just the reverse. It was entirely conditional. She had as much as told me so, back during the war, when we had the ghastly row that separated me from her forever. Yet, he *was* my father, and he was literally *begging* for my approval. I *did* want him to be happy. I simply didn't honestly believe that Edwina was the one to help him achieve that. After all, I had known Edwina much longer than Papa had and longer than anyone in the family had.

However, after many conversations with Spence, and Dr. Avery, I decided that I would try very hard to accept the decisions Papa was making, and would make a great effort to have, if not a friendship, at least a civil relationship with Edwina. I tried to keep my mind away from the fact that Papa and Edwina were going to be seeing one another again, and did so by concentrating all of my time and attention upon my own life. Staying busy seemed to be the key to not thinking too much about them. Thus, I began part-time volunteer work at a mental health clinic not far from *Tunbridge Wells*, which also counted as an internship for my Doctoral degree. I worked three days a week, from noon until six-o'clock, and found it very rewarding. Most of my clients were women, who were leaving abusive marriages, or trying to work through personal issues with parents or children. Though it had taken years, due to the war, Dr. Hausfater and I had finally completed our textbook project, and it was in the process of being edited, in preparation for publication. So, I also was in London one day a week, helping to design the cover for the textbook. I was proud of the work I had done, and it motivated me to finish what I'd begun. Spence was extremely supportive. We talked more about the possibility that I might work alongside of him, now that he had completed his training and was a full-fledged psychiatrist. I was very excited at such a prospect. We had the long-term dream of perhaps someday operating our own mental health facility. For the time being, he was continuing on with his work at Maudsley, as he was badly needed there, but we both knew that he didn't intend to be there indefinitely. The more I worked with Doctor Hausfater and my co-workers at the clinic, the more my confidence grew. I was so tremendously interested in the field, and felt that I brought a particular strength and compassion to it, because I had dealt with so much in my own life. My own experiences made it far easier to understand what might otherwise have been simply theory. To me, the theories were reality.

In May, Papa called to tell me that Edwina was visiting him again for the week, and I was rather at a loss to know how to handle the news. I simply couldn't bring myself to act happy about their newfound relationship. Still, Spence sat me down and told me that I had to learn to let go, and that I needed to do what was right. Dr. Avery was in agreement with Spence. Both tried to help me understand that what Papa and Edwina did with their lives should not be a concern of mine, and that any promise I'd felt obligated to make to Mummy, did not have to be adhered to. Both explained over and over that to let go was the healthiest way for me. By not letting go, I was continuing to allow them to have power over me, and I did clearly understand that. The larger question, at least to me, was *what, indeed, was right?* I was still grieving my mother's death, perhaps even more than I had when she'd passed away, although there were probably many people who wondered why in the world that would be so; I still harbored anger over what Edwina had done to betray our friendship, and to tear the Somerville family apart. How could I simply forget all of that, and act as though it had never happened? Edwina was not the same person I had giggled and shared intimate secrets with when we were young girls at *The Ashwick Park School*. Too much had happened between us, and I couldn't fathom ever being Edwina's friend again. And to top everything off, there was the bit about Kippy, her son. Whose child was he? Edwina had become pregnant in 1939, while married to Dieter Schoen, the German military officer she had wed while having the affair with Papa. She had absolutely refused to tell even Papa who the father was. Supposedly, she didn't know, since she'd had sexual relations with both of them on the same day. The mere thought of that still disgusted me, and I didn't completely believe that she wasn't absolutely certain about the identity of Kippy's father. I was terrified that it was Papa, which would make Kippy my half-brother, and Isabella's uncle!

I'd learnt that Edwina took Kippy to America, after Mummy discovered the truth of the affair, and threatened to ruin Edwina forever. Edwina had a sister, Grace Crawford, who had married an American and lived in

Greenwich, Connecticut. Apparently, that is where she had settled, finding work after the war with a fashion designer in New York. She'd left Kippy behind with her sister, while paying visits to England to see Papa. I doubted that Kippy even remembered England, or the Somervilles, although he and his mother had stayed with us at *Willow Grove Abbey* during the war, until the revelation of her affair with Papa. Of course, Kippy had only been a baby then. He would only be seven years old now. That was hard to imagine. Of course, our Isabella was ten years old, and that was hard to grasp as well. She had no recollection of Kippy or Edwina either, and we never spoke of either of them. I did not intend to tell her about our past relationship, even if Papa and Edwina did end up wed. I was in a terrible quandary. Spence was an incredibly level-headed man, and was *such* a good person. He simply couldn't understand holding a grudge, and I so wanted to be like him. Was it my continued need for approval? In any event, I vowed to try to accept the situation, albeit reluctantly. When I accepted my father's telephone call, I couldn't help but notice that he sounded like a giddy, school-boy. I knew, right then, that Edwina had managed to manipulate her way back into his heart, or very possibly into his bed. I also suspected that it would only be a matter of time before I began to hear talk of marriage. I wasn't certain that I could bear such a thing. When Papa went so far as to put Edwina on the telephone, forcing me into a conversation with her, it was all I could do to keep from bursting into tears. It was clear that neither of them had the slightest understanding of how difficult the entire mucked up mess was for me. Edwina and I didn't have a lot to say to one another, and it was a strained conversation.

"I understand that you're earning your Doctoral degree, Sophia," Edwina began.

"Yes. It seems that it's taken forever. I'm volunteering part-time at a mental health clinic near our home, and also finishing up the textbook project."

"Psychology is it, then?" She asked.

"Yes. I want to practice on my own, or perhaps in partnership with Spence someday."

"Somehow, I never took you for a bluestocking, Sophia. But then, to each his own. It's just that I've always thought that those who immerse themselves in psychology are trying to find solutions to their own problems."

"Well, that's probably true, Edwina. God knows, I seem to have had my share," I retorted. My hands were clenched into fists.

"Well, yes, indeed you have. But, it all turned out for the best, didn't it? I'm sure you'll be splendid at whatever you choose to do. I've always thought you could be anything you wanted."

"Really?" I responded. "I never knew you felt that about me. I don't recall ever discussing anything but the necessity for me to find a 'suitable man,' and your passion for fashion design and Paris." It was a rather nasty bit, that, but I wasn't feeling warm and fuzzy. I truly didn't remember Edwina ever being particularly concerned with anyone's goals but her own. When we were growing up, all I ever heard about was Edwina's designing career, and now it seemed she'd turned her attention to becoming Countess Somerville, with the same passion. I knew that my response had been abrupt and somewhat clipped, so I tried to soften my tone.

"Have you been working these past few years?"

"Yes, I have. When I arrived in New York, I visited several of the fashion houses. Many of the top designers moved to the States, due to the war footing over here. I went to work for *Bonnie Cashin,* who has become a major sportswear designer. It was all very exciting. We designed a year-round wardrobe, comprising an overcoat, suit, blouse, and day dress. *Vogue* praised the fact that clothes conceived by top designers are now widely available. It's quite a positive triumph." I couldn't' help but marvel at the fact that while a world war had swirled about her, Edwina had been consumed with fashion. Always fashion. Only fashion.

"That does sound exciting, Edwina. I'm glad you're using your talents," I replied. "So, you and Kippy have been in the States the whole while, then?"

"Yes. I thought you knew that. But then again, I'm not certain why I would have thought so. At any rate, yes, we stayed with my sister and her husband in Connecticut until I was established with work, and then I leased an apartment in New York City. Kippy is attending *The New York Collegiate School,* and soon he's off to *Groton.* I'm sure you know that's a wonderful preparatory school, and naturally, he'll be boarding. I know you must be thrilled to have Spence home again. Your father has been telling me of his latest endeavor. Spence seems to have fared much better than he would have had he continued with his plans to marry to Charlotte Ross."

"Edwina, you're well aware that he broke off with her shortly after you and I saw him in Paris, soon after Isabella was born. He told me he had never really loved her." Edwina knew that Spence had been engaged after he and I had broken off our relationship, because I had been in Paris with her when we ran into him one night at Deux Magots restaurant. He had announced at that time that he was engaged to Charlotte, who was also an alumna of *Ashwick Park*.

"Well, yes, I knew that. It's just that it makes one wonder whether he foresaw a wish to continue with his education, and the cost of such a venture. I know that Charlotte did not come from a lot of money," she retorted. "So, he is now on a new path, toward becoming a psychiatrist? Won't that be interesting? The two of you sitting around picking apart people's brains," she laughed. "Your father tells me that Owen's money is helping to finance this endeavor. That is *so* nice. I'm sure you appreciated that you were able to continue living a nice life while Spence is in training, and I'm sure Spence appreciates it too." It was perfectly clear that she meant to intimate that Spence had broken it off with Charlotte and married me for money. I decided it was best to simply ignore her rude comments.

"Yes, it's all going very well, and Spence feels that he's making a wonderful contribution. I'm very proud of him."

"Yes, well, I'm sure you should be," Edwina replied. "I'm enjoying being back in England tremendously. Am thinking I might return permanently. Things are so different now."

"You mean what with the war having ended?" I asked.

"Yes, well, that and other things. "

"Such as my mother having died?"

"I suppose that does carry some weight, regarding what I might do in the future."

"Yes, I imagine it does, Edwina. But, it's a big decision to move across the pond again. I'd think it through carefully."

"I already have, Sophia. Well, let me hand you back to your father. It was nice speaking with you."

It was a strangely formal conversation, for two women who had known each other as long as Edwina and I had, and it was certainly filled with barbs. But what else could it have been? I didn't draw out the conversation with my father either, since it was clear that he wanted to get on with devoting his attention to Edwina. I didn't actually have anything else to say. When I hung up the telephone, I slammed my hand down on the desk, and then put my head on my arms. I simply couldn't believe what was happening, and there was absolutely nothing I could do to stop it. I intended to try to accept the situation, but I was furious. I was hurt, and part of me couldn't help but think about how my mother would have felt if she had known what was happening. It was impossible *not* to think of Mummy. I had promised her that it would not happen. But, I was helpless to stop it. Edwina's comment about Owen's money was completely over the top, and it was just about impossible for me not to be offended.

I had literally *been* Mummy for a good part of my life. That sounds enormously odd, I know. But, because she was such a dominating force, and I had so much fear of her, as well as my almost desperate need for her love and approval, I'd had almost no identity of my own. If I agreed with her outlook on life, and tried to replicate her behavior, I had a much better chance of earning her love. If I were faced with the choice of being myself, and acting according to my own values, or acquiescing to Mummy's values, I always caved in, and did what she wished. I lived for approval from her, from both of my parents, really. Now, I was beginning to realize that I was still trying desperately to win my father's good opinion. I'd never had my mother's. I continually fought a battle between what *I* genuinely believed, versus Mummy and Papa's values, which were, in truth, vastly different from my own. I had converted to Catholicism when I married Spence, much to my parent's dismay, and from that point forward I'd begun to develop deeper spiritual values and beliefs. And there was no question that those values and beliefs were hugely unlike Edwina's.

Nevertheless, in the case of Edwina, I believe that Mummy and I would have been in complete accord, although perhaps for different reasons. Edwina hadn't been Mummy's best friend, as she had been mine, although she *had*, indeed, been extremely close to Mummy. Actually, Mummy often had compared *me* to Edwina, wishing that I could be more like her. That was another reason it had nearly destroyed Mummy when she'd learned of Papa's dalliance with Edwina. I wasn't angry with Papa if he wished to re-marry. I quite understood that he would want some happiness, after years of Mummy's rages and extremely wearying behavior. Mummy, of course, would never have understood that. I even quite understood why he was so taken with Edwina, since he'd spelled it out so clearly, when he didn't think he'd find himself in the position of trying to convince me that she'd make a splendid stepmother. *"She is a wild-woman in bed,"* he'd said during the war. What I *did not* understand was why he could not step outside of himself and *see* the pain that he was causing. He had to have been an idiot to ask me to accept my former school roommate and best friend, who had lied to me repeatedly, as a mother figure! Edwina, who betrayed my deceased mother, who caused me to miscarry, which led to my inability to have any more children, who'd deceived me in the worst possible manner. It was beyond the pale. Had he come to me and expressed understanding of what I was feeling, I might have been better able to cope with the entire muddle. However, both he and Edwina were defensive, and all I heard, repeatedly, was *their* definition of unconditional love. *Where*, I wanted to ask, was their unconditional love towards me? Shouldn't they have loved me, and accepted my feelings as valid, if they expected the same under-standing from me? It all seemed so terribly hopeless, and I couldn't help but give my emotions free rein, sobbing into my arms, and pounding my fists upon the desk. Spence found me in that position when he returned from the hospital. Thank Goodness, Isabella was playing with friends and staying at their home for supper. "Sophia, what in the world is the matter? Spence exclaimed, as he came upon my tear-streaked face and hunched-over posture. " You're obviously devastated. What's happened?"

"Oh Lord, Spence, I've just spoken to Edwina. She's at Papa's for the week. I'm sorry. I simply *cannot* endure this. These sorts of things don't happen in real life. Well…yes, yes, I know…you say they do. But, it all seems like a nightmare. I don't know how I'm going to cope with this. Spence, I really believe he will end up marrying her."

"I've always been of that belief," he answered. "I hate to think of it, but that is probably what's going to happen. Do you think it would help to talk with either of your brothers?"

"I doubt it very much. Blake will be all for it, and I just don't know about Drew? He once told me that if anything like this happened he would stand firm with me against Papa, but who knows? I certainly don't feel comfortable ringing Blake. Perhaps, I might try Drew. I don't think he will be thrilled at this latest news. I don't know, Spence. Perhaps he already knows that she is here in England visiting him. What do you think?"

"Give him a ring, Sophia. It just might help."

Thus, I rang Drew, and told him what the current situation was. He sounded very peculiar, as though he hadn't time to chat with me. Finally, he told me that he, too, had received a letter from Papa, and had already spoken with him. He told me that he thought Edwina would be good for Papa, and didn't think I should interfere. He said I should give it to God, and get on with my own life. I couldn't argue. I knew, deep in my heart, that he was undoubtedly correct, but there was also the matter of Edwina having once been my school roommate and dearest friend. It was impossible for my brothers to understand how that affected me. When I rang off, I made the decision once again to try and follow his sound advice. There was no point in getting into any sort of uproar. At least, not until this thing had progressed further, which was surely going to happen. I told Spence that I was growing to mistrust nearly everyone except him. I even worried that Drew would immediately ring Papa and tell him everything that I'd said. "I don't mean to sound paranoid, but I think there is a real possibility of that."

"Sophia, it's not paranoia when it *is* a realistic probability," he smiled gently. "I know it isn't much help, but all I can tell you is that I love you, and that what your father does or doesn't do, regarding Edwina, shouldn't affect our lives. Drew loves you, and I don't think he will play any manipulative games where you are concerned. I doubt that deep in his heart he is terribly thrilled about this news. He is a good person, and is undoubtedly going through his own personal struggle with this. And, don't forget, he, and Blake for the matter, scarcely ever knew Edwina…certainly not the way you did. They were both pretty much in the dark even when it came to the affair. *You* were the one Edwina told all of the vile details…and your father too. I doubt he ever told them that his tremendous attraction for her was that she was a 'wild woman in bed', and I know with certainty that there is no way on earth that she ever told them that she had her first orgasm with him."

"I understand what you're saying. I'm sure you're right. Neither Blake nor Drew knows half of what I know. I guess I shouldn't expect their feelings to mirror mine. We all have different perspectives, don't we? Nevertheless, Spence, it will affect our lives…and Isabella's. He is her only grandfather. What is she to think if he marries Edwina? How am I to explain that my former best friend and *Ashwick Park* roommate is now my stepmother? How am I supposed to visit in the home where I grew up, and see Edwina holding court as the 'Mistress of the Manor?' And Spence, we have never even told Isabella that Papa is seeing Edwina again. Plus, she knows nothing about the horror of the affair and how it affected me, and you, and her Grandmother. I don't *want* her to know about all of that. If Papa *does* end up marrying her…oh Dear God, I so hope and pray that won't happen…knowledge of all of the things that preceded this would be overwhelming to Isabella. I'm not sure she would ever consent to seeing her Grandfather again. She has been raised so completely differently. We've brought her up in the Catholic Church. She completely believes in living a Christian life. I don't think she would look very favorably upon Papa marrying Edwina, especially if she knew the entire story."

"Sophia, please, let's take one-step at a time. Perhaps your father will keep his word about not re-marrying. As far as Isabella is concerned, let's just keep mum about all of this for now. She doesn't remember Edwina, or Kippy, or any of the past angst. Let's just hope that this all blows over. Nigel is older now than he was then, and he may realize that having Edwina around isn't the smashing good time that it was."

"I sincerely doubt that," I replied. "He's besotted with her. It's so obvious. He sounds like a sixteen year old on the telephone," I replied. We set about eating our evening meal. I tried to concentrate upon other matters, and when Isabella returned home, we didn't discuss it any further. Nevertheless, when I went to bed, I lay awake far into the night, trying to sort through the muddle of my emotions, and asking God to bring me peace. Finally, I realized that it wasn't up to God to bring me peace. It was up to *me to* let go of my anguish, but I couldn't do it. Not then.

Chapter Six

MARCH, 1947
OVERHEARD CONVERSATION

At any rate, God was not receptive to my pleas, for it was only three weeks later that exactly what I was so frightened about actually came to fruition. That time, instead of calling, Papa wrote me another letter. He knew what my reaction would be, and I'm sure that he didn't want to hear it. The letter was a mish-mash of tripe about how much he wanted to be happy, and about how Edwina had told him that she 'had been his mistress once, and that it had nearly killed her *and* that if he wanted her again, he would have to marry her.'

How innovative of her. She knew exactly what Papa's response would be to such an ultimatum. By the time his letter arrived in our post box at *Tunbridge Wells*, he had already bought her a five-carat, heart-shaped diamond engagement ring! I nearly died at his lack of taste, but was much more upset at the news that they were planning to marry. He did not give a date, but I suspected it wouldn't be a long engagement. I was heartsick. Spence smiled sadly when he heard the news, and said that Papa should have told me before he bought that ring, because I could have offered Mummy's to him. After discussing the latest happenings with Spence, the decision was made that I would drive to *Willow Grove Abbey*, under the auspices of retrieving my mother's blue Wedgwood Queensware. I'd had the ring she left me appraised, and learnt it was a terribly inferior grade diamond…filled with flaws, and almost yellow, although certainly not a Canary. It was valued at fifty thousand dollars under the amount that she had told me it was worth. Which meant it was not worth very much. At any rate, the Wedgewood china was to be mine, and the planned visit to *Willow Grove Abbey* would provide an opportunity to speak with Papa, face-to-face. I knew from his letter that Edwina would not be there, as she had returned to New York to wind up financial affairs there. I assumed that meant she was giving up her position at Bonnie Cashin and also her apartment. Naturally, she also had to tell Kippy of her forthcoming marriage. I doubted that he would be coming to England for the marriage, as he was at boarding school.

On the following Friday, I drove to *Willow Grove Abbey*. Upon arrival, at about five o'clock, I was looking forward to one of Nan's excellent dinners. The first shock I received was that Nan was not there. Papa had let her go. After over forty years of service, he'd simply cut her loose. The reason he gave was that Edwina was going to want to select her own help, and did not want servants who had been loyal to Mummy. I was furious, but tried to keep my temper under control, as I didn't want to start the visit with an argument. Joseph was also gone, for the same reasons. Edwina was planning to interview new prospects, and in fact, had contacted an agency in London already. All of the other servants, except the gardeners, had been given a leave, so that Edwina could decide whom she did and did not want to keep. Therefore, there was no one at the house except Papa, other than outside laborers, which meant that I would be doing whatever cooking was called for. I didn't mind that so much, but it was such a shock not to have Nan's familiar face greeting me at the door, or Rose's short, round little body in the kitchen that I felt like bursting into tears. I asked Papa where Nan had gone, and he said that she was in *St. Ives, Cornwall,* with her sister. Papa had, at least, given her six months' pay, but that seemed precious little to me, after a lifetime of loyalty. I meant to contact Nan, as soon as I returned to *Tunbridge Wells.* Joseph already had another position, which didn't surprise me, as he was a first-rate employee. He had joined the Royal family's household, and later became Princess Margaret's driver, so, I suppose in Joseph's case, Edwina did him a favor. I threw two chops in a pan, made up a salad for dinner, and searched round for a bottle of good wine, as I knew I would need a bit of fortification to see me through the evening. When we sat down at table, Papa commented upon my culinary skills, and seemed to be trying to be as pleasant as possible. I tried too, but it was difficult. As we ate, sitting in the large, old kitchen, I tried to coax more information from him. "So, then, when are you and Edwina planning to make this legal?" I asked him.

"Oh, we'll wait a bit. I don't want people thinking I've not done the proper thing in observing a decent interval following your mother's death. Nevertheless, on the other hand, Sophia, I'm not getting any younger, and I don't want to wait a long time. We are discussing January of 1948." I knew exactly why they were planning on marriage in January. It was so totally obvious. Mummy had passed away in October of 1946. Supposedly, Papa and Edwina had begun to see one another again in February of 1947, although I suspected it was earlier than that. At any rate, by waiting until January of 1948, it would be a new year, which made it sound as though there had been a more lengthy time between Mummy's death and Papa's remarriage, although it would really only have been 14 months, if that.

"I really don't understand what the rush is, Papa. I know you said in your letter that Edwina refuses to be your mistress. That was rather confusing to me. After all, one is only considered a mistress when the gentleman's wife is living. Since Mummy is deceased, wouldn't Edwina simply be considered your companion?"

"Well, technically, that's true, Sophia, but Edwina had to endure quite a lot of scorn due to her past relationship with me. I want to make up for that, and I want to make an honest woman of her."

"From whom did she receive scorn? Other than Mummy and me?"

"Well, that was quite sufficient, wasn't it? She felt rather beaten up at the end of that ordeal."

"I don't suppose either of you ever gave any thought to whether Mummy or I felt a bit beaten up?"

"Well, of course we did, Sophia. But, you got what you wanted, didn't you? And so did your mother. Edwina had to begin her life anew, alone, with a young child, in a strange country."

"Those were the consequences of her decisions, Papa. She might have returned to her *own* family, if loneliness were truly an issue. The Phillipses always acted as if she'd hung the moon."

"She didn't want to burden them with her troubles."

"I see." I took a bite of my chop, and there was silence while we both sipped our wine. "She didn't mind burdening our family with her troubles," I continued.

"Sophia, your unkindness is very uncharacteristic of you. I do so want this to work. Won't you please try a bit harder to keep a civil tongue?"

"I am trying, Papa. But, it isn't easy. I wish you would just go on living with her…I know that you two *are* living together. Why must you get married, and so soon?"

"Well, if you *must* know, Sophia, Edwina refuses to allow me any marital privileges until we are legally married," he shouted. Frustration (*Lack of sexual satisfaction?*) combined with the excellent wine we were drinking, had loosened his tongue.

Ah ha! That explained it. "No matter, Papa. I'm sorry I asked." I changed the subject. "I'm assuming that you will go on living here at *Willow Grove Abbey?*"

"Yes, of course. Although, Edwina has spoken of looking at properties in the south of France, now that the war has ended. She adores France, as you know, and feels the change of climate and lifestyle would be good for me."

"You don't mean that you would sell *Willow Grove Abbey?*"

"No, no. We'd be thinking of a second home."

"Papa, I'm going to ask you something that would be none of my business, under normal circumstances, but you and I have never minced words with one another, and I don't think by any measure this could be considered a normal situation."

"You can ask me anything, Sophia. I shall answer if I can."

"*Willow Grove Abbey* is my childhood home, as it is Andrew and Blake's. We've always assumed that it would remain in the family. Now, I'm concerned that your impending marriage to Edwina could change that. What provisions have you made concerning the house?"

"Well, Sophia, Edwina will, *of course,* inherit the house. That's only right. I'm asking her to give up her home, and move here, and she most certainly deserves security. She will be my wife, after-all. She will be the Countess Somerville."

I could no longer stay calm. "Edwina will inherit this house! How could you possibly do such a thing? This property has been in our family for generations. For eons! It's always belonged to a Somerville heir. Now, you are telling me that Edwina will own it, if you pass away?"

"To begin with, Sophia, you are forgetting that when I marry Edwina, *she* will also be a part of this family. Blake will never return here to live. He is quite happy and content in Scotland, and with the townhouse in London. Andrew doesn't choose to be Vicar at our chapel. He and Annie are finding *Wraxall* a delightful village. They seem quite happy. You and Spencer won't be returning here. Now that Spencer has completed his training, I'm certain he'll want to go where there are opportunities for him to use his newly honed skills. That leaves Edwina and Kippy."

"Do you mean that it will be hers outright, and that if she should pass away, our childhood home would be Kippy's?"

"Yes, that's precisely what I mean."

"But, Papa, Kippy, as far as I know, is not a Somerville. Do you mean to adopt him?"

"That is what Edwina would prefer."

"What do *you* prefer?"

"I haven't reached a final decision on that matter. I have another option, actually. The house can be left to Edwina for her natural lifetime, in Trust, and then revert to you children upon her death."

"That would seem eminently fairer to me, but the whole thing just turns me upside down. I cannot imagine that Edwina might own this house. Plus, Edwina is *my* age. By the time she would be expected to be of an age to pass away, your biological children could well be gone. What does that mean? Would *Kippy* inherit, or would your eldest grandson, Blake Jr.?"

"Oh Sophia. You make everything so complex. I really don't know. My thinking is that Kippy would inherit. If I adopt him, he would be a son, and a son would take precedent over a Grandson."

"Papa, this just is not right. I don't understand your thinking at all."

"I've explained my reasoning to you, Sophia," Papa answered, in a rather superior tone.

"I'm having trouble with a lot of your reasoning at the moment, Papa, but I'm trying very hard to respect your decisions. How can you know that one of us might not want to come back here, in time? I've always thought that was precisely what Spence and I might do. It isn't such a far distance from Bristol, or Bath. One could even commute to London, via train. You know how much I have always loved *Willow Grove Abbey*."

"What are you so concerned about, Sophia? Are you worried about money? I'd hate to think that we're going to have a falling out because you're greedy about your inheritance. If money is the issue with you, then you should have considered that before you married someone who wasn't landed gentry."

At that, I stood up, grabbed my plate and put it into the sink. My heart was pounding and I was afraid I was going to start weeping. I also felt sick to my stomach. "I think I'm going to retire to my rooms, if you don't mind, Papa. This has been a long day for me, and I don't think we should continue this conversation at the moment. Perhaps things will seem different in the morning."

"That's fine, Sophia. I understand," he replied. "I need to ring Edwina, anyway."

With that, I climbed the stairway to my familiar bed chamber, and for the first time since Mummy's death, I would have given anything if she had been down the hallway in her own rooms. It was inconceivable to me that such a thing was happening. I was obviously still coming to grips with the reality that Mummy was gone, and now I was being faced with the shock of my father's intention to marry Edwina, and leave the family home to her! As I reached the top of the staircase, I could hear Papa already on the telephone with Edwina, sounding jovial and enraptured. He appeared to have already forgotten that I was there. I scarcely slept all night, and lay awake rehearsing over and over the points I wanted to make when I spoke to him the next morning. I was up and dressed early. I knew his usual routine, and went to the kitchen to find him there, reading the *London Times* and drinking a cup of tea. I sat down next to him at the table and joined in a cup of Earl Grey. I don't remember now what the first few innocuous comments spoken were, but what I *do* remember is Papa saying, "How are you feeling this morning, Sophia? Did you sleep well?"

"Not terribly, if I'm to be honest Papa. This is such an awful lot to take in, you know. Plus, I fretted half the night about your comment regarding money and my marriage to Spence. I would have thought that was settled long ago, Papa. I'm perfectly happy with my circumstances in life, and am not in the least worried about how much I shall inherit. But, if I'm to be completely honest, I have to say that I think any normal person would find it hard to accept that the woman who caused so much heartache to me, and to my mother, might inherit one pence of your money."

"Sophia, let me tell you about Edwina's wonderful idea," he said in an almost manic tone. It seemed as though he hadn't heard a word I'd said, and had been waiting with bated breath to tell me about the latest conversation with his beloved. "We discussed it last night on the telephone," he continued. "She told me that she wants to be an asset to me, not a liability." He had a wide smile on his face, like a child.

"How nice," I responded. "How does she intend to accomplish that?"

"She has suggested that I give her the inheritance that I would normally be leaving to you, Andrew and Blake, and that, in turn, she will gift it to you after my death, which would save a tremendous amount of money in taxes."

All color must have drained from my face. "You cannot be serious, Papa," I exclaimed.

"I'm very serious. It would save a great deal in death taxes, which means it would also be saving you children money."

"Wouldn't Edwina be giving up her own lifetime tax exemption to do such a thing?" I asked. "Why would she do that?"

"Because she loves me," he replied. Again the school-boy smile.

I leaned back in my chair and took a deep breath. "Papa, I don't want to sound paranoid, but if you were to enter into such an agreement with her, there is no way you could do so in any sort of a written, legal document, since to do such a thing *would* be illegal. You cannot gift money to another person with any strings attached. You would simply be relying upon her word. You would have no guarantee that she'd follow your wishes. No one would be foolish enough to do such a thing, Papa." He seemed surprised at my knowledge of the law, and of gift tax implications, and apparently had forgotten that when I married Owen Winnsborough, and later became his widow, I inherited a good sum of money, and spent quite a bit of time schooling myself on such matters, in order to be a good steward of that estate. I had even taken a course once on '*Wills and Estate Planning*'.

"There isn't a mean, deceptive bone in Edwina's body. If she promises she'll do something, then she'll do it."

"Papa, even if that is so, which I do not believe, please, I beg you, *please* do not leave me under Edwina's control when it comes to my inheritance. That's simply grossly unfair. She should have nothing whatsoever to say about such matters, and surely, you can understand why I wouldn't want to be beholden to her in any way for even a shilling of my inheritance? I don't believe either of my brothers would want that, either."

"Well, there you are wrong. Your brothers both think it's a brilliant idea."

"I don't believe you. But, if it should happen to be the truth, then let them participate in this illegal scheme. I want no part of it."

"What would you expect me to tell Edwina?"

"Tell her the truth," I answered."

"I'm afraid she'll be offended. She'll think you don't trust her."

"She'll be correct," I replied. "After what she has done to this family, I've no reason to trust her."

"Sophia, I don't even have to be discussing this with you, you know. This is really between Edwina and me, and it isn't actually any of your business."

"Oh Papa. That would be comical, if it weren't so sad. There have been many things through the years that weren't my business. It wasn't my business whether Edwina was a 'wild woman in bed,' and it wasn't my business that she had her 'first orgasm' with you. I could go on and on. So, forgive me if now I feel that something that actually affects me *is* my business."

"I wish I'd never told you anything about my relationship with Edwina."

"And I wish you hadn't either, Papa, but you did. You told me many things, as did she, and I'm not one to easily forget, especially something like that. Do you honestly believe that this situation has any semblance of normalcy?"

"I think that a person deserves to be happy in life. Actually, I thought that it would be easier for you to accept my marriage to Edwina, than if she were a perfect stranger. At least you *know* Edwina. Why, she was practically a member of this family for years."

"Papa! *That* is the *heart* of the matter. Can't you begin to understand how I feel? Yes. You're absolutely correct. I certainly do *know* Edwina. No one knows her better than I. That is the whole problem."

"Well, you certainly thought she was a wonder when you were friends at *Ashwick Park,*" he nearly shouted.

"We were children, Papa, and I trusted her. Don't you see how she betrayed me? Why would you expect me to trust her now? Edwina is a narcissistic, self-absorbed person."

"Oh, well, now there you go with your psychological jargon. Perhaps you need to learn the power of forgiveness in your life," he said, in a rather righteous manner.

I jumped from the table and started to cry. Later I would be angry at myself for losing control. It was too reminiscent of what Mummy would have done, except that she would have smashed everything in the room. "I wish Mummy had never died," I cried. "She could be beastly, but I don't believe she would ever have put me through something like this. I'll learn to forgive Edwina, when she admits the pain she caused to so many other people."

My father was very stoic and unemotional, which only served to escalate my own upset. "Well, that isn't what happened, Sophia, and it isn't what is going to happen. Your mother is dead, and nothing will bring her back. Edwina does not owe you, or anyone else an apology. She and I have every right to be happy. You're now trying to run my life, the way your mother always did, and I'm not going to have it. You can either accept the fact that I'm going to marry Edwina, and be happy for me, or suffer the consequences."

"What consequences?" I cried. "What can you possibly mean by such a cryptic threat?"

"Well, obviously, if you won't accept Edwina as my wife, I think she will have every right not to want you in our home."

"What? What are you saying? That you'd allow Edwina to bar me from my childhood home? Are you daft?" I was close to screaming, between great sobs. "Papa, I never, ever thought you could be this cruel."

"Sophia, I even paid a visit to our Vicar at the village church, and had a long talk with him about my difficulties in obtaining your approval for my wish to marry Edwina. *That's* how far *I've* been willing to go to try to find a solution to your stubbornness."

"Really, Papa? Did you tell him that you had a ten-year love affair with her, and that Edwina was my former school roommate and dearest friend? And that Mummy welcomed her into our home and treated her every bit as nicely as she treated her own daughter."

"Well, *of course not*, Sophia. Don't be absurd."

I thought I must be losing my mind. "But, Papa, if you didn't *tell* those things, then the Vicar hasn't all of the primary facts. Those two things are the heart of the matter. You're just running around trying to get people to feel sorry for you, and to paint me as a wicked, little money-mad daughter."

He just sat there and looked at me. There wasn't one minuscule sign of emotion. He was implacable. I had never seen this side of him before. *Or had I?* I took another deep breath and tried to bring my emotions under control. Screaming and crying wasn't going to accomplish anything. I knew Papa's tendency toward playing the victim. I could just hear him saying to Edwina, and probably my brothers, *'Well she screamed, and yelled and said beastly things, and I just sat there and took it.'* It was clear to me by that time that my father intended to stop at nothing to have his way, and that he meant to destroy anything or anyone who got in his path. Moreover, he didn't simply want to marry Edwina…He wanted *everyone's* blessing. It was so reminiscent of the conversation I'd had with Edwina in the hallway at *Willow Grove Abbey* during the war. That was when I realized that Edwina would stop at nothing to get what she wanted. My father and Edwina were two of a kind, apparently. If there was even one person in the family who wasn't supportive of his decision, it was clear that he was afraid persons *outside* of the family would question his actions, and he cared immensely about what others thought. His narcissism was incredible.

"Papa, I haven't asked you not to marry, Edwina. I know that would be futile. I can't and won't pretend to be happy about it, but I've accepted that it will happen. I'm simply trying to get straight how things will be, and attempting to make you understand that *anytime* there is a second marriage, where a large estate is involved, and children by the first marriage, it's only prudent to have legal documents drawn. *Any* solicitor would tell you the same thing."

"I should think that I know a bit more about this sort of thing than you do, my dear child. What have you ever done except live off the proceeds of someone else's money? First mine, then Owen Winnsborough's, and now Spencer's. One could make a case for the fact that it's you who seek out marriage for profit, not Edwina, who has worked and supported herself for years."

"What a low, despicable thing to say. How could you? All of my life I was taught that the only appropriate choice for me would be to find a suitable husband. If I had wanted a career, both you and Mummy would have forbidden it. The more I accomplished in life, the more Mummy seemed to hate me. And you never told her that she was being unfair."

"She felt that you acted superior to her."

"Rubbish! I'd like you to give me one example of my *ever* showing superiority to *anyone,* ever! That is total, complete poppycock. Part of Mummy's problem was that she always felt such incredibly low self-worth. No matter what I'd accomplished, she would have thought I felt superior to her. She could have accomplished much more in her own life, so that she wouldn't have had to feel inferior to anyone, but she chose not to, for fear of failure. The only people she was ever fond of were those who had never accomplished anything. That's why she didn't encourage me to be successful. All she ever wanted me to do was find a husband. Neither of you *ever* showed the slightest interest in seeing me choose a career and make my own way, independent of a husband. This is very interesting knowledge to have now. Why wasn't I told this in 1931, when I went away to school?" When my University Professor, Doctor Hausfater, asked me to become his co-author on the Adolescent Psychology Textbook? You showed absolutely no belief in *my* talents. In fact, both you and Mummy might just as well have laughed at me. You certainly didn't encourage me. It's amazing that I accepted his incredible offer, and now, you criticize me because I haven't been a career woman."

"I left that part of your up-bringing to your mother."

"You left *all* of my upbringing to Mummy. You stood by and watched her do beastly things to all of your children, and never stood up for any of us."

"Oh, am I now to receive a lecture on how I ruined your life?" He actually laughed.

"*I didn't say you ruined my life!* Quit turning around what I am saying! But, I *am* saying that there were many, many times when your support would have meant the world to me. If you had stood up for me when I wanted to marry Spence, in the beginning, I would never have gone through the ordeal with Owen."

"Perhaps it's a good thing you did. It certainly enriched you considerably."

"Papa, that's a beastly thing to say, and I wonder if it's really your true belief. Are some of these comments coming from Edwina?"

"Edwina knows you very well, Sophia"

"Yes, that's true. And, if there's one thing Edwina knows, it's that I was madly in love with Spence, and did everything I could, including marrying Owen, to protect him from the threats that Mummy made, and that you didn't argue with."

"Well, I'm sorry I wasn't the perfect father, Sophia."

"I feel totally helpless, Papa, and I don't even know how to converse with you anymore. You've never been like this. I've protected you all of your life. Now, you act as though I'm some stranger. I feel like the moment that Mummy died, you felt like you could relax, and quit worrying that I might tell her the truth about you. So, now you don't have to even pretend to be kind to me."

"Protected me?" Papa said, with a perplexed look.

"Yes, protected you. You know very well that's true. There have been so many times that I could have told Mummy things, and didn't, as I knew you would be the recipient of her wrath. I could enumerate scores of times when I kept my mouth shut. I did not tell her things you did. You know *exactly what I am talking about.*" I was shouting and weeping again, and when I stopped talking, I felt out of breath and light-headed. I put out my hand and held onto to the kitchen counter to steady myself. I was gasping.

"Are you speaking about my relationship with Edwina?" He asked, with a complete tone of innocence.

"That and other things." He knew precisely what I was referring to, but for some reason, I could not find the courage to state the facts about the vile episodes when I was a child. *Nevertheless, he knew.* There was no question that he knew. He'd as much as said so years back, when he had made the statement about choosing Edwina for his lover because it was the closest that he could come to me!

"I suppose you have told these fantasies of yours to Edwina?" He asked. It was clear that there was fear in his voice. *He was a frightened little boy.*

"No, Papa, as a matter of fact I never have, which is bloody amazing. Blake is the only one who knows, and of course, since he thinks you are a God, he's chosen to make me out to be the liar. Spence, of course knows. That is why I am seeing a psychiatrist. Moreover, please, please stop calling them 'fantasies'. You know as well as I do that I'm not fantasizing about anything."

"And, from what you're now saying, I have to assume that you're threatening to blackmail me into submitting to your wishes. I see that you intend to ruin me," Papa replied. I always have been worried that you would dream up some lie about my having performed unspeakable sexual acts with you."

"What are you saying? I said nothing about ruining you. I said nothing about 'sexual acts.' It's interesting that you have been worried about something that supposedly never happened. I do not intend to ruin you. I'm simply speaking the truth."

"I have no recollection of such truth. I think you've been reading too many of your psychology textbooks, Sophia. Perhaps you've developed some sort of mental disease yourself. I don't know."

"Oh Papa, this is sad. You know the truth. My God! There are just the two of us here. I do not intend to repeat this conversation. Don't you know that it would go a long way toward healing, if you were to stop this denial, apologize to me for your behavior, and take responsibility for your actions?"

"Ever since you began this bloody psychology of yours, I've been concerned and worried that it would plant some foolish ideas in your head. It obviously has."

"Papa. I guess I should have known. You know…. *you know*…. that what I'm saying is true. And you're now pretending that nothing ever happened and I'm the one who's crazy? We had this conversation once before in Bristol, after your heart attack. You admitted it was the truth then. Don't you remember that?"

"This is really a most distasteful subject. Do you honestly think that anyone would believe that I would do the things I'm being accused of?"

"What am I accusing you of, Papa?"

"Ah…Sophia we both know."

"Yes, I *certainly* do know what happened," I shrieked, with tears falling in streams down my face. I was four years *younger* than Isabela is now! *Think about that!* It continued, until you came to my room. I was just a child. *A child!* I've never forgotten a moment of any of it. *Never.* It was revolting to me, and it is amazing that I am able to have a normal relationship with my husband because of what you did. I could have cried out and told Mummy. I don't know if she would have supported me or not, since she was so demented. I went to Blake and told him everything, but he said I was lying and would not help. So, I took matters into my own hands, and put a chair in front of my bedroom door every night, with a chest of drawers behind it."

I was almost hysterical. Papa's cruelty was unbearable, and I felt at that moment that I was the same little girl again, being over-powered and controlled by my father. I knew I had to get myself under control, or I was in danger of breakdown. I whirled and walked out of the room, and then ran up the stairway to my bedroom. Throwing things haphazardly into my valise, I quickly prepared to leave. In the back of my mind, I thought that perhaps Papa would come upstairs and try to stop me from leaving… would put his arms about me, hold me, and beg my forgiveness. It was complete idiocy on my part to even give credence to such a foolish idea. Neither my mother, nor my father, had *ever* shown that sort of compassion for any of their children. I finished packing and carried my bag down to the front doorway. Of course, there was no Joseph to carry it to the auto for me. I meant, at least, to bid a farewell to Papa, and try to end the horrific ordeal on a better note, but when I went in search of him, I found that he was in the library on the telephone with Edwina. I stopped outside of the partially open door, and listened.

"Sophia has gone round the bend. I can't talk any sense to her. She's disturbingly jealous of our relationship, and also of you receiving any of my money. Now she's gone so far as to accuse me of doing things when she was a child, which are too morally reprehensible for me to dignify by repeating." There was a pause, while he obviously listened to Edwina's reply. "Oh, I know Edwina. I suspect that the majority of this is anxiety about losing her inheritance. You know, Sophia has always been a fearfully dependent person. I have spoken with Blake and Drew about this, and they feel that she has always been too spoiled and needs to get out of her head that she is going to inherit everything." Another silence followed, during which I was certain that Edwina added great insight to the conversation. "Yes, Yes. I see. Well, you certainly know her very well, Edwina, perhaps better than I ever have. Friends generally *do* share things with one another that they'd never tell a parent. I tell you, I'm really very concerned about her mental state. She seems ready to stop at nothing to destroy me. You know, I've told you this before, but it's becoming more and more clear to me that while Pamela had a violent temper, Sophia is simply *crazy*…yes, yes…I'll tell her that you think she should get off any medication that she is on, and stop this ridiculous psychotherapy."

I had heard all I cared to hear. I didn't even bother to say goodbye… Simply walked out of the house, got into my automobile, and began the drive to *Tunbridge Wells*. I could scarcely see the road, for the tears in my eyes. Papa didn't slap, scream vulgarities, throw things, or rip my clothing to smithereens; he only tore my insides apart, and played with my mind. I'm not certain which was worse.

Chapter Seven

JULY, 1947
A PARTY

When I finally reached *Tunbridge Wells*, I was incredibly relieved. Spence saw me pull into the drive and came out to meet the car. I was so terribly glad that he was home. I opened the car door, and literally fell into his arms. My eyes were terribly swollen and I must have looked a fright.

"I gather your visit with your father was rather unproductive," he murmured, as he held me to his chest.

"Yes, you could say that," I cried, real tears escaping from my stinging eyes. "It was beastly. Just beastly."

"Come into the house, darling. Let's have a cup of tea, and you can tell me everything."

"Isn't Isabella here?" I asked.

"No. At Holly's. Holly was Denise's daughter, as well as Isabella's dearest friend. I sat down in our lovely parlor, and leaned my back against the chair. "Oh, that feels so good," I sighed. Spence brought me a cup of tea and a handkerchief. "Oh, where to begin?" I said.

"At the beginning, Sophia."

"All right," I sighed, and wiped my eyes. "I arrived at *Willow Grove* only to discover that Edwina has let go both Nan and Joseph! And the rest of the servants have been given time off, while she decides who she will or will not retain. It made me sick. Spence, there are cottages on the property just for the purpose of providing homes for long-time, loyal employees, who consider *Willow Grove* their home. Nan came to work for the family when she was just fourteen years old. Thirty-five years ago. I know she planned on staying there until the end of her life."

"What were Edwina's reasons for doing such a cruel thing?" Spence asked.

"Nan and Joseph were too attached to Mummy. At least according to Papa."

"That is absolutely abominable. Wretched. Edwina wasn't there, was she?"

"No, no. She's off to New York. I'm certain that she is winding up all of her affairs in New York, in preparation for her forthcoming marriage. I wonder if she's telling all of her American acquaintances that her fiancé is seventy-five years of age, and that she had a ten-year affair with him. Also that his daughter was her schoolmate. I suspect that is being left out."

"What about Kippy? Is she bringing him back with her?"

"No. Not yet. He's about to start boarding school at Groton, and has been excitedly looking forward to it, so she's decided to let him continue with those plans."

"That's probably good. I don't see your father wishing to raise another youngster at his age."

"It will be enough that he's raising Edwina," I replied, sarcastically.

Spence couldn't help but laugh. "So. It was just you and your father, then?"

"Yes. It was terribly uncomfortable from the start. Of course finding Nan and Joseph gone was a ghastly shock. But, I do think we both made an effort, at first, to be civil. I retired early, as the conversation was becoming more uncomfortable. It had turned to my inheritance, and he'd informed me that Edwina will be his sole heir, including *Willow Grove Abbey*."

"*Willow Grove*? He is going to leave her your ancestral home?"

"Yes. He says that it's only fair, and that, after all, she will be Countess Somerville when he marries her, and thus a member of the family. He has it all figured out that neither Drew nor Blake, nor you and I would ever want to live there, so he desires that Edwina pass it on to Kippy."

"Kippy? It has no meaning for Kippy. That is insane."

"Everything Papa says or does is insane, Spence. He did say that there is a possibility that he will reconsider and leave it to Edwina for her lifetime, and then have it revert to his natural children. That would probably mean that at least one of Blake or Drew's children, or Isabella, could own it someday. Except that he says Kippy would still be his heir, or I suppose a child of Kippy's. All of this is bad enough, but wait until you hear his next brilliant idea. Or I should say, Edwina's idea."

"Whatever else is he contemplating?"

"She has suggested that he gift to her all of the inheritance ear-marked for Blake, Drew and me. The idea is that he would be saved heaps in inheritance taxes, and she would gift it back to us over a period of time."

"Surely he understands that such an action would be illegal? I'm no accountant, Sophia, but I know that you can't gift money and then tell the recipient how to use it, or to re-gift it."

"He knows that. I made certain he knows that. I even explained that he cannot put anything like that into writing, and he said that didn't mat-ter, because 'there isn't a mean bone in Edwina's body and that he trusts her implicitly.'"

Spence just shook his head, sadly, and put his face into his hands. "Well, you've done your best, darling."

"But, Spence there's more. I confronted him about his sexual abuse of me as a child. I never have told you, but I confronted him once before, after he had the heart attack when Blake had him at the hotel in Bristol since Mummy wouldn't let him return to *Willow Grove* when he was released from hospital. You were at war, and I wasn't about to upset you with their childishness."

"Wasn't that right after I'd been home, following your miscarriage?"

"Yes. He was released from hospital one week after I was released. I travelled to the hotel in Bristol to have him sign some tax papers on *Willow Grove,* and Blake and I got into it. He was acting a fool, as usual."

"Did your father own up to what he did, when you were a child?"

"He did to me, alone. I went into his bedroom to talk to him, after he had overheard the row between Blake and me. I'd reminded Blake of how I had run to his bedchamber when I was seven, begging him to listen to me, and asking for his help. All he said at that time was that I was a liar, and that if Papa had done anything like that, it was because he needed affection."

"Yes, I remember your telling me that part when you were in *Twigbury* that weekend of November, 1935."

"Well, now Papa totally denies anything like that ever happened. He says it is some fantasy I have dreamed up from studying psychology. Worse, still, I heard him distinctly tell Edwina on the telephone that while he knew that Mummy had a violent temper, he is absolutely certain that I am *crazy*. How many times do I have to hear that, Spence?"

Spence put his arms about me, and held me close. "My adorable Sophia. You and Drew are the only truly sane persons in your family. I am so dreadfully sorry you had to go through this. I shouldn't have let you go down there alone."

"No matter," I answered, wiping away tears. "Perhaps it's a good thing. I believe I know what I'm in for now."

"What do you mean, darling?"

"Spence, I know I sound ridiculous, but I truly believe that Papa is frightened that I am going to tell the truth to everyone, and he intends to take the initiative, and manipulate this so that I end up seeming mentally ill."

"No one who knows you could ever believe that. All of your friends adore you, and know what a good person you are. Please don't worry about such a thing. I really don't believe that your father could be that evil."

"I'll try to put it out of my mind, Spence, but I do intend to be cautious."

"You know that I'm always in favor of that where your family is concerned," he answered, smiling.

Things didn't improve over the coming months. In fact, if anything, they worsened. I had a brutal letter from Drew, saying all sorts of nasty things. Drew! My special, beloved Drew! He viciously attacked the discipline of psychology, telling me that psychoanalysts weren't worth the "powder to blow them to Hell." I found the letter truly disturbing. Drew had always been so gentle, and he was, after all, a clergyman. I didn't answer it, but Spence did. Unfortunately his missive accomplished nothing and instead created even angrier feelings. I reached the point where I just didn't care. In fact, it felt very nice for my husband to stand up for me. I was still corresponding and speaking by telephone with Papa, but the conversations were so ugly. They always ended with me in tears. My father was, at least in my opinion, acting like an imbecile. Since I had last seen him, he'd bought a villa, sight unseen, in Cap d'Antibe, on the French Riviera. He'd contacted a property agent in that area, who'd found the villa, telephoned Papa, told him that it was a wonderful bargain, and that he should grab it immediately. Instead of going to Cap d'Antibe to see the property, first-hand, Papa gave the agent permission to make an offer on it, and of course, the offer was accepted. I was stunned. Such behavior was pure recklessness. Edwina, of course, was beside herself that she was going to have a home on the Riviera.

Next, Papa announced that he'd be spending Christmas with Edwina's family, in *Bury St. Edmunds*. That was terribly surprising to me. Foolishly, I had merely assumed that I would see my father sometime over Christmas, if not on the actual day. I had even been silly enough to hope that he might come to *Tunbridge Wells* to be with us. Another fantasy. Edwina had never shown any tremendous interest in spending a lot of time with her own family, and suddenly it looked as though the Phillipses were going to be an integral part of Papa's new life. In addition to Christmas, Papa told me that both he and Edwina were flying to Spain to attend the wedding of one of her nieces. Last, but not least, they intended to spend New Year's Eve, 1948, in Monte Carlo with Blake and Susan.

I continued with my weekly visits with Dr. Avery, and tried to put the whole sordid mess out of my mind. I was working very hard on my dissertation for my Doctorate, and it consumed a huge amount of time and energy. One evening, after I had returned from London and University, and Spence was home from Maudsley, we sat down in our parlor and talked a bit about pleasant things. We spoke in depth about how we wanted to mark the occasion of my receiving my advanced degree, in July. Spence wanted for us to have a party at *St. James Road*. I was in favor of his idea, since I questioned how much longer we would be living there. Spence had finished his Residency and obtained his M.D. in Psychiatry, so now seemed such a perfect time to commemorate both of our accomplishments. Papa and Edwina were in Cap d'Antibe, and I have to admit that I was rather glad, as I suspected they would not have wanted to be a part of any sort of celebration.

"Why don't we think about a garden party in July? It will be summertime, Spence, and the gardens are so lovely then. We could even have it catered. What do you think?" I looked up at him anxiously.

"Splendid idea, Sophia. I'll give you free rein to do it up top drawer. How many guests are you thinking?"

"Not too terribly many. Of course, all of our friends here at *Tunbridge*. Also, all of the people you have met at Maudsley. Dr. and Mrs. Hausfater, and of course I shall write to the Winnsboroughs, if you don't mind. Papa and Edwina are going to the south of France at their new property there, so I'm rather happy that they don't present a problem. What do you think I should do about Blake and Drew and their families?"

"Why don't you invite them, and see if we can't set about making amends. It would be awfully healthy if the children in this family could all stand together in the face of what is coming with your father and Edwina."

"Well, I guess I can do that. I'm a bit apprehensive, but what can it hurt? They can always send their regrets."

"One other thing, Sophia. I want to give you something very special to observe what you've accomplished. What would you like, darling? Or shall I use my own judgment?"

"Spence, you needn't do that. A party will be enough. I cannot imagine anything in the world that I don't already have."

"Would you like to build a Conservatory onto the house?" He asked.

"Spence! Whatever are you thinking? We don't even know if we'll be here that much longer."

"I know, but I don't think that really matters. If we move, it will only add to the value of the house. You love to garden so, and with a Conservatory, you would be able to grow all of your lovely blooms even through the winter months."

"That is such a beautiful thought, Spence. Of course, I would adore a Conservatory, but can we afford one?"

"Yes. Absolutely. My income is going to grow substantially now that I've finished up training. You have been such a frugal little wife during this time. I'd like to splurge on something you would love."

"I love *you*, darling!" I laughed, and kissed him.

On July 5, 1947 I took my oral examination for my Doctorate Degree in Psychology. I passed with flying colors. Then, on July 10, I received my actual degree. Of course, Spence and Isabella were there, as well as Dr. and Mrs. Hausfater. I was so proud when the Dean of the College of Arts placed the hood around my neck, symbolizing that I was a full-fledged psychologist. It was a tremendously important moment in my life, and one I had never dreamed would become reality. None of the rest of my family was present.

And so, I set the date for the party for the 30 of July, which happened to fall on a Saturday, and Spence was able to make arrangements to have the day off from his work at Maudsley. We also invited Sir Aubrey Lewis and his wife, as I had met both, and learned that I liked them immensely. Surprisingly, Blake and Susan sent an acceptance, and I was pleased. They were bringing their three little girls, Emma, Gabrielle and Alexandra. I'd only seen them once at Mummy's funeral, which wasn't the best place to become acquainted. It would be nice for Isabella to get to know her cousins. Drew also had another son named Ian. His older son, Nigel, after Papa, was now six years old. Then, there was also Pippin and Blake, Jr., and Blake's former wife, Elizabeth. I invited them all. On the day of the party, our family was in a very festive mood. It was sunny and warm outside, and tables were scattered under the lovely old trees beside our magnificent gardens. Everything was blooming gloriously. I'd had the bakery in *Tunbridge Wells* do a special cake, topped with a diploma. Isabella looked precious in an adorable pale pink sundress, with her dark curls tumbling down her back. She was still an incredibly beautiful child. Still petite, with a winning smile, and those sapphire blue eyes. I wore a sundress too, in my favorite white linen, appliqued with daffodils. I had worked a lot in my gardens all summer long, and my skin had turned a golden tan, due to my Mediterranean ancestry. I accessorized my dress with a lovely gold bracelet and necklace, and I felt like a summer princess. Hairstyles had changed after the war, and were trending toward either quite short, or shoulder length. I'd had mine cut for the party. I was a bit frightened that Spence would not approve, but he loved it. Because it was naturally curly, it looked tousled and carefree, with tendrils of bangs on my forehead. Isabella said I looked '*gamine*', which was a French word she had picked up somewhere. Even Spence looked summery and relaxed…a rare thing for him at that time in our lives… in a white linen shirt, with the sleeves rolled to his elbows, and casual trousers. He reminded me of the picnic we had taken to Hyde Park in that gorgeous summer of 1935. So much had happened since then, and yet in spite of the war, and stressful happenings in our own lives, he had changed very, very little. He was still that handsome gentleman I'd met on the night of my debutante Ball.

Both of my brothers arrived at almost the exact same time. It appeared that they had arranged to follow one another. Perhaps Blake had gone to *Wraxall* and stayed with Drew and Annie, and then they left from Drew's house. Everyone seemed cordial when they arrived. The young children seemed a bit shy at first, but before very long they had joined with the large group of others who were playing in the backyard. We grown-ups were enjoying gin and tonics, , and the children were gulping gallons of lemonade. We had hired marvelous caterers, and the meal they were serving was divine. I requested a repeat of the picnic lunch Spence and I had that summer day in Hyde Park, when he had first kissed me, along with several other delicious dishes. There was Cold Chicken, Caviar on Toast Points, French Potato Salad, Liver Pate on Water Biscuits, Chilled Shrimp Cocktail, Cucumber Sandwiches, Nicoise Salad, Oysters Rockefeller and Artichokes with Hollandaise Sauce. Spence had even splurged on two cases of Dom Perignon champagne. We circulated among the guests, alternating between watching how adorable the children were, and catching up on news about friends. I warmly embraced the Winnsboroughs, who were beginning to look just the slightest bit frail. It moved me that they had made the effort to come to our party. After we chatted a bit about inconsequential things, the Duke and Duchess took me aside and said they would like to chat privately with me when I had a moment. I told them that I would be happy to *make* a moment for them, and we went into the house, telling Spence I would be back in a tick. Sitting in the parlor, the

Duke spoke first. "Sophia, we won't take long, as I know it's important that you not abandon your celebration," he said.

"No matter. Spence has everything in hand. Don't feel rushed," I answered.

"The reason we wanted to speak with you privately is because we wanted you to know that we've made a decision regarding *Winnsborough Hall* that affects you, and it only seems prudent that you should know."

"A decision that affects me? About *Winnsborough Hall*? Whatever can that be?"

"We have decided to establish a Trust, and name you as the Custodian. We would like you to use the home for some worthy purpose. As a school perhaps, or hospital. Whatever you think would best honor Owen's name. The only restriction we place on you is that whatever you decide to do with it, please let it bear Owen's name."

"Oh, my Heavens! Are you certain you want to do this?"

"Yes. We've thought it all through very carefully. There is no one we want to leave the house to, and the expenses for upkeep would be quite a drain for anyone. Of course, we will target a goodly part of our finances for whatever endeavor you decide to undertake. But, if it becomes a non-profit institution of some sort, there would be charitable funds as well."

"I am simply overwhelmed. What a lovely, lovely thing to do for Owen's memory. This would mean so much to him. He loved that home."

"Well, we're terribly pleased that you like the idea," the Duchess smiled. "Owen Sr. will look after getting all of the legalities underway then."

"Yes, indeed, I shall. I feel very relieved. We know we are putting the old place into good care."

"You know I shall think long and hard before making any decision, and whatever it is, I shall ring you at once and let you know." We exchanged embraces and kisses on the cheek, before rejoining the celebration, which was in high gear. I couldn't wait to share the news with Spence, as I already knew what *my* preference was regarding conversion of *Winnsborough Hall* into a lasting memorial to my former husband. A few moments later, Blake, Susan, Drew and Annie approached me. I complimented all of them on how nice everyone looked, and how precious their children were, as well as making certain I thanked each of them for coming. Everyone did look splendid. Both Blake and Drew wore dark blue blazers, with grey trousers, and their wives were equally proper, with lovely summer dresses. Blake, however, looked at me with the sneer that only he was capable of.

"Did you purposely plan this get together so that Dad and Edwina wouldn't be able to attend?" He began.

"How absurd, Blake. Not at all. I only received my degree this month. Spence wanted me to mark it in a special way. I didn't even know when they were leaving for France, when I would be graduating. Just that it would be sometime this summer. It seems more likely that since they knew the date was approaching, they purposely left the country."

"We've been kept up-to-date on the trouble you've been causing for them," he continued.

"Trouble? What trouble? Papa and I had words when I was last at *Willow Grove*, but I certainly wouldn't say that I was causing any trouble. If anyone was, it was Papa and Edwina."

"I imagine this little party is costing a bloody fortune," he stated rudely.

"That really is no concern of yours, Blake. Why are you in such a foul mood? It's a lovely day, and I would like to think that our family could get together and enjoy one another. Can't we try to do that?"

"Sophia, we actually have nothing in common. At least for my part, I'm only here to stand up for Dad."

"In what way? Why does he need defending? And, what sort of comment is that you just made, about having nothing in common? Isn't your being my brother enough commonality?"

"We have no interests in common. You lead a very different life from Susan and me. At any rate, we are all well aware that you are blackmailing Dad."

I felt dizzy. Could he be serious? "Blackmailing him? Are you telling the truth?? What on earth are you taking about?"

"We heard that you and Spence are planning to add a Conservatory to the house, "Drew said.

"We've thought about that, yes. You know how much I adore gardening, and if I had a small Conservatory on the back, I could do potting and so forth year round. How on Earth did you even hear about that?"

"Dad told us, Sophia. How would you pay for that?"

"What is all of this sudden interest in our finances? And I still want an answer to Blake's comment about 'blackmail.'"

"Dad told us all about it. He told us that you have threatened to say he did distasteful, really quite abominable things to you when you were just a girl, if he didn't start sending you a portion of your inheritance every month. I imagine those are the funds you are counting on to build your Conservatory."

"He said what?"

"You heard me. He says that's how you can afford to add on a Conservatory. Are you denying this?"

"My God! Of course I'm denying it. It is an abysmal lie. A wicked, disgusting lie. How could you ever believe such a thing?"

"We don't believe Dad would make something like that up." Drew said.

"Drew. You know I'm not a whit like that. I would never do such a thing. Don't you see what Papa is doing? Drew, I've never told you, but Blake knows that Papa did molest me when I was a young girl. Tell him, Blake. You know that's true."

Blake laughed. "I don't know any such thing, and this isn't the first time I've heard you make such an accusation. Dad is worried about your mental health and it's pretty clear he's right."

"Blake, you are a disgusting liar. I will not stand hear and listen to any more of this. And Drew, I really would have thought better of you. Annie, don't tell me that you are believing this rubbish too?"

"I don't know who or what to believe, Sophia. If your father is lying, then he *would* be daft."

"Yes, that's absolutely correct. Think about it. Look at the way he's behaving. Would it totally surprise you if that were the case?"

"I just don't know, Sophia," Annie replied.

Susan, in the meantime, never opened her mouth. She had been there in Bristol. She *knew* the truth.

"You know," I began, "I invited all of you here today because I hoped it would be a new beginning for all of us. I wanted your children to know Isabella, and vice-versa. I wanted to have a close relationship with my brothers. Obviously, that was a beastly mistake. I would sincerely appreciate it if you would just leave now, before Isabella hears any of this, or Spence does. I can tell you right now, Spence will be very angry, and he seldom, if ever, becomes angry. Thank you for coming to the party."

I spun about and walked hurriedly away. From a distance I saw my brothers and their wives rounding up their children and putting them into their respective autos. All of the poor, little things were crying, as they'd been having fun, and didn't want to leave, but they were told to hush, and doors were slammed. Even Blake's first wife, Elizabeth, and his two eldest children left. I didn't feel that they left so much because of any angry feelings, but undoubtedly felt that they would be uncomfortable if the others were not there. I didn't even wait until they drove off. Instead, I found Spence, and asked for another gin and tonic. I was beyond furious, but there was a myriad of guests and I had to push my feelings aside. Suddenly, across the way, I spotted the one person I had hoped would attend the party more than any other, and my spirits soared. I'd invited Nan, and she arrived at just the proper moment. I was so pleased to see her.

"Oh Milady, I'm so 'appy to be with yer again," Nan exclaimed. "I've missed yer like the Devil. How is yer father doin? There ain't a day goes by that I don't think about him and yer Mum. I were awful fond of 'im, yer know."

"I know, Nan. I never would have thought that Papa would let you go. I'm sure it was horrid for him, but you know how it is now, what with Edwina about to become his wife."

"Yes, Milady, but it's still mighty 'ard for me to believe. Oh, ain't the Countess rolling over in 'er grave, God Rest 'er Soul?"

"I can't even begin to imagine, Nan. It was Mummy's worst fear, and now it's coming true."

"When are they doing it? Bein' married?"

"Supposedly in January. Or this fall. No one tells me very much. For all practical purposes, they might as well be married now. I'm fairly certain that she's living there. Also, they have purchased a home in the South of France…that's where they are now." Nan looked aghast. She couldn't imagine that Papa would do something so foolish. Neither could I, for that matter. "Nan, what are your plans?" I asked, changing the subject.

"I don't 'ave many, right now, Milady. I s'pose I'll find another place. I just 'ate the thought of starting all over with a new family. But, I 'ave to go on till I get me pension. You know I was with the Somerville's for 36 years…. A long spell. It don't seem right, somehow. You was like me own family."

"I know, Nan. You have always been family to me. I don't remember a time when you weren't there with us."

"I was there when you was born. You was the prettiest baby…such long lashes on them eyes of yours. You never did lose them, neither."

I grinned. "Well Nan, how would you like to come to work for Doctor Stanton and me, here in *Tunbridge Wells?*" I asked.

"Milady, are you bein' serious? Why, I'd just love it. What with the little one, I'm s'posin you could use the 'elp."

"You bet I could, Nan. You'd have to act as sort-of an all-round person, since you'd be our only help. You'd live in, of course. We've plenty of room, that's for certain. I'd need you to be flexible Nan. You'd be watching Isabella sometimes, acting as the housekeeper, and cooking occasional meals."

"Why, I could do all them things, all of the time, Miss Sophia. In this puny little 'ouse, why it wouldn't take no time at all to clean top to bottom."

I laughed. "Well, compared to *Willow Grove Abbey*, it *is* a puny house, but there still seems a lot to be done. Isabella demands a lot of my time. My other nanny, Martha—you remember her—got married, after the war, so I've not had anyone since. Moreover, I've just received my graduate degree in psychology from the University of London, and I plan to begin searching for a job where I can make use of it. Spence finished his training, so I'll probably wait to job seek until I know where he is going to work. But, I *am* doing volunteer work three days a week now. It would be heavenly to have you here to keep things running smoothly when I can't be home."

"Milady, I'd be 'onored to be part of your 'ousehold. When would you be wantin me to begin?"

"As soon as you're able, Nan. Of course, I understand that you'll have to move your things up from Cornwall. We shall be happy to pay the expenses involved."

"Oh, there's not all that much. Just my few clothes, uniforms and some personal items. Everything I 'ave fits in one grip. I could make the trip back, pack up what I 'ave, and return the next day. What do you think about next week, Monday?"

"That would be wonderful, Nan. I'll give you a key, in case I'm not here, although I should be. I'll show you today where your rooms will be, and give you a tour of the house, so you know where everything is."

"That would be just fine. Oh, Milady, I'm just so 'appy to think I'll be working with you again. I always did think you was the best of the bunch."

"Well, thank you Nan. We'll enjoy having you here. Spence will be awfully glad. It's been a bit mad around here, what with my classes and all."

Thus, my problem regarding household help, and specifically the wrong that had been done to Nan, was solved and I knew that Spence would be pleased, as he'd been very much in favor of the idea. I intended to give Nan a nice raise in wages too, as I suspected that my father hadn't done so in quite some time. By the end of the day, I was tired and really rather glad to see the party come to an end. I was happy to kiss Isabella goodnight and relax. Finally I was able to sit down and talk with Spence about the conversation I'd had with my brothers. When I did so, Spence became very angry; probably angrier than I'd seen him in a long while. He thought my brothers had been completely out of line, and said so. I was less angry than I was hurt. It seemed that, in one fell swoop, I was losing my entire family. Mummy was dead, Papa was marrying Edwina, and both of my brothers had hostile feelings towards me. It was hard for me to understand what I had done to bring it all about. Of course, Spence talked about the family dynamics involved, and intellectually I understood what was happening, but emotionally I was devastated.

All communication with my brothers ceased, and conversation with my father diminished to a bare minimum. He rang me occasionally, but they weren't pleasant conversations. I did not bring up the 'blackmail' accusation, as I knew beyond any doubt that Papa would simply deny it, or tell me that my brothers had misunderstood. There was no overt fighting, but when we spoke, it was very strained. I also began to receive letters from people who'd been friends of my parents, particularly of my father, and each was an attempt at convincing me that I should accept the forthcoming marriage. I didn't answer most of them. Many referred to the fact that Edwina had been an "old family friend" and I knew that Papa hadn't told the truth about the fact that she'd been my school roommate. Others referred to her age as being some ten years older than reality, which made it clear that he was lying about that, too.

A woman who had been a close friend of Mummy's, rang me up and told me that Papa had arranged to have dinner with her, and her husband a few weeks before he and Edwina left for France. This wonderful woman had been one of the very few persons whom Mummy had told of Papa's affair, and as a result, she disliked Edwina intensely. Apparently, when Papa met them for dinner, he was on a quest for approval. From what Mummy's friend said, it was obvious that he'd been on a mission, contacting and seeing each of his and Mummy's old friends, in the hope that he could charm them into accepting his new marriage. There was no doubt that Edwina had instigated such an undertaking, as she didn't want to start her married life at *Willow Grove Abbey* with people saying negative things about her, and London overflowing with nasty gossip. Whatever the reason, Papa's exercise wasn't successful with regard to Mummy's dear friend. She was extremely angry about the entire fiasco, and said as much. At one point, she asked Papa why he didn't pursue someone else's school roommate, besides his daughter's! She told him that there was no way she could condone what he was doing, and finally, Papa became rather angry, and told her that he didn't care if she condoned it or not. Therefore, that was that, and I was very certain that my father was disappointed that his charm offensive hadn't succeeded. I was exceedingly proud of Mummy's friend. It was clear to see what was taking place, and I saw no way to fight against it. People believed what they wanted to believe, and Papa had always been a tremendously admirable figure in most people's eyes.

Of course, in the end nothing made any difference. On 12 January, 1948, Edwina and Papa were married, in the parlor of Edwina's parent's home at *Bury St. Edmunds*. I didn't know that the ceremony was going to take place until the night before, when Papa rang me. There wasn't much I could say. I told him that I hoped he would be happy, and I *meant* it. It was a short call, during which he told me that none of our family was going to be present and that one of Edwina's brothers, Eugene, was to act as 'Best Man', and a sister was to be 'Matron of Honor'. When I hung up the telephone, I rang a florist in *Tunbridge Wells*, and wired a large arrangement of white roses to be delivered the next day. I felt I needed to do *something,* although it seemed more like a funeral than a wedding. Then, I took to my bed, and wept until my head felt ready to burst. Nan and Spence both tried very hard to console me, but I just couldn't deal with the reality that Edwina was going to be Countess Somerville in less than twenty-four hours.. I lay on the bed, scrunched up like a fetus, first beating the pillow with my fists, and then burying my face in it, weeping buckets of tears, until the linens were soaked. I felt I had broken the promise made to my mother, and a lot of the anguish stemmed from never having grieved her death properly to begin with, although I didn't realize that at the time. Certainly, Mummy had not been an exemplary mother. Nonetheless, she *had* loved me, in the only way in which she was capable. I also couldn't help but wonder how much of Papa's untruthfulness through the years had contributed to Mummy's behavior? Which came first? Mummy was always obsessed with the fact that Papa had fallen in love with her and married her so quickly, and she'd presented to the world that their marriage was the 'stuff of fairytales'. I knew that there was no way that my mother would ever have admitted that there were problems in her marriage. So, I wept for her too, and the sadness of it all. However, mostly, I wept for myself. I had lost my family and my dearest friend, and that friend had become my stepmother! At that moment, I couldn't see how I was ever going to endure such changes in my life. I lay there on the bed, sobbing and think-ing, trying to get hold of the enormity of what had happened. I thought back to when Edwina and I first met, and remembered wonderful, happy times, and then I jumped ahead to the fact that Edwina was going to be married to my father the next day. It was excruciating.

Papa rang the following morning, but I didn't speak to him. Spence answered, and had a very brief conversation, during which Papa told him that he and Edwina were, indeed, husband and wife, and that they 'felt very good about it.' He also thanked us for the flowers. They were leaving again that afternoon for Cap d'Antibe, and would be returning in April, so would be gone for 3 months. I was glad that they would be far away. I didn't hear from either of my brothers, nor did I expect that I would. I suspected that they would be visiting Edwina and Papa in France during their stay, and I was correct. I learned later that they traveled to France

as a foursome, and spent two weeks there in March. That didn't matter
to me either. Nothing did. In fact, I slid into a terrible depression. At my
lowest point, I even considered suicide. Papa laughed when I told him I
had those feelings, and later said he knew I'd never do it. It was cruel. I
suspected that Edwina had convinced him that any mention of such an act
was simply some sort of manipulation on my part. The problem with that
sort of thinking was that nobody could have cited any possible reason I
might have for such manipulation. Was I supposed to be threatening such
a horrible act with the hope that it would keep my father from marrying
Edwina? Was it a means to frighten my family? Or, was it a true cry for
help to the people I wanted to understand my pain? I've grown to learn
that such cries for help are never to be taken lightly. I believe that I had
reached a point where I had no desire whatsoever to die, but the pain of
living was becoming too hard to bear. It was wonderful luck that I was
already seeing a psychiatrist, as I certainly needed one. Plus, the additional
blessing of having a husband who understood my ghastly problems made
an enormous difference. Still, it all took time.

Chapter Eight

APRIL, 1948

ILLNESS

In April, I felt strong enough to attempt to see my father. I had literally lived in a bottomless pit for four months. As I talked out my feelings with Dr. Avery, I grew stronger, and my resolve to once again be the cheerful, strong, resilient person I had always been returned. I rang Papa upon his return from Cap d'Antibe. He seemed genuinely glad to hear from me, and I was hopeful that we might be able to resume some sort of rapport. I knew it would be a long and difficult road back, and I had no illusions that we could have more than a polite, but hopefully friendly relationship. Spring was upon us, and summer was fast approaching. That had always been my favorite season. As trees began to bud, and flowers poked their heads through the ground, I realized that the England of my youth was still there…that Hitler's wish to ruin us, and to take away the splendor that defined our delightful country had failed. We had suffered and we had faltered, but we had never fallen and matters were improving daily, both for me and for my country. I suggested during my conversation with my father that he and Edwina meet Spence and me in London for dinner and theatre.

"Sophia that's very thoughtful of you, and I wish we could," he replied. "But, I've been experiencing some health problems, and I'm afraid I'm not able to travel at the moment."

"What do you mean, 'health problems?" I asked.

"Toward the end of our stay in France, I was about to cross the street one day, when my legs just went out from under me. They felt rubbery, as though they were going every which way. I couldn't control them. I sat down for a few moments on a bench, and then my entire left side went numb. I was not able to continue. Edwina rang for an ambulance. According to the French doctors, I suffered a small stroke.

"Have you seen a physician back here in England?" I asked, with concern in my voice.

"Yes. When I returned to England, I contacted Dr. Hardwick. He has done some tests."

"What does he have to say?"

"Just that apparently I *did* suffer some sort of disruption in blood flow to my brain. It was probably a small stroke."

"What sorts of tests did he conduct?"

"Oh, nothing much. Strength tests. He listened to the sides of my neck with the stethoscope. You know I don't understand this sort of thing, Sophia."

"I know, Papa," I replied. "Few people do." I was well aware that no one in my family was terribly knowledgeable about medical matters, and certainly Edwina would be of no help. She was a fervent non-believer in medicine, and didn't believe there was any such thing as illness. Mummy and I had always been the ones in the family who'd had a knack for medical subject matter. Then, of course, I was married to a physician. Probably one reason Papa was so pleased to hear from me, though he would never have admitted it, was that he was somewhat frightened and wanted reassurance from someone who knew something about medicine.

"Would you like me to have Spence ring you?" I asked. He seemed surprised that I would offer to have my husband ring him. Perhaps he thought Spence was completely fed up with him. If so, he truly didn't know my husband, and his tremendous capacity for forgiveness.

"That would be splendid, Sophia, if it wouldn't be too much of an imposition," he said.

"Not at all," I replied. "I'll have him ring you tonight.

"And, how have you been?" he asked.

"All right", I answered. "I'm seeing a psychiatrist in London for depression, and it seems to be helping."

"You're still feeling blue?"

"Papa, depression is more than the blues. It's really quite debilitating. It's difficult to explain. I have no energy, and nothing is appealing to me. Even Isabella doesn't give me the usual enormous joy. I don't sleep well, or I sleep too much, and the future seems very bleak to me."

"You shouldn't feel that way, Sophia. You have a good life. You need to think more positively."

"Papa, if it were a matter of simply thinking positively, I wouldn't need a psychiatrist."

"Well, does he say that you are mentally ill?"

"No, Papa. Not everyone who sees a psychiatrist is mentally ill. He says I am suffering from depression, brought about by happenings in my life. It is termed 'reactive depression.'"

"I suppose I'm the cause of this."

"I didn't say that, Papa. The causes are undoubtedly multiple, and I'm sure they go back a long way. There is no one to blame, and I'm getting help. I feel much better than I did."

"I don't think Edwina will think that you should be seeing a psychiatrist. She doesn't believe in such things."

"Papa, that is really of no concern to me. Perhaps you don't need to share this information with Edwina?"

"Oh, I couldn't do that. I share everything with Edwina."

"That's fine then, Papa. I don't care one way or the other."

"Well, I do hope that you'll be feeling better soon."

"Yes, thank you," I replied, rolling my eyes. We spoke of a few more innocuous things, like the weather and politics, and then the conversation ended. There is no question that I must have been doing far better emotionally, as I did not burst into hideous tears the moment I rang off. Instead, I rang Spence and told him the symptoms Papa had related to me. He said he couldn't tell much without knowing the results of tests, and suggested that I ring Papa back and ask him to contact Dr. Hardwick to give permission for Spence to contact him to discuss the case. I did so, without delay.

When Spence came home that evening, he said that he had spoken with Dr. Hardwick, and had a better idea of what we were dealing with. We sat out in the garden, as it was a lovely spring evening, and I was so enjoying being out-of-doors again. The daffodils and hyacinth were blooming, and Isabella played a game of jump-the-rope with her friend Holly.

"So, what did Dr. Hardwick say?" I asked.

"He told me of some other symptoms. In particular there is one which has him concerned."

"Which is that?" I asked.

"Your father has a heart murmur, and also the sounds in his carotid arteries, the ones in your neck on both sides that carry blood to the brain, don't sound as clear as they should. He also has an involuntary tremor. In other words, he shakes. Particularly his hands shake, and he cannot control the movement."

"What is that indicative of?"

"He may have Parkinson's disease, and also could be in danger of another, greater stroke?"

I felt fear grip my heart. "Oh my God, Spence. Isn't there something they can do to lessen the chance of that happening?"

"Not a lot. Dr. Hardwick will probably put him on a medication that thins his blood, which will help to ensure against blood clots. There is no treatment, Sophia. I imagine his diet will be altered significantly. No salt. Lots of fluid. Also, he should probably increase his exercise."

"Oh My God! If Papa suffered a severe stroke, it would be ghastly."

"Yes. It could cause total paralysis, speech impairment, any of a variety of handicaps, or, of course, death."

"What about the Parkinson's?"

"Gradual deterioration. Speech would eventually become impaired. Also movement."

"Spence, this is too much to bear. He was certainly terribly fatigued after Mummy died, and then he began to race round like a possessed person when he took up with Edwina again. I think he's never wanted to admit to himself that he isn't her age, and she's always been extremely high energy. The last thing he would want is for her to think of him as an old man."

"Sophia, I know it's tempting to place blame on Edwina, but there's just no way that's valid. If he has suffered a stroke, and is at risk for another, it's more likely due to hereditary factors. Do you know what his parents died of?"

"Not really. Heart problems, I think."

"Yes. That would fit. For the time being, I think you need to be circumspect when you speak with him. Dr. Hardwick is his attending physician, and he'll ascertain when the time is right to talk to him about what treatment is going to be followed."

Thus began a period of great difficulty. My relationship with Papa and even Edwina improved because I made certain that it did. I telephoned at least once a week, and tried very hard to be nice and amiable when speaking to both of them. If it was true that Papa was facing the very real possibility of another stroke, as well as the dastardly effects of Parkinson's disease, it was not a time for family in-fighting. The only trouble I had with Edwina during that time was that she still refused to believe that there could be anything physically wrong with Papa. She did not believe that disease existed, so it was useless to try to talk to her. The summer limped along in such a fashion, and I knew that Spence and I needed to go to *Willow Grove Abbey* to see my father, but I suddenly became very avoidant, and kept thinking of excuses for why it would not be a good time to visit. Perhaps I too, did not want to know the truth. Finally we made the decision to visit Papa in November. It had been over a full year since I had seen him and my first visit since his marriage to Edwina. Thus, Spence and I drove down to *The Abbey* on a raw, windy November day. The trees were barren, the landscape bleak, and my feelings matched the scenery about us. We left Isabella in Nan's care, since we weren't certain of Papa's condition or whether or not he would be up to having a teenager in the house. When we arrived, it felt very strange to walk into the house for the first time since Edwina had made it hers. *She had definitely made it her own.* Gone were the pale, pastel colors which Mummy had so loved, and the lovely puddle draperies of taffeta, silk and velvet. Edwina's decorating style went toward the very modern, and there really was no one color scheme. The windows were hung with pleated drapes of chartreuse linen. There were still some pieces that had belonged to Mummy scattered throughout the house, including several French Bibelot cabinets, filled with her collection of Lalique crystal animals. I had been with my mother when many of them were purchased. There was also a lovely, old marble topped console table in the Great Hall, which had been in the family for generations, as well as the Waterford Crystal chandelier that had adorned the entry hall for as long as I could remember. I tried very hard to be friendly, but seeing Papa for the first time was hard. He didn't look at all well. He'd aged terribly in such a short time, and was walking with a cane. When we sat down to talk, it was clear that he had some difficulty pronouncing certain words. He was worse than I had expected, and had obviously been putting up a good front when I had spoken with him on the telephone. I now learned that he had suffered several more small strokes.

We had arrived at just about tea time and Edwina had the cook prepare a nice meal. Papa had little appetite, and Edwina was watching her weight. I noticed that no particular attention seemed to have been paid to altering the salt level in the food; in fact, we had a starter of French Onion Soup, which was *quite* salty. After we ate, Papa went to bed early and Edwina, Spence and I sat in the drawing room, talking. I was extremely uncomfortable, but tried hard not to show it. Edwina poured herself a martini, and asked what Spence and I would like. Spence asked for a glass of Port, and I, a glass of Sherry. The conversation was satisfactory, but for the fact that Edwina had a bit too much to drink, and got somewhat belligerent. She began to tell me about *my* grandmother, Mummy's mother, and of how she was a difficult woman, who made everyone's life a living Hell. I was angered by her comments, but bit my tongue. I had loved my Gran dearly, as had all of the children in our family, and had no recollection whatsoever that she was the difficult person Edwina was describing. This had to be another tale of Papa's. *In addition, who in the world was Edwina, to be telling me about my own grandmother?* Then the subject changed to, of all things, alcoholism. Edwina considered herself an expert on the subject, because an acquaintance in France had been so afflicted. According to her, it was a weakness of the spirit, which could simply be overcome with more positive thinking. That is what *all* disease was. Neither Spence nor I argued, as it would have been pointless. Next, the conversation turned to the 'wonderful, fabulous year' that Papa and Edwina had enjoyed together. This was a bit unrealistic, given that he had been ill for at least a third of it. Apparently Edwina wasn't letting that get in the way of their happy life.

They still kept social engagements, following a full schedule, and it had to be terribly hard for a man who had such difficulty getting about and conversing. Still, I knew that Papa would never have said that he didn't feel up to socializing. Finally, Spence put an end to the evening, saying that he was tired from having worked all day, and then driven some three hundred kilometers, so we gracefully retired.

The next day was Edwina's birthday, and we were planning to dine out. We slept late, and then had brunch in the dining room. Edwina and Papa were already up, so it was just Spence and I in the dining hall, for which I was thankful. We spent the day lounging about the house, looking at old photo albums and pictures from the new villa in France, which looked lovely. I didn't mention my brothers, nor did Papa or Edwina. At about five o'clock we all dressed for dinner. I wore a crème colored silk dinner dress, with a jewel neckline, cap sleeves, wide belt, and very full skirt. It was a new Dior, and the look was fast becoming the rage all across the globe. Edwina complimented me on it. She also wore a Dior, with polka dots on a white silk background, with a halter top and cinched-in waistline. I vowed to try my hardest to make it a nice evening. Papa and Edwina took us to a club in Bristol, to which they belonged. The setting was lovely, beside the sea, and we had a table where we could watch the waves lap upon the shore beneath the windows. Papa started the conversation by asking Spence what he was going to do now that his Residency at Maudsley was ending. That time had arrived.

"Sophia and I haven't spent a great deal of time talking about it. Of course, I could stay on at Maudsley, as Sir Aubrey needs help desperately. The hospital is growing by leaps and bounds, and this new National Health Service scheme is really going to put the work load on them. But, I've a mind to strike out on another adventure."

"What sort of adventure, Spence?" Edwina asked.

"Well, my ideal would be to direct my own mental health facility. I'd like to put into practice everything I've learned under Sir Aubrey, and some other theories that I'm keen on. I'd particularly like to concentrate my efforts upon mental issues that men are still suffering from the effects of the war."

"Is that a possibility?" Papa asked.

"Yes Sir, it's possible. I may be offered a Directorship at a Hospital. In fact, I suspect that I shall be, but I don't want to get into solely doing administrative work. I never want to lose my ability to work with patients, which is what brought me into the field to begin with."

"I should think there's more money to be made in administration." Papa commented.

"Perhaps, but that isn't my only motivation, Sir." Spence answered. Papa frowned, and turned his attention to me. "Sophia, I know you don't like to talk about Blake, but I have to tell you that I was very impressed a couple of weeks back, when he had a group of his old school chums visit him, and brought them here to the Abbey to see me. You know, each and every one of those boys has been very successful in life. I don't believe that there is one who hasn't become a millionaire."

"That isn't necessarily my definition of success Papa," I answered, wishing we could stay away from the subject of money.

"Well, Sophia," said Edwina, "We are talking about money making a person successful. That's what your father is trying to tell you."

"I understand what he's trying to say, Edwina. I just don't happen to agree with his definition of success. I think Spence is a far greater success than any of Blake's friends, and believe me, I know all of them." I didn't mean to sound negative or hostile, but I was so very tired of hearing about money being equated with success. Every time Blake and Papa got together all they discussed was the size of their stock portfolios. It always seemed that they were trying to outdo one another. Spence had told me that he got very tired of listening to them. Then for some unfathomable reason, I tasted a spoonful of vichyssoise, and began to weep. I honestly didn't know why I was weeping. Later, Dr. Avery told me that it probably wasn't just one thing, but rather a combination. It was the first time I had been with Papa and Edwina socially; it was Edwina's birthday, and I remembered ones we had celebrated together at *Ashwick Park*; happy times, when we were young. Now, there was the usual talk of money, which grew so very, very tedious, and through it all, there was Edwina sitting at the head of the table, being addressed as 'Countess Somerville' by the waiter. I got up, excused myself and went to the ladies room. Of course, Edwina followed.

"*Now* what is the matter with you?" she almost shouted, while she pounded her fist on the top of the sink basin.

"I'm sorry, Edwina. I wouldn't ruin your birthday for anything. It just seems such an untenable situation. Suddenly I felt overwhelmed."

"Look, Sophia, *deal with it*! I'm tired of your sniveling. The only important thing here is your father. It doesn't matter what I think of you or what you think of me. We both care about him. I think we have to make a bigger effort to put aside our differences and concentrate upon him." It was one of the few wise things that Edwina ever said, and I certainly could not disagree with her.

"I'll try harder, Edwina," I answered. I powdered my nose and we returned to the table. However, no sooner had we sat down, but the weeping began again. Edwina looked disgusted and even Spence seemed a bit put out with me. I felt absolutely ghastly. We finished the meal in silence and left the Club. All of the way home no one spoke, and when we entered the house, everyone went their separate ways. Spence and I collapsed into bed and he was asleep before his head touched the pillow. I, on the other hand, didn't sleep a wink all night long. I tossed and turned, trying to analyze why I had acted so beastly. I was angry with myself, and felt very guilty. When dawn lighted the windows, I tiptoed into the bath, washed my face and brushed my teeth. Then, I slipped into a dressing gown and went in search of Papa. I knew that he would be awake reading the *Times*, probably out in the garden. Sure enough, there he was, sitting at a table in the garden, concentrating on the newspaper. I went to him and kissed his cheek.

"Good morning, Papa," I greeted him.

"Good morning, Sophia," He answered, in a flat, emotionless tone.

"Papa, we need to talk," I said. He continued with his reading, and did not look up.

"I don't know what we have to talk about," he replied.

"Papa, please. Did we ever have these bad times until recently?" I asked. My purpose was to go on and tell him why I thought the entire family was falling apart, and I had no intention of placing the entire blame on Edwina. Nevertheless, he wouldn't give me the chance to speak.

"I recall that you called me 'beastly' and pushed me, and that was long before Pamela died."

He was referring to the time when I had visited my parents to discuss the possibility of a thirty-fifth anniversary party for them, when Mummy had called me '*crazy*' and Papa had taken her side. "Oh, Papa, why do you do this? That is so unfair. You know what the circumstances surrounding that incident were." Just at that moment Edwina rounded the corner of the house, where she'd apparently been hidden all along, listening to our exchange. I looked up and asked if she would mind leaving me alone with my father for a few minutes. Edwina stunned me when she answered.

"Yes, I should mind very much," she said.

I simply sat there, staring at her. After a few moments, I regained my poise and answered back. "Well, it appears that the person I tried to talk to back at *Willow Grove Abbey*, when Mummy learned of your disgusting affair, has returned."

"Yes," she replied. "And I'm in charge now, so you'd better get used to it."

"In charge? In charge of what?" I asked. "I'll speak to my father whenever and wherever I want, Edwina."

"Then I'll throw you out of my house," she replied. Papa had obviously put Willow Grove Abbey into her name. Her comment was proof of that.

"You can't keep me from seeing my father," I shouted. "You'll see me in a Court of Law."

"Ha! Try it. You won't have a leg to stand on. Everyone knows you aren't stable."

"Edwina," I said, trying to regain some self-control, "I came out here this morning because I wanted to apologize to Papa for my behavior last night. I don't even know why I started to cry. I have not slept at all, and I wanted him to know that I'm sorry. Why is it necessary for you to monitor every conversation I have with my father? Am I *always* wrong?"

Edwina didn't answer, and stormed into the house. I turned back to my father and said, "Are you just going to sit there and let her speak to me this way?"

"She's just protecting me," he answered.

"Protecting you? I'm your *daughter,* not some evil intruder! Papa, how can I possibly have a relationship with you if you won't listen to me, when it is absolutely clear that this nonsense about my not being 'stable' is being batted about? I'm perfectly stable. I've had some difficulty with depression. I wasn't given any time at all to grieve my Mother's death, and I admit that it's been very, very difficult for me to accept the enormous changes that have occurred in my life, but I'm sane and perfectly normal."

The door opened, and Spence came out, followed by Edwina. "Sophia, what is going on?" Spence asked. "Edwina came to our room and awakened me, saying that you're out here causing trouble." He was frowning deeply.

I was infuriated. Standing up, I shouted at Edwina. "Damn you Edwina Phillips. You are a liar and a sneak. You had no right to disturb my husband, and I am not the one who is causing trouble. If you'd simply left me alone with my father, everything would have been fine." Then, I turned to Spence and explained, word for word, what had taken place.

He scowled at Edwina. "What in the world possessed you to say such a thing to Sophia? That was totally uncalled for." He moved to my side and took me by the hand. "Come, Sophia. This isn't going to work out, and I think we'd better leave." I followed him into the house, to our room, and swiftly packed our belongings. When we came down the stairway, I could hear Papa and Edwina's voices in the library. I took a deep breath and walked to that room, feeling that I couldn't leave without saying a goodbye to my father, as he was ill, and I didn't know when I would see him again. As I entered the library, Edwina stood and faced me, hands on hips.

"By the way, Sophia. My name is *not* Edwina Phillips. It is Countess Somerville. *Do not* forget it."

"Edwina, you may be a member of this family, as far as my father is concerned, but I shall never think of you that way."

"Then you'll be barred from the door."

"That means a lot", I retorted, "Coming from "the 'wild woman in bed'""

"What is that supposed to mean?" Edwina asked.

"Ask my father, Edwina. He's the one who told it to me," I answered. I knew that I should not have said it, but Edwina had pushed me to the limit. Now, it was Papa's turn to be infuriated. He did not like Edwina being told something that he'd said about her when he thought their relationship was over. I never had any doubt that it was true, and was sure Edwina knew that Papa had said it.

"That's enough, Sophia. You keep your mouth shut," he shouted.

"I'm sorry, Papa. However, this is very unfair, and I don't understand why you expect me to take any arrows Edwina wants to sling in my direction, without striking back. Spence and I are leaving. I came to say goodbye. I love you, and I'm worried about you. I hope that I'm able to see you again without this kind of row. Nevertheless, I'll never set foot in this house again as long as Edwina lives here. I shall come to *Bedminster-with-Hartcliffe*, but stay at an Inn." I leaned over, kissed him, turned, and walked out of the room and out of *Willow Grove Abbey*. I wept all of the way home. It seemed that all I did during those days was weep. Spence was a brick, as usual, but there really wasn't much he could do. I could tell that he was angry by the firm set of his jaw, but he stayed calm and spoke reasonably.

"Sophia, the important person here *cannot* be Edwina. Your father is ill, and he's undoubtedly going to get worse. You don't want to be placed into a position where you aren't able to see him. We don't know how much longer he'll be able to communicate by telephone, and I can assure you that he'd not be able to write very well now."

"Oh God, Spence. What am I to do? He's married to that little money-grubber, and she won't even recognize that he's ill. I feel so helpless. And, there's no sense in calling Blake or Andrew, as you know what that situation is like."

"I know darling. Things just couldn't be much worse, could they?" He replied, reaching over and patting my arm. We drove the rest of the way in silence, but when we arrived home, we learned that things could, indeed, get very much worse.

Chapter Nine

May, 1948-July, 1948

More Illness

I did not hear from either Papa or Edwina for several weeks. I tried to ring them, but was always told that they were out, or resting. Then, one day as I returned from running errands, the telephone was ringing as I walked into the house. Isabella was upstairs taking a bath and Nan was undoubtedly in her own rooms. I ran to the telephone and answered. It was Edwina's voice.

"Well, Sophia. You'll be delighted, I'm sure, to hear the latest news," she began.

"What on Earth are you talking about, Edwina. What news?"

"It seems the doctor has found a mass on my x-rays."

"Whatever do you mean? When did you have x-rays taken? This so surprised me, as Edwina was known to never have seen doctors and to my knowledge she had never had a complete physical examination. Moreover, no one had said a word about her health or any x-ray examinations.

"Your father made me go to the doctor some weeks ago, as I've been experiencing some pain in my arm at night. I think it's nothing. I've been doing gardening and probably overdid. Nevertheless, Nigel made me go, and Dr. Hardwick took x-ray pictures of that area and my chest and I don't know what all."

"And you say he's found a mass? What sort of mass? And where?" I asked, aghast.

"It's all up and down my chest area. He says it wraps around my aorta, whatever that is, and covers most of both of my lungs. He wants to see x-rays I've had earlier in my life, so that he can compare them, but I've never had any done."

"For God's sake Edwina, this could be very serious. Did he explain what could be the cause of what he's seeing?"

"He just says that there's a mass, and that it shouldn't be there."

"What does he suggest you do about it?"

"He's sending me to some sort of a specialist. I think this is all a bit overblown. I feel perfectly fine. He took about a gallon of blood from my arm."

"Edwina, can you put Papa on, please?" I asked.

"Yes, yes. He's right here."

"Papa? Papa, are you there? "

"Yes, Sophia." He replied, speaking very slowly, and slightly garbled.

"Papa, what is going on with Edwina? This sounds very bad. Have you spoken to Dr. Hardwick?"

"Yes. I was with her when she got the x-ray results." He seemed unable to say much, because apparently Edwina was right next to the telephone.

"Papa, are they suspecting that what they've found is a tumor?" I put my hand to my forehead, as the beginning of a headache emerged.

"Yes, Sophia. Almost definitely."

"Do you think it may be lung cancer?" I asked, shivering as I said the word.

"It seems likely, and very advanced."

"Oh Papa, what can Spence and I do to help? Where is Dr. Hardwick sending her?"

"To a specialist in London. I don't think I'll be up to making the trip with her. Perhaps you could accompany her. She'll need someone who can understand the medical jargon."

"Yes, yes, of course, I'll go with her. When is her appointment?"

"The day following tomorrow. She can drive over to your place, and then perhaps you could drive to London."

"That would be fine, Papa. On the other hand, if she doesn't feel up to driving, I'll be glad to fetch her. Just let me know what you want me to do." We concluded the call, and I turned to Spence. I was white as a sheet.

"What is it darling? You look as though you've seen a ghost," he said.

"Spence, you aren't going to believe this. That was Papa and Edwina. Papa made Edwina go to the doctor a few days ago, as she's been complaining of a pain in her arm. Apparently, the doctor telephoned just a while ago. Unbelievably, she has never undergone an x-ray of her chest or lung area."

"I believe it," Spence replied.

"Well, believe this! They've found a mass that sounds enormous, taking up most of her chest cavity. My God Spence, could she have cancer?"

"It's entirely possible. You know she's a heavy smoker. I've always thought bloody cigarettes are a trigger in some people. I'm very glad I quit after the war. At any rate, what is Edwina going to do?"

"Dr. Hardwick has recommended a specialist in London. I assume a cancer doctor. And then, well, who knows? I offered to help in any way I can. I guess I'm going to take her to the specialist, since it's terribly difficult for Papa to get round."

"My God, Sophia, what next? No one would have dreamed something like this would happen in a million years. Here is your father, dealing with the after-effects of a stroke, with the very real fear that another one could strike, plus the added diagnosis of Parkinson's, and now Edwina has possibly been afflicted with cancer."

"Spence, if this tumor is that large, how long could she have had it?"

"There's no telling, without knowing what type of cells they are, or what the primary site of origin was. My guess would be that she's had it a long time."

"I know this is a stupid question, but what do you think the odds are of her being cured?"

"Darling, I haven't the foggiest, given the small amount of information we have. But, you know as well as I do that cancer is the one of the least treatable of all diseases. If it's inoperable, I suppose they might try some radiation, or some of the new chemotherapy that's being done with some success. It depends on whether it's metastasized to other organs."

I began to weep. "Oh God, no matter what Edwina has done, and no matter how angry I've been at her, I never would have wished something like this upon her," I sobbed.

"I know that darling, and so does Edwina. Now put that sort of thought right out of your head. You've offered to help, and we both shall, and then all we can do is pray that it isn't as bad as it sounds right now. You know how Edwina tends to dramatize and be somewhat histrionic. Let's wait and see what the doctors say."

Two days later, I retrieved Edwina from *The Abbey* and we headed to London, to see a Doctor named Eccles, who was supposed to be well known and highly thought of in the field of oncology. Edwina seemed in remarkably good spirits for someone who had very probably been handed a death sentence, but then, she was the girl who did not believe in negativity. When we arrived at the physician's office, I parked the car and met Edwina inside of the waiting room, where she was filling out a myriad of forms. Most required that she answer questions about her past medical history, and of course, she had none. I knew that the doctor was going to find her a challenge, to say the least. I asked the nurse if I could accompany Edwina into the examining room, and the nurse said that would be fine. I was glad that I could be present, as I suspected, rightly so, that Edwina would simply not understand the gravity of the situation she faced. After she had undressed and slipped into a simple cotton gown, the doctor entered the room. He was in his middle fifties, with gray hair and horned rimmed glasses. There was a kindly look about him. After shaking hands and introducing himself, he sat down and looked at the x-rays that Dr. Hardwick had sent to him. Then, he stood, and began to manipulate Edwina's upper chest area, paying particular attention to the area around the lungs and heart. He also checked underneath her arms and along the sides of her neck. Then, he had her lie down, and he felt of the various internal organs in her abdominal cavity. Finally, he said he wanted to get some more x-rays, and she was shepherded off down a hallway, where they took pictures of her lower torso, as well as the chest area again. When all of this was finished, she returned to the small examining room, where I waited. Shortly thereafter, Dr. Eccles re-entered.

"Countess Somerville, we have quite a dilemma on our hands, I'm afraid," he began.

"What sort of a dilemma?" Edwina asked.

"My dear, you have what appears to be advanced cancer. I should say most likely stage four carcinoma of the lungs, and also a large mass, probably also stage four, on the kidney. I don't know which the primary site of origin was. In other words, it may have begun in the lung and spread to the kidney, or vice-versa. Or, more rarely, but possibly, we may be dealing with two separate cancers."

"What difference does it make?" Edwina asked.

"Different sorts of cancers are known to respond to different forms of treatment. Unfortunately, we have no good ways of knowing what sort we are dealing with, unless we go in and do exploratory surgery, which I think we will probably have to do in your case. But, it has to be done gingerly, as sometimes surgery can cause the cancer to spread more wildly."

"Can't you just cut it out?" Edwina asked.

"It's not that simple. The tumor in your chest area has completely filled the cavity, and is wrapping itself around the main artery that leads to your heart; the aorta. There's no way we can remove it with surgery."

"Well, I have two lungs and two kidneys. Can't you take one of each out, and I'll just get along with the other? Doctor, I simply need to know what my 'down-time' is going to be. How long will I be out of commission?"

"Madam, I don't think you grasp the seriousness of your situation. We are talking here of seriously advanced cancer, which, in all probability has spread to other organs as well."

"Do you mean that it's going to take a long time to recuperate?"

"I mean, Madam, that you are quite possibly terminal."

"Terminal? You mean you think I have a disease that is going to kill me?"

"That is absolutely correct. We may be able to buy you some time with surgery, radiation and chemotherapy, but I have to be honest with you. The chances of a cure are very remote."

"Well, I just don't accept that. I simply don't. I don't believe in negative thoughts. Just do whatever it is you have to do, and I believe that I can bring my body back into its natural harmony and it will right itself."

"Countess Somerville, I think you need to be referred to someplace where the very latest treatments are being tried. I can get you into an experimental program. I would suggest Sloan-Kettering, a clinic in New York City."

"New York City? That's half way round the world! Are you mad? Surely we have doctors here in Britain who can do the same thing."

"Not necessarily, Madam. At the clinic in New York they are trying some new and innovative techniques. After you've had a series of treatments there, I can continue on with the treatment here in England. But, you would have to go there initially, to be enrolled into an experimental program."

Edwina got up from her chair, as though terminating the conversation. "Well, I'll have to think about all of this. I don't know that I can be traipsing all about the world. I have a husband who's ill, and I need to be home."

"Countess Somerville, if you do not get the treatment you need, you are not going to be at home or anyplace else. I don't know how much more clearly I can state that."

"Come, Edwina," I said. "We're taking up this man's time. We'll discuss this with Papa and Spence. Perhaps they can make you see what needs to be done," I said, putting out my hand and motioning for her to follow me. I thanked the doctor, and told him we would be in touch with him in a short time. He looked rather disgusted. When we were back in the car, Edwina began to rant about how she didn't believe that she had cancer.

"How do they know? Just from looking at some fool image? It could be anything. Maybe I have some sort of allergy. They haven't actually looked at the tissue. It could be perfectly normal." She was in complete denial.

"I think they see enough of this, Edwina that they know what they're talking about. But, that's why he wants you to go to New York. Apparently, they are the best in the world. I imagine they'll do a biopsy. They'll take some of the tissue out and study it under a microscope. Edwina, you must take whatever chance you have. It's daft not to go to the best, when you can afford it. I'll be happy to make the trip with you."

"Oh, yes I'll bet you would. I'm sure I can count on *you* to take care of me. *You'd* like nothing better than to see me dead. For all I know, you put this curse on me. You wished negative thoughts about me!"

"Now Edwina, that's plain nonsense. You know better than that. I'd never wish this for you or anyone else. I've made no secret of the fact that

I was greatly hurt by your deception and betrayal, but I would never, ever, want you to be ill. I can't believe you'd even say such a thing."

"Well, it seems pretty strange to me that I've never been sick a day in my life until now."

"Edwina, I'm not going to argue this with you. When we get to *Willow Grove Abbey* please listen to what Papa suggests. You know that he'll want what is best for you. Do you promise you'll do that?"

"Yes, I'll listen to what Nigel says, but who's going to take care of him while I'm in New York?"

"Edwina, we can always get a nurse to come in. Of course, I'll do all I can too. You'll be gone just long enough to get on with the treatment regimen you require. If more help than I can provide is needed, we can always get a nurse.'""

We arrived at the *Abbey* and Edwina exited the car almost before it had come to a halt. It was clear that she had no intention of asking me to come in. I would have to ring my father later, to make certain that he'd been told the entire story. Back at my own home, I paced the floors, trying to absorb the beastly situation the family was facing. Chances were ninety nine percent to one that we were going to lose both Edwina and Papa. It almost seemed like a race against time, as to who would be the first to go. Spence was at the hospital, and I wanted to know more about the options available. Therefore, I trudged down to the small branch library in our village, searching amongst the shelves until I found medical journals dealing with strokes, cancer and Parkinson's disease. I felt that I had a fairly decent understanding of stroke, but was still totally ignorant about cancer, and also knew very little about Parkinson's. I especially wanted to know what the prognosis was, in terms of survival time. I found a medical journal article focusing on the latest research done. It was not encouraging. Stage four cancer was the worst, and carried a very grave prognosis. A lot seemed to depend upon the types of cells involved. I also was not at all reassured by what I read about Parkinson's. I left the library empowered with more information, but feeling extremely despondent. That evening, Edwina rang me, and said that she'd decided to make the trip to the States. Apparently, Papa had been able to get through to her. I told her that I would accompany her, but she said that she wouldn't need me, as her sister, who lived in Greenwich, Connecticut, was meeting her in New York and would be with her. I had to admit that I was relieved. I hoped that Edwina's sister had a decent understanding of medical matters, as I knew that the poor American doctor was in for a difficult time. Edwina left two days later. It was three weeks before Christmas. I took her to Heathrow and stayed until she boarded her airplane. Then, I headed straightaway to *Willow Grove* to have a chat with my father. I didn't know how many opportunities I would have to do so in the future. When I arrived at my old family home, I found my father in the library, sitting in his wheelchair, reading the newspaper. He'd just recently made the transition to a wheelchair and detested it. I tried to put on a sunny face upon entering the room.

"Hallo, Papa. I got Edwina on her way safely, and thought I'd pay you a short visit before returning home. How are you feeling today?"

"About the same. I'm not going to feel better." He sounded despondent.

"Papa, if you will follow all of the doctor's advice very stringently, I think there is every reason to believe you will improve. It isn't good for you to just sit all day. Do you try to go outside at all? Are you staying away from salt?"

"No, Sophia. Edwina doesn't believe in changing our routine. I'm more concerned about Edwina than I am for myself. It's just unbelievable that this has happened. Of course, she keeps herself in a constant state of denial, and I just go along with it, but I'm worried sick. It's inconceivable to me that your mother died of cancer, and then I marry Edwina, who is so much younger than I am, and now *she* has it."

"Papa, she'll be getting the best help available. If anyone can help her, they'll do it in New York. They're starting to do some interesting things. Unfortunately, Edwina waited such a long time to see the doctor. You know her views on medicine. I'm afraid that's her biggest deterrent at this point. It may be too far advanced."

"I don't think there is any question that it is. I hope that they can buy her some time, but I suspect that I'll lose her before I go. I made all plans regarding my estate with the thought that she would certainly outlive me. Now that seems very unlikely. Remember, I've been through this before. Your mother died less than two months after her diagnosis."

That comment surprised me. "If you believe that Papa, you need to be making arrangements for what you'll do in the eventuality that you lose her. Of course, I hope you know that you're welcome to come to Spence and me."

"I would go to Blake. Not that I don't appreciate your offer, Sophia, but Blake was never able to spend as much time with me because of your mother, and I want him to have that opportunity now."

"Papa, I don't want to sound insensitive and please don't misunderstand what I'm saying, but I'm concerned about *Willow Grove Abbey*. I assume that you have put it into Edwina's name. If she should die, what will happen to the house?"

"It will come back to me. It's set up so that if I die first, it will be hers, and if she dies first, it will be mine. Then, if she should die after me, the house will revert to you children. That is an agreement we have between ourselves." This was not an easy conversation. It was not a pleasant subject. Of course, we'd had the horrific conversation about this once before, and I loathed the notion of once again discussing it. Plus, it seemed rather crass, considering the circumstances. However, I was always worried about when I would next be able to speak with him alone.

"What do you mean that you have an agreement between yourselves? Do you mean it still isn't written down?"

"No, it isn't. We decided that after I became ill. We saw no reason to re-do the entire Will."

"Papa, I don't mean to pry, and you can tell me that it is none of my business, but at one time you told me that you'd considered leaving *Willow Grove Abbey* to Kippy. From what you're saying now, I assume that's changed?"

"Yes. He's just a small child. It would be years before he would be able to assume the necessary responsibilities. In addition, after a lot of thought, I believe, as you do, that one of you older children may decide that you want to live here. Of course, if Kippy should want to live here someday, that will be his prerogative, as well. I'd expect any of you children to honor that wish."

"Have you ever come to a conclusion about whether Kippy is your son or not?" I asked.

"No Sophia, I haven't. There is just no way to know. He is a fine young chap though, and I would be very proud to have him as a son. Whatever you may think of Edwina, she has been a fine mother to him."

"I know that she loves him very much. What do you think she'll do regarding Kippy if something happens to her?"

"She will have her sister in the States adopt him. They are fine people, with good moral values and she would want him raised with the proper start in life. Of course, I intend to make certain that money is no object for Edwina, and Kippy will have the best of everything"

"Papa, I know you probably don't believe it, but I would take Kippy and raise him as my own, if that's what Edwina wanted. However, I suspect she wouldn't trust me to do that."

"Well, you must admit, you've beaten up on her quite badly at times, Sophia."

"Oh Papa, I'm not going to start this discussion again. Whatever has been is in the past. I'm not going to pretend that I like what Edwina did to this family, but I'm not so cruel as to take it out on an innocent child."

"Kippy will be fine if he is adopted by her sister. I think it might be better for him to have a fresh start in the States, where no one knows all of the history."

"Yes, you could very well be right there," I answered. "Papa, I'm sorry for any pain that I've caused you during this last year. It wasn't intentional. I just have had a very difficult time with the whole situation."

"I'm sorry too, Sophia. I should have listened to you more. You weren't wrong about everything. I've made mistakes."

I really did not know what he meant by that comment, but decided not to press for more details.

"There are things I've done in my life that I'm ashamed of, Sophia, and for which I need to ask forgiveness. I think you know what I'm talking about." I was stunned at his words. There was no question that he was referring to his abuse of me, and I didn't know how to answer him.

Finally, I replied. "Papa, I have loved you all of my life. As for forgiveness, well, I must say that your accepting responsibility for incidents I've never understood makes me feel much more able to give that."

"I know that, Sophia. I've never understood some things either. Perhaps the good Lord will help me to figure them out. *I am* sorry if I hurt you in any way."

I had tears in my eyes as I heard those words. Words that I'd never thought he would speak. "Well, I guess we've both hurt each other, at times, haven't we?" I answered. "I do want you to understand that I feel my love for you has been completely unconditional. I long ago forgave you, and have always loved you. But, your apology to me means more than mere words can ever say. You are ill, Papa, and I have no intention of going through it all again. There have been so many things I haven't and still don't understand. I believe I do have a much better understanding now, than I did even during the war years. More than anything you did to me as a child, I have had so much difficulty understanding why and how you could intentionally say and so some of the things you did, to my brothers, and to others, including Mummy, about my character, Papa. You've always known I'm not crazy as you've termed it. Yet, that word has found its way over and over down through the ranks of this family. If there is one question I wish you could answer for me, it would be that one."

"Sophia, I once told you that I'm a survivor. Perhaps you were right when you said that my strong wish to keep my reputation, was not what should have been termed survivorship. Not, when I was willing to let you suffer so that persons might not learn the truth about some of my evil actions. You were one hundred percent correct. I *was* terrified that you would tell your mother and everybody the truth about what sort a person I was am. And I was willing to paint you as mentally unstable, in order not to suffer the consequences of my actions. That was horrifically wrong."

"Papa, if you had come to me and been honest about your fears, I could have laid them to rest. While I couldn't and wouldn't have lied anymore about my feelings about Edwina and the appropriateness of your marriage, I would have assured you that I had no intention of smearing your reputation. I believe you, and everyone in this family, see me as a loose cannon. Perhaps my honesty has always been too much for this family. But, at no time did I have any desire to cause pain to anyone by being honest. Because of all of the pain from my past and from Mummy's actions too, I have a very difficult time coping with those sorts of feelings. If only we had learned somewhere along the way to learn to really talk to each other, without rancor and discord. At any rate, I'm sorry Papa if I added to your consternation. I could not lie anymore."

"Sophia, you don't need to apologize to me for anything. I've had a wonderful, wonderful life. I know that you think I haven't, what with your mother and all, but that isn't true. I loved her, and it wasn't all a lie. She did wear me down after a while," he mumbled, with a wry smile on his face, "But there were many happy moments. Don't ever feel sorry for me. I really don't know why I chose to marry Edwina. Had I known what I would be facing, I never would have done so. Part of the reason was that I knew I had disappointed her in the past. I made promises I couldn't, or perhaps didn't want to keep. I had hurt her badly too. I knew by marrying her after your mother died, I could at least rectify that wrong. Even persons who knew of my affair would likely think better of me if I married the person I'd been involved with. It seemed a good way to right a wrong. Edwina would be happy, and I would be looked upon as a gentleman again. And, I can't negate the fact that I did not want to be alone. Knowing that Edwina did love me, in her own way, I also knew that I could have a peaceful married life, which I had never had. Does any of this help you to understand better? I want you to go and live your life now." Tears filled my eyes and spilled over onto my cheeks, leaving shiny tracks.

"Oh Papa, I do feel better. Thank you. But, I don't want to lose you."

"Sophia, the Bible says that there is a time to be born and a time to die. My time is approaching. You won't be losing me. I shall be right here watching you blossom even more. You have grown into a beautiful woman. You have a top-drawer husband, and you're the most honest person I've ever known. You are wonderful mother and I am proud to have been your father. We'll be together again, Sophia." I bent down and put my arms around him, hugging and crying.

"Papa, from the way you are talking, I am getting the impression that you are becoming more spiritual. I should love to think that is true. I cannot imagine facing illness and advancing age without God to help you."

"Sophia, there is no question that I have become a strong believer. Your mother was never very keen on religion, you know. Even when Drew decided to become an Anglican Vicar, she was proud of him, but didn't really understand his beliefs. You know how your mother was… it angered her if she thought that someone felt like they were better than she, and she always felt awkward around Drew, or anyone who spoke about religion. She had a child's view of God. As though he knew she was not a Godly person. Which, of course, was true. But, I can honestly tell you, without trying to sound like too much of an evangelist, that I have definitely accepted Jesus Christ as my Lord and Savior. I hope I didn't start believing too late."

"Papa, as long as you have a breath left in your body, it is not too late. It makes me feel so much better to know that I will definitely see you again. Perhaps on the other side, we can get things right. I'm so sorry for the time we wasted. I should have let you do as you wished with Edwina. It all just hurt so badly. But, Papa, it still is not too late, here and now. If you would only follow the doctor's orders more stringently. Please. Whether Edwina does or does not believe in illness, what in the world can it hurt to try to change your diet, and make an attempt to walk a bit each day?"

"It's just that it takes a lot of energy to argue with her point of view. It's easier to agree."

"Papa. Edwina has been wrong about a lot of things. You know that. Can't you just understand that she is wrong about your illness too?"

"I know, I know. But you have no idea how stubborn she can be."

"Oh, but I think I do," I laughed ruefully. There was a length of silence. "Papa…is there no way that you can make my brothers understand that I am not the evil person they make me out to be?"

"Oh, Sophia. I don't know. I really don't feel like getting into all of it again. I don't think they really follow the entire story. I'll try to have Drew talk to you at some point. He is most likely to listen and understand."

"I would greatly appreciate that, Papa. It hurts terribly to know that my family thinks I am a wicked person, when I am not. Can't you make Edwina understand that her actions caused terrible, terrible pain? If she could only grasp how what she did hurt me. Don't you think it's possible for her to fathom that?"

"What she did was selfish and wrong. However, it was done. I'll make a bigger effort to ask the cook to prepare less salt in my meals, and I shall try to take a bit of a walk every day. But, Edwina has a lot to face now, and I am asking you to be there for her. I simply can't get into everything that went before. Perhaps if you try very hard to show her that you forgive her, she will stop being so defensive. She doesn't trust you, Sophia. Please don't disagree with her, or tell her that her thinking is wrong. She believes that causes her stress." There was no hope that anything would change.

"All right, Papa. I'll do whatever I can to help. If she had only gone to the doctor sooner. You know, the amazing part of all of this is that she always considered her mother to be such a fount of wisdom, and yet, in the end, it's her mother's negative beliefs about medicine that may kill her."

"That's absolutely right, Sophia, and it's a terrible tragedy. Edwina is not a bad person. She is misguided and places her emphasis upon material things that in the end are not very important. She is also still terribly immature. But, I'll stand by her, and try to be there for her as I promised, til death parts us."

Chapter Ten

Junе, 1948
A Dire Prognosis

While my conversation with my father was a big step in the right direction, I must admit that I was a little bit skeptical of everything that he had said. It was very unlikely that he had made such an abrupt about-face, and that he had become so deeply committed to God and confession of past wrongs. If I were to be completely honest with myself, I'd have to say that I believed there was a modicum of manipulation involved in what he was saying to me. Papa knew he was dying. No matter how much his wealth and power had insulated him against the truth, there was no way those blessings could help him now. He was still frightened that I would tell people the secrets he had so carefully protected, after he was gone. A way to avoid that happening would most likely be an apology to me, a plea for forgiveness, and acceptance of a Christian philosophy. He knew very well that I was capable of a good deal of forgiveness. There was no way of knowing whether what I suspected was true, and it really didn't matter anymore. For his own sake, I hoped that what he had said was sincere.

Edwina returned home from the States twelve days later. I met her at Heathrow, and she looked very good for someone with such a grave illness. She was dressed in an obviously new, black wool ensemble with a huge fringed hip sash, by Balenciaga. I complimented her upon it and she said that she'd spent a day shopping in New York before her return trip. I had passed the point where anything Edwina did surprised me.

"Were you able to see Kippy?" I asked.

"No, no. I don't want him knowing anything about this until I find out just what the future looks like for me. He is happy in school, and there is no reason to upset him, if it doesn't need to be done. I did have a long talk with my sister Grace, and her husband, Craig, and they both readily agreed that they would be thrilled to adopt Kippy if that is necessary. Kippy scarcely remembers his life in England. I don't want to upset his world, by dragging him out of school, and moving across the pond just so that I can have him nearby."

"Kippy is certainly aware that you have married again, and that you are a Countess, isn't he?"

"Yes, but not all of the details. I mean, not everything that has taken place up until now. I would prefer he not know everything. I don't want him growing up with hard feelings toward you, or your father, or anyone. If I get better, then he won't ever have to know those things. He only knows that I married an Earl, whose first name is Nigel. I never even mentioned that his name is Somerville. I don't believe Kippy will ever even meet Nigel. He's going downhill so rapidly, and I don't want my son to go through being expected to mourn for someone he never even knew."

"You wouldn't have Grace and Craig adopt him until you were no longer here, would you?"

"No. But, I've told them to go ahead with adoption proceedings immediately if anything should happen to me. That will also be left in my last instructions. He is going by the name of *Crawford* now, because they are the ones who oversee his needs at school, and to whom he returns on holidays now, and I want him to have a home where there is a father and a mother. Even if I beat this stupid cancer thing, I think he would prefer to be like the other boys, and have the same last name as his father. He doesn't really even go by 'Kippy' anymore. Apparently that isn't really an American name for Christian. Most of his friends call him Chris."

"So, what have the doctors in New York told you, Edwina? We've all been so terribly worried. What was their assessment of your condition?"

"They think its primary lung cancer that's spread to the kidney. I still question whether they aren't all wrong. I feel perfectly fine, for someone whose body they're wringing their hands over. They did some surgery, took some tissue for examination, and performed all sorts of tests, with strange, gruesome machines. They even had a machine that looked at the inside of my brain."

"Your brain? Do they suspect that the cancer has spread to that area?" I asked.

"I don't know. They're going to send a report to Dr. Eccles, in London. When the man was administering the brain test, he asked me if I'd ever had a stroke. Of course, I told him that I had a stroke awhile back, so if he was seeing something in my brain that was probably it."

"What? Edwina, you've never had a stroke! What are you talking about?"

"Yes, I did, a few years back. It's of no account. It was a 'good stroke'."

"What is a 'good' stroke?" I asked, practically ready to tear my hair out at Edwina's obtuse answers. "Did you go to a doctor at the time? Was there any permanent damage as a result of this stroke?"

"No. As I said, it was a 'good' stroke."

"Edwina, please tell me exactly what happened," I said, gritting my teeth as I maneuvered the car through a roundabout. Edwina sighed, as though the question was inane. "It was when I was in New York City, after I'd left England with Kippy. I was brushing my hair and felt a strange sort of buzzing in my head. I had a lie-down on the bed for a few moments, and it passed. Then, I got up and placed a call to my mother. I asked her what she thought it might have been."

"Why would you have called your mother? Why not a doctor?"

"Sophia, you know better than anyone else that our family has never believed in illness. Therefore, we have never gone to doctors. Mum has always been the knowledgeable one in the family about such matters."

"I see," was all I could manage as a response.

"And so, Mum said that what I'd experienced was a 'good stroke.' Of course, she's frightfully knowledgeable about the human body and symptoms that can result from lack of harmony. It was a release of negative energy through the top of my head."

Oh Dear God in Heaven! When did Edwina become a demented person? Was this the cancer speaking?

Of course, I didn't argue with her. Instead, I changed the subject to whether the doctors in America felt that they could help her situation.

"They've started me on a treatment regimen. I will have to go weekly to the doctor here, and he will put medicine into my arm through a needle drip. I'm not at all happy about this, Sophia. They told me that I'm probably going to lose all of my hair."

"Edwina, that's infinitely better than losing your life," I answered.

"Yes, I suppose so, but just the thought of being bald makes me sick. I suppose I'll have to have several wigs made."

"Yes, that would be a fine solution," I replied. "Do the doctors feel that this treatment has a good success rate? Are they optimistic, Edwina?"

"Well, it's experimental, you see. I don't think they really know. Apparently, it has shown promise. Honestly, Sophia, I still believe that if I can just avoid all stress and put my body back into harmony, everything will be fine."

"I know you believe that, Edwina, and I'm sure it's very good to think positively, but I'm terribly glad that you're in this program, as well."

"Well, it can't hurt, I suppose, although I don't like the idea of such poisonous drugs being put into my system."

"Sometimes things like that are necessary," I responded. We traveled the remainder of the way to Willow Grove Abbey in relative silence, for which I was thankful. When we arrived, I enquired as to whether Edwina wanted me to come inside with her, but she waved me off.

"No, No. You've done quite enough. I can deal with things from here. I'll explain everything to Nigel.

Poor Papa, I thought.

When I arrived back at St. James Road, Spence was already home and I was so glad to be able to talk everything over with him. He just shook his head when I related my conversation with Edwina.

"Spence, I don't remember Edwina being like this when we were younger. If she'd talked such odd thoughts, I don't think I ever could have been as close to her as I was."

"Perhaps the cancer has spread to the brain," he answered. "But, Sophia, I have to say that I never found Edwina to be a mental giant. Surely you must have always been aware that you run circles around her with your intelligence. Not just intelligence, but common sense, as well. "

"Yes, I suppose. My performance in school was always better, at any rate."

"Sophia, I suspect that the sorts of things young girls talk of don't include the kinds of topics we're now dealing with. Much of what I recall from your early relationship with Edwina was silly, girlish chatter. I don't mean to be demeaning, darling, but you know what I'm saying."

"Of course, you're absolutely right. We didn't have many deep conversations, now I think back. You know, I never even remember speaking to her about anything to do with religion."

"Sweetheart, you were young girls. I don't completely disagree with Edwina's belief in the power of thinking positively, and of avoiding stress and the like. The human mind can do wonders. Sometimes patients are given up as hopeless, and because of strong belief, they miraculously end up cured. It's good that she thinks in a positive manner, but I do think she carries it to a bit of an extreme."

"Oh, I certainly agree with that," I smiled. "I'm not certain where she comes by her beliefs. She never was a great reader. Not Edwina. From what I've seen, since she has lived at *Willow Grove*, there is *one* new book in the house, and it is a coffee table book on 'Chocolate.'"

We both looked at one another sadly, and ruefully smiled.

Isabella came into the parlor at that moment, and we changed the subject. Our little girl was fast becoming a young lady. She was about to turn twelve years old, and it was clear that she was going to be a beauty. She still had that lovely, dark, thick hair, falling in masses of shiny curls, and her sapphire eyes were riveting. She'd always had high color in her cheeks, and her lips were the shade of pink rosebuds. She was still tiny, but was beginning to show signs of developing breasts. Isabella smiled when she entered the room and kissed me.

"Hello, Mummy. I didn't think you'd returned yet. How is everything at *Willow Grove Abbey*?" She asked.

Oh Isabella, not at all well. Grandfather has had to go to a wheelchair, and I'm afraid his wife is ill now too." I hadn't told Isabella anything about Edwina's condition, as I'd felt it better to wait until we knew more details.

Isabella knew very little about Edwina, just that her grandfather had re-married a younger woman. She had never even met her. She sat down on the sofa next to me, and I reached over and pinched her cheek. "I love you, beautiful, young lady," I smiled.

"Thanks, Mummy. I love you too," She answered, tossing her long hair over her shoulder.

"What have you been up to?" I asked.

"Well, actually, I've wanted to talk to you and Papa about something, but you've been so busy with Grandfather's illness, I haven't wanted to bother you."

"Darling, Papa and I are never too busy to talk to you, I hope you know that."

"I do, Mummy, but, still, it's been a rough patch, I know…"

"What do you want to discuss, Isabella?"

"Well, I want to talk to you about going to *Ashwick Park*. I know we've talked about it before, but no decision has been made."

"Darling, do you *want* to go to Ashwick Park?"

"Yes, Mummy, I do. Alexandra Stewart is going, and so is Holly Parsons. We've talked about it together. I think I'd be happy there." Alexandra and Holly were two of Isabella's closest friends and their commitment to *Ashwick Park* practically assured that Isabella would want to follow suit.

"You don't think you might become homesick, having to live away from Papa and me?" I asked.

"Of course, I'll miss you, but it isn't as though you'll be an ocean away. I can come home on weekends if I want."

"Yes, I suppose that's true."

"Papa, what do you think?" Isabella asked, turning to Spence.

"Isabella, you're only just turning twelve in August. Your mother didn't go away to boarding school until she was fourteen. If you go now, that will mean you'll spend six years away from home, before you leave Ashwick and go on to University, or whatever you intend to do. Are you certain you want to do this so soon? I think you should do whatever you truly want. But, I don't want you to go away to school because that's what your friends are doing. Nevertheless, if you truly want to experience what it's like to be at a boarding school, I've no objection to it. Ashwick Park is a fine school. Look at your Mummy." Spence smiled, glancing over at me, with great love in his eyes. I returned the smile. "I'd just like to see you wait at least a year."

"Oh, I'm not thinking of going until next year. That's when the others are enrolling. I'll be thirteen then. Do you think that would be all right? The school has a wonderful reputation, and I'd like to think I was carrying on a family tradition."

"Have you been in contact with the school," I asked?

"I wrote them and they sent me brochures and an application. I don't think I will have any problem with admission. My academic work is very good and I'm considered a legacy, what with Mummy having graduated from there. But, they don't take girls younger than 13, so I couldn't go until next year anyway. But, if you don't get your application in very early, it's very likely someone else will get your spot."

I thought about Isabella's going away to *Ashwick Park* and had to admit that it brought a lump to my throat. It seemed only yesterday that I was making the same plans. Isabella had not led the sheltered life that I had, but she was still so young and seemed terribly naïve. I wanted to keep her close and protect her from the pain that the world could offer, but I knew that she had to experience life on her own.

"Well, darling, then, if you're certain this is what you want, Papa and I will look over the brochures and application. We will do whatever is necessary for you to be admitted for the fall term in 1949."

Isabella jumped up and hugged me tightly. "Oh Mummy, you're the best. I hope I'm just like you when I grow up."

I hugged her back. "No Isabella, I want you to be just like *you*. You're special and unique. I want you to be your own original self. Go and enjoy a wonderful stay at Ashwick Park, but don't try to duplicate my school years. This is *your* time." I don't think that Isabella truly understood what I meant, but she nodded and then ran to her Papa, hugging him.

"This is so exciting. I'm going to ring Alexandra and Holly, this minute. They'll be so happy." With that, she skipped out of the room, black curls bouncing in her wake, and Spence and I smiled at one another. We were both thinking about another young *Ashwick Park* girl, and a summer night after she was presented at Court. He got up and walked over to me.

"You are still as lovely as you were when I met you, you know," he said, in a dreamy voice. "You're still the *Queen of Ashwick Park* as far as I'm concerned."

"I suspect not, darling, but I appreciate your saying so," I giggled.

"I think, that perhaps we should have a lie-down and discuss this further," he laughed, kissing me on the neck, and taking me by the hand. I, too, thought it a lovely idea, and so I called to Isabella and told her that her Papa and I were going to take a short rest, and we disappeared up the stairway. No matter what other problems we faced, we were still very deeply in love.

Meanwhile, on the twenty-fourth of June, a major international crisis began. During the multi-national occupation of post—World War II Berlin, the Soviet Union blocked the Western Allies' railway, road, and canal access to the sectors of Berlin under allied control. Their aim was to force the western powers to allow the soviet zone to start supplying Berlin with food, fuel and other aid, thereby giving the Soviets control over the entire city. In response, the Western allies organized the Berlin Airlift to carry supplies to the people in West Berlin. Aircrews from the United States, The RAF, The Royal Canadian Air Force, the Royal Australian Airforce, and the South African Airforce flew over 200,000 flights in one year, providing up to 4,700 tons of necessities flights in one year, providing up to 4700 tons of necessities daily, such as fuel and food to the Berliners. It was marvelous to see what our brave men were still capable of, and we shouted our encouragement aloud as we heard reports of the missions.

We began trying our best to be there for Edwina and Papa. I made trips back and forth to *Willow Grove Abbey* trying to see that both of them were all right. Thank God they now had a bevy of servants to look after them and all were true angels, for most had not been with them long, yet each performed their chores with more than the requisite energy necessary to collect a paycheck. The new Housekeeper's name was Mrs. Madison, and she seemed very competent, but nothing like our dear Nan. She was quite strong in her tone, and the other servants appeared to almost jump when she came into the room. The entire staff was very serious about the English unspoken rule that servants should 'not be seen nor heard.' In other words, they were somehow supposed to be invisible. Interestingly, there was a new butler, named *Sanford*, and also a Lady's maid named *Vera*. Apparently Papa's fortunes had risen again. Or Edwina's needs were much more important than Mummy's. No matter. I was quite glad to see a new and larger staff, as there were two ailing persons in the household. Papa had also added a new chauffeur, named *Winslow*. In my heart, no one would ever replace Joseph, but again, I was glad that there was someone who could drive to their doctor's appointments and other obligations. Of the two, Papa was definitely the one who required extensive assistance, since he continued to deteriorate, almost on a daily basis. Edwina, didn't look like she was ill, except that once a week she traveled to London to take her experimental treatments, and she *did* lose all of her hair. Of course, she immediately had several high quality wigs made from a fine establishment in London. One would not have known that anything was amiss, unless one knew her intimately, as I did. I was glad that Kippy was away at school, as it would have been a difficult thing for a child to observe, and it would have made matters more complicated if there'd been a young boy in the home.

One day, when Edwina was outside in the garden, I had another opportunity to talk with my father in private. It wasn't a long conversation, but it turned out to be profound. I entered the house and found him in his wheelchair, sitting by the fire, simply staring into the embers. I felt so badly for him, as it was not even possible for him to read anymore. He had difficulty turning the pages of a book, since his hands shook so. Finally, after an untold number of other tests, the doctors had reached the definite conclusion that not only had Papa suffered many small strokes, but that he was afflicted with Parkinson's disease. I hoped that Edwina was reading to him. The wireless was on in the room and that was his best form of entertainment in those days. Spence was looking into a new form of electronic media, called the television, and if it looked to be promising, we planned on making certain that Papa had one.

"Hallo, Papa," I said as I entered the room, bending down to kiss him. I never failed to be shocked at the change I saw from week to week and even day to day. It was so extreme. He looked terribly old and withered, and his eyes had a glazed, vacant look. He shook and trembled terribly. I knew, in my heart that there was no way he was going to live a great while longer. He smiled, as much as he was able, and I placed my hand on one of his. I had stopped asking how he felt, as I almost felt it an insult. It was just about completely impossible for him to speak anymore. I'd spoken with Dr. Hardwick, our family doctor in *Bedminster-with-Hartcliffe, and* asked his opinion of a prognosis. He told me that a recent, fine study, in keeping with Papa's age group, revealed that many patients only lived for months after presentation of symptoms. In fact, Edwina told me herself that the Neurologist that he had seen in London had rung them, and that Edwina had spoken to him. *That* doctor had said that he would probably die within sixteen months from the beginning of his symptoms! Edwina became very angry, and apparently told the physician that under no circumstances did she want Papa told that information. She believed it would take away all of his hope. *It also might have caused him to change his Will.*

"I saw Edwina in the garden," I remarked to him now. "It seems she's enjoying the nice weather. Your roses are breathtaking."

He tried to say something, but it was very difficult for me to understand him. I had to ask him to repeat it. Very slowly, he formed the words. "I…want…yellow roses…on my…casket," he said. I swallowed hard, and only just managed to stop the tears that formed behind my eyes.

"Then, you shall have yellow roses, Papa," I managed to say. He smiled. There was silence.

"Papa, you don't need to answer me, but I just need to tell you that I'm concerned about Edwina's mental state. She said some strange things to me when I collected her from Heathrow. She said she'd had a 'good stroke' years back, and of course, that is total foolishness. I'm only bringing this up because I fear the cancer is affecting her brain more than we know. If you have noticed similar oddities, then I need to make your nurses aware, so that they know to be wary of any orders she gives."

"Ahhhh…. Sophia. I've…heard…that…for…years," he managed to say in his garbled manner.

"You've heard it for years?"

He nodded his head. "You mean she's said this before…Has said it for years?

He nodded again. "Papa, didn't you realize that was insane talk?" I asked, in absolute amazement.

He nodded his head in assent. *Then why did he marry her? If anyone had told me that they'd had a 'good stroke,' I would have gotten far away, very quickly. Why, Why, Why??*

Nevertheless, it was not the time to ask such questions. The time for answers to questions such as this was over. He just shrugged his shoulders, as if to say 'It's beyond me'.

"It's all right, Papa. It doesn't matter now," I said. "Is there anything I can get or do for you?" I asked, although I knew it would be hard for him to tell me if there was.

"Elicitor," he replied. I could not understand what he wanted.

"Elicitor? Papa, I don't understand. Can you be clearer?"

Very, very slowly, he formed the word. "Solicitor"

"You want to see your solicitor?" I asked.

He nodded, yes.

"Is there something you want him to change in your Will?" Again, he nodded, 'yes'.

"Then I shall call him immediately" I answered. "I'm certain that he'll be happy to come to *Willow Grove Abbey* to see you." I had no sooner gotten those words out of my mouth than Edwina entered the room, carrying a crystal vase filled with roses from the garden.

"Nigel, aren't these simply divine? I thought they would perk you up a bit and give the room a spot of life. I've invited the Woodbridge's over for cocktails, and thought we needed a bit of the outdoors in here."

I was dumbfounded. Before I could stop myself, I blurted out, "You've invited company to the house, when Papa is feeling so dreadful?"

"Sophia, people are the best thing in the world for him. He simply lights up when there are others in the room."

I marched across the room and grasped Edwina's arm, tugging her into the hallway. "Edwina, he can scarcely speak," I said in an astonished voice.

"I understand him perfectly," Edwina answered.

"That's because you never let him talk."

"He likes to hear me tell him of the day's events. He likes to entertain. We are not letting his illness interfere with our lives. That would be negative. In fact, I'm doing a fine job of training him. I'm impressed with his progress."

"Training him?" I echoed. "What do you mean, 'training him'?"

"Oh nothing terribly hard. But, I think it's positive for him to be expected to say and do certain things."

"For instance?"

"Well, for instance, unless he says 'Please', I don't let him have a glass of water."

"Have you gone daft? He is desperately sick, Edwina. He can scarcely speak. He has to be frightened and anxious and he's surrounded with strangers and you make him say 'Please' before he can have a drink of water?" I wanted to slap her.

"Sophia, I don't need this sort of stress in my home or in my life. My husband and I are getting along perfectly fine. Now will you please leave?"

"Yes, of course, I'm leaving Edwina. I *am* sorry if I upset you. It only surprised me that you were having guests." I was simmering inside, but wisely kept still.

Just as she was turning to go, the nurse wheeled Papa into the room. While Edwina was arranging the roses, he opened his hand and there was a balled up scrap of paper in it. He obviously meant it for me, and I took it without comment. Then, I had no choice but to go. It was one of the hardest things I had ever done. I wondered if I shouldn't have simply taken Papa and left that house, bringing him back to *Tunbridge Wells* with me. There he could have had a drink of water without saying 'Please'.

Chapter Eleven

July, 1948

Another Funeral

I never saw my father again. I still had the tiny scrap of paper he had managed to give me during my prior visit to *Willow Grove Abbey*, and I had read it, of course. One could scarcely understand his handwriting, but it was clear enough. He had written that he wanted to add a codicil to his Will. As to what that might have entailed, we never knew. I could only surmise from the conversation we'd had during my last visit that it related to his desire to put into writing his wish that *Willow Grove Abbey* revert back to his children upon Edwina's death. But, he never saw the solicitor, and those wishes were not followed. The events leading up to learning of the shocking information contained in his Will were another of the heartbreaking events in my life. I had just recently returned from that last visit to *Willow Grove Abbey* earlier in the week. Spence and I had gone to our room, and were both reading in bed when the telephone rang. It was *Western Union* making certain that we were home, as they had a telegram to deliver. I couldn't imagine who would be sending a telegram. I dressed in a casual outfit, and was ready when the delivery arrived. I took the yellow envelope into the Great Hall, and opened it.

PAPA IN HOSPITAL. STOP. APPEARS GRAVE. STOP. AT NATIONAL HOSPITAL FOR NEUROLOGY AND NEURO-SURGERY. STOP. QUEEN SQUARE. STOP. LONDON. STOP.

DREW

I ran up the staircase and threw the telegram at Spence. I was weeping, and all undone. "Spence, Papa is in hospital in London. Read what the wire says. Why didn't the family ring me? Why wait to send a wire. I think they hoped it wouldn't arrive in time. This is inconceivable. We must prepare to go to London at once. How long do you suppose he's been this bad? Oh, Spence, I'm all undone!"

"Sophia, let's first call the hospital and see what his current status is. That's the sensible thing to do."

"Yes, yes, of course. Where is the London directory? I know I have one up here in this room. Did I put it in a drawer? Where is it?"

"I have it right here, Sophia. It's on my bedside table. I'm searching for the number now. Here it is." He immediately rang the hospital exchange, and asked for an update on the condition of Lord Nigel Somerville.

I couldn't understand the conversation. From Spence's end, there were only "ahh's and "I see's. Finally he rang off. "Sophia, sit down here by me, please."

I did as he requested, my pulse racing. "What is it, Spence? How is Papa?"

"Sophia, your father passed away an hour ago."

I screamed hysterically. "That damned family of mine. Why didn't they call me when he was taken to hospital? I would have been there in time. Why, Spence, why? I cannot believe they would be this rotten to me. They knew he was bad off!"

"Sophia, I would imagine Edwina preferred not to have you there. And, your brothers have certainly acquiesced to her wishes, ever since your father married her. I understand your upset. This was a ghastly way for them to treat you. One would really think that a family could be considerate of each other at such a time."

"Not *my* family, Spence. I suppose I should telephone one of them, perhaps Drew, since he is the one who sent the wire. Don't you think so?"

"Yes. Absolutely. Do you want me to call?

"No Spence, but thank you. I need to speak to him, and find out exactly what happened, and what in God's name they were thinking!

"I have no idea, Sophia. I don't know that they *were thinking* very clearly. I doubt they thought he would pass away so quickly. Still, it was terribly insensitive not to inform you immediately of any deterioration of his condition. Please, if you speak with any of them, try hard not to become upset."

'I shall," I answered. "If I let go my feelings, I'll be in a mental ward." I managed a weak smile. At that precise moment, the telephone rang. I answered, and it was Blake

"Sophia, its Blake. I have some very sad news."

I didn't say a word.

"Dad died tonight."

Finally I spoke. "Yes, Blake, I finally received Drew's wire. Spence rang the hospital, and received the ghastly news. What happened? How long was he in hospital?"

"We were at *Willow Grove*. All of us. Dad began to have trouble breathing. It progressively worsened, so we called an ambulance, and had him taken to London."

When was this?

"The day before yesterday?"

"And no one saw fit to ring me?"

"We thought we should wait until the doctors had seen him, and given us their prognosis."

"And, what was their prognosis?"

"That he had little time left. He was terminal. We set into motion plans to bring him home and let him pass away around his family and his beloved *Willow Grove Abbey,* just as had been done with our mother. We didn't think he would go so quickly. "

"Are Spence, Isabella and I not part of his family?"

"Of course Sophia. We were just about to ring you. The doctor's gave us every impression that he would live a week or more."

"Didn't you think I would have wanted to see him as quickly as possible?"

"Sophia, do you ever think about anyone but yourself? It was a terribly difficult time for us, and a shock. We couldn't do everything according to your timetable."

"All right, Blake, go on." I was trembling all over.

"Well, we were with him all day. We listened to a soccer game on the wireless with him. Then, we decided to go out and get a bite to eat that night. He was resting well, and the nurses said it would be perfectly fine."

"Didn't the hospital have a cafeteria?"

"Yes, of course. But, you know how beastly hospital food can be. We took a taxi to Claridge's and had a good meal. In the middle of dinner, we were told we had a call at the front desk. I went to answer it, and it was the hospital telling us that Dad had died."

"Well, I'm certainly glad that you got a good meal in," I answered snidely. "Did Papa ever mention me at all?"

"Yes as a matter of fact, he did. When we first reached hospital, he said that you had told him that you thought he should have been on oxygen."

"Yes, I did. Quite some time ago. I mentioned it to Edwina, as well."

"He also asked Drew to ring you. Actually, his exact words were, 'Talk to your sister'."

"Then why in God's name didn't he do it, Blake?"

"Well, Sophia. It was difficult for him. You know we hadn't seen you since the unpleasantness at your garden party. He felt more comfortable sending a telegram."

"Blake, you have always been beastly, but I would have hoped for better from Drew. In other words, Papa was in hospital three days before any of you decided to notify me, and then only after Papa asked Drew to ring me. And then he *still* chose not to ring."

We didn't think he would die so soon. And he didn't tell Drew to *ring* you, simply to *talk* to you."

"You knew he was terminally ill. You didn't have a crystal ball. Anyone would know it could have been any time. Obviously, nobody in the family wanted me there. How cruel of you."

"Well, that's the way it was, Sophia. I'm *ringing* you now. Do you want to know the plans for the funeral?"

"Yes, of course." At that moment I was capable of murder.

"There will be a viewing here at *Willow Grove* in two days, and then a funeral in the Chapel and burial in the graveyard here at St. Edward and St. Mary on the following day. I've taken care of the obituary in the *Times.*"

"Papa told me the last time I saw him that he wanted yellow roses on his casket."

"All right. I'm glad to know that," he answered.

"Is there anything else that I can do?" I asked.

"No, I believe everything is under control. Edwina still has some things to accomplish, but we are here to assist with anything she has to do."

"Shall I come to *Willow Grove* now?"

"I don't see any reason for that. Why don't you plan on arriving the day of the viewing?"

"That will be fine, Blake. Thank Drew for sending the wire and thank you for ringing me," I answered in a flat tone. I replaced the receiver and sobbed into my husband's arms.

Chapter Twelve

JULY, 1948
HEARTBREAK

Spence, Isabella and I arrived at *Willow Grove* on Thirteen, February 1949. I literally killed myself trying to be nice to my family, but I must say that I was in unbelievable pain because of my family's ghastly behavior leading up to Papa's death, and the planning of his funeral. Besides the yellow roses, which I'd requested, no one asked my suggestion for any other additions to the service. It was all planned by Edwina, Drew and Blake, and I suppose Susan, who considered herself the last word in etiquette. I had taken a gold cross from a bracelet of mine, and placed it in Papa's suit pocket in the casket. Then, I was shown that there was a small drawer at the end of the casket where people could put any memorabilia, or a letter they had written to Papa. I had no knowledge of it ahead of time, so was the only member of the family who didn't have a letter written. Susan prattled on about how how wonderful the family had thought the casket was, because it had a small drawer in it. 'How lovely of them to make certain I was at *Willow Grove* to help select the casket. When I was led into the viewing room, I nearly fainted. I screamed out in pain and sorrow. My legs began to shake and I was weeping as I cried out "Papa I should have been there." Various members of my family paced up and down in the room, instead of leaving me alone for a few moments with Papa. No matter. All I did was weep, and thank God that I had Spence there to hold me in his arms, and my sweet Isabella, to comfort me. Susan also told me that the day they took Papa to the hospital, a gentleman from the Parkinson's Foundation had come to the house to speak with them, at the request of his physician. Up until that time, they had not even been aware that there was such an organization. I had joined it the moment I learned of Papa's diagnosis. Susan said that this very nice man spoke with Papa for a few moments, and then took them all into a separate room, and told them that Papa would be dead within a week. She again jabbered on about how dreadful Papa's eyes had looked, all glazed, like he was already 'half dead'. I so appreciated her descriptive details. Drew told me that Papa had spoken with him alone for a moment, and that was when he'd said to Drew, 'Talk to your sister.' I suspect that Papa wanted Drew to know the truth about everything, and that was why he worded his request in such a manner. No matter. What was done, was done, and I tried to keep my emotions under control.

Literally hundreds of people attended the viewing, and I saw many old friends whom I had not had any contact with since before the war. I couldn't believe that I actually enjoyed seeing them, though of course, I still felt miserable. I have no recollection of speaking with any of my family members during that event, other than occasionally to introduce someone who asked to meet one of them. Many had not met Edwina at all, so she was the one I most frequently had to introduce. Edwina did not look either fashionable or well. She wore a quite unflattering navy blue dress, and her color was ghastly. Naturally, she wore a wig, which was most unflattering, and absolutely no cosmetics. Of course, I hadn't expected her to look stunningly attractive, but it almost seemed that she had gone out of her way to look uncharacteristically drab. Even though she had cancer, it was entirely out-of-character for her. I couldn't help but wonder if she knew she would be meeting many admirers of Papa's, who had heard of her, but hadn't ever seen her, and she did not want to appear to be a tart. She kept a stiff upper lip throughout the whole affair, and although I should have felt badly for her, that was not easy to do. I was embarrassed, as I'm certain my brothers were, that she continued to take photographs of my father in his open casket throughout the viewing. If she had wanted such photographs, it seemed to me that it might have been more appropriate to take as many as she wished before there were hundreds of people in the room. Still, I did try exceedingly hard to be kind to her, and made certain that she rested periodically, and had water near her at all times. I didn't even make her say 'Please'.

When the last person departed, I asked Edwina if she wanted to join Spence, Isabella and me for dinner, but she refused, saying that she was dining with my brothers and their families. That was perfectly acceptable to me, and we went our separate ways. I didn't see or speak to any of them until the next day at the funeral service. Surprisingly, the event was sparsely attended. It was my suspicion that many, many people knew of Papa's affair with Edwina, and all of the untoward events surrounding it, and by not attending the funeral, it was their way of sending a message of antipathy. I felt much more upset that morning, than I had the evening before. To begin with, I found myself seated next to Edwina, with Spence on my other side. She didn't shed a tear, and simply stared straight ahead during all of the moving hymns and eulogies. I sobbed uncontrollably. I'm certain that everyone present thought I was so desperately weeping because of the loss of my father, and of course, that *was* part of the reason. I am also certain that most guests knew there had been difficulty between Papa and me before his death. Of course, no one knew of the close chat we'd had that last time we saw one another. Not even Edwina. Most knew the details surrounding his marriage to Edwina, and that he'd had an affair with her for so many years, and that she had been my school roommate. One person mentioned to me that they understood Edwina was a very old family friend, particularly of Mummy's! It was clear from the beginning of the service, that I had purposely been omitted from any participation. Both Blake and Drew spoke. Drew read a passage from Corinthians pertaining to love. He seemed a bit uncomfortable when he read the passage which said 'If I speak in the tongues of angels…but do not show love…I am but a noisy gong…clanging in the wilderness'. I couldn't help but wonder if it wasn't directed at me. Perhaps I really *was* becoming paranoid. It just seemed like a passage that did not have a lot of relevance to the setting and purpose for our gathering. I had never heard it read at a funeral service before. When Spence had written his angry letter to Drew many months before, he had made reference to the fact that I was very articulate. Was the message meant to say that I might have been good with words, but I had no love for others…particularly my father? It seemed very unlike Drew to be so insensitive. I suspected it was more likely Susan's suggestion, as I was, and still am, positive that neither Blake nor Edwina knew any passages from the Bible. Weren't any of them able to understand that if I hadn't love for Papa, I would never have protected him so, and allowed my own needs to become subjugated to his? Blake performed the last eulogy, following two men who had known and worked with Papa. And it was absolutely incredible. Blake was a wonderful public speaker, and he did a superb job. Everyone laughed, cried, smiled and sobbed. When the last hymn was sung, 'Thine Be the Glory', and the pall bearers carried the casket out, there wasn't a dry eye in the chapel. Except both of Edwina's.

When the services were over, we all went back to *Willow Grove Abbey's* enormous dining room, where a tremendous spread of food was on display, and a very fine wine was offered. We arranged ourselves into a receiving line, and thanked the congregants for their attendance. No one in the family spoke to me, but for Blake's young daughters, as well as Annie and Pippin. Of course, Spence stayed by my side, as well as Isabella, who really didn't know her uncles or cousins at all well. Although Isabella had known Edwina when she was just a wee child, she had no memories of her. Kippy stayed in the States and wasn't present. I hadn't seen him since he was a bit over two. I was really very happy to see Pippin, as she had developed into a truly beautiful young lady. She was extremely slender, with very long taffy-colored hair, and the prettiest smile. I wished we might have been able to talk longer. She had been immensely close to Mummy, and I knew that she was grieving terribly, now that she had lost both of her grandparents. I'd heard that Edwina's sister, Grace, and her husband had formally adopted Kippy, when Edwina learned she had stage four cancer. I wondered what, if anything, Kippy even knew about his real father, Dieter Schoen, the German. I knew that he had survived the war, since apparently he once made an attempt to find Edwina in 1945, and it was then that she had filed for a divorce. After that time, no one had any idea to where he had disappeared. I'm not certain that Kippy even knew of his existence.

Spence, Isabella and I did not linger long at the reception. We drove around the area surrounding the *Abbey*, reminiscing about places in my childhood memories, and finally returned to *Tunbridge Wells*. I had hoped to return home with my parents precious, little Terriers, which my mother and father had made me promise that I would take if something happened to either of them. That had always been my intent. In fact, in the earlier will that my father had written up by his solicitor, before his marriage to Edwina, the dogs were specifically mentioned as a bequest to me. I adored those little dogs, and had been with my mother when both were chosen. In fact, one was even named after my childhood name, *Sissy*. I asked Edwina if she would like me to take the dogs earlier that morning, and she flatly said 'no.' She'd never had a pet in her life, and just didn't have the same deep love I had for animals. I couldn't understand why she wouldn't let me have them, unless it was just one more way to hurt me. After she turned down my request, I simply asked her to please make certain that the little dogs were mentioned in her will, if anything should happen to her and she agreed.

Time moved on. The decade ended, and the 1950's were ushered in. Their arrival signified the end of our country as one of the great powers in the Western world. That was the Britain where persons who had served their country during the war were still prominent. So much changed later. During the early Fifties, we were all still so proud to be Brits. Tradition still mattered, church played a part in most people's lives, and we all sang 'God Save the Queen' before school began. I tried to pay visits to Edwina at *Willow Grove* as frequently as possible. She continued with her treatment regimen, and she neither seemed better nor worse. Immediately after Papa's death, her entire family transferred themselves to *Willow Grove Abbey*, to look after her. Although it was hard not to be somewhat irritated, when thinking of the Phillips living at my lovely, ancestral home, I did have to admit that it was thoughtful of them *to* show such kindness toward their sister. After all, the house belonged to Edwina now, and I had no right to say anything about who lived there and who didn't. All I could hope was that she would keep the promise Papa told me she had given to him, to return it to the Somerville children, if she didn't survive the cancer. I still had no communication with either of my brothers, so I had no idea what might have been happening with them. Blake was the executor of Papa's estate, but he never sent me a copy of the will. I assumed that everything had been left to Edwina, until after her death.

As summer flew by, and fall approached, it became apparent that I was no longer welcome at my ancestral home. Every time I visited, there was a distinct coolness. Edwina's brother, Eugene had literally taken over, and now gave all the orders. Finally, one day when I was visiting, he told me that he would prefer it if I no longer came to see them. I was aghast. He explained that Edwina seemed to be getting worse, and that the family felt it was because my presence caused too much stress in her life. I countered that comment.

"Eugene, I never, ever make any reference to difficulties Edwina and I have had between us. I treat her with respect, and try to show my very real concern about her health. How can I possibly be causing her any stress?"

"Well, you see, Sophia, the mere fact that you refer to her health causes stress. None of us believe that Edwina is seriously ill. We all believe that her body is out of harmony, and that she will be fine, once the harmony has been re-established. Continually bringing up her health only causes more stress. Plus, I'm sorry to have to say this, but she doesn't trust you. She feels that you wish her dis-harmony, and that your presence could be the reason she is out of harmony to begin with.

"You have to be joshing," I nearly shouted. "I've never heard such idiocy in my life. Does she speak to her doctor about these nonsensical beliefs?"

"No. She is frightened that the doctor will refuse to continue treating her, if she tells them she is at odds with the diagnosis."

"Well, she might be correct on that score."

"Sophia, you are entirely too negative to be in this home. You bring your negative energy into our home, and it causes stress."

"It's quite interesting that my husband and I live quite happily in our *own* home, and there is not a whit of stress. How do you account for that, Eugene?"

"You don't have hostility and jealousy toward Spence, as you do toward all of us, especially Edwina. You don't send him negative vibrations."

"Oh, good gracious. I'll be most happy to stay out of your lives. No matter. Frankly, the person who has suffered untold stress from all of the madness that Edwina caused has been me, not you or Edwina. I'm not comparing that to the stress of her illness, Eugene, in case you wish to twist that around." I gathered my belongings and automobile keys, and without another word, marched out of my childhood home, past my mother's baby grand piano, a glass display cabinet filed with Lalique crystal, the incredible Waterford chandelier in the Great Hall, and my parent's two little terriers, looking up at me with soulful, innocent eyes.

I really was perfectly happy to bring an end to my visits to Edwina. At the least, they had been stressful for me. I returned to my preparations for Isabella's approaching departure for *Ashwick Park*. We had such fun shopping for clothing, and packing her enormous trunk. The school sent us a long list of necessary items. I knew I was going to miss her dreadfully, but was also terribly excited for her. She'd had a much freer life than I'd been allowed at her age, but I still knew that this was an enormous watershed moment in her life. I had never talked to her at length about the fact that Edwina had been my roommate at *Ashwick Park,* as it seemed unnecessary information for her. I was interested to see who the school would match her up with, and prayed it would be someone utterly different than Edwina.

Finally the day arrived. Spence and I packed the auto, and made the trip to *Ashwick Park,* where we unloaded her belongings and settled her in. There we *did* meet her new roommate, a sweet young lady whose name was Ruth Riverton. She seemed rather shy and quiet. It was obvious that she was quite scholarly, and we discussed her interest in medicine. She was hoping to be a physician, and was delighted to learn that Spence was a doctor. I breathed a sigh of relief, as she couldn't have been more different than Edwina. Our Isabella was quite talented in design and architecture, and hoped to go on to study that field at University. I thought the two girls would be well suited, and would spend a good deal of time in the library. And so, Isabella was off to *Ashwick Park.* It was September, 1950, and Spence and I rattled about the house, ringing our daughter every other night, out of loneliness. Isabella went off without a backward glance. Every letter we received was brimming with enthusiasm over the choice she had made. She loved everything about the school, and loved the village, just as I had. She loved her roommate, Ruth, whom we learned was from Mousehole, Cornwall. Of course, her letters brought back memories, but I tried to push the bad ones aside, and to recall only the happy times. After all, the bad times had come much later. It didn't seem that a great deal had changed at *Ashwick Park* since my graduation. Students were still required to wear the beastly uniforms that Edwina and I had so reviled, and rules were still quite strict. Spence and I were glad for that, as we didn't have to worry about Isabella making unwise choices. The *Ashwick Park* girls couldn't ride in automobiles, which was another thing we appreciated.

Isabella had turned thirteen in August. She was such a lovely girl and had shown no signs of going through a difficult teenage period. Not only was she lovely, she had such a sweet personality, and had definitely inherited her father's intelligence. Spence and I traveled to the school for Parent's Weekend, a special two days devoted to introduction of the school to the student's parents. When we arrived, it was just as I remembered, with hoards of girls everywhere, giggling, pushing, shoving and generally acting like fools. Isabella was no exception. We took a group of her friends to dinner, and it was a lot of fun to be with them, listening to their dreams for the future. Things *had* changed in that regard. Each girl spoke in terms of continuing her education beyond *Ashwick Park*. Most were planning to earn a university degree, and some even dreamed of being physicians and barristers. A few were going on to finishing school in Switzerland, and some wanted to try their hand at art or drama school. No one seemed to be looking for the '*suitable man*', and I was pleased that in the twelve years since I had left, there had been a gigantic leap forward with regard to the aspirations of young women. Oh, most still made off-hand comments such as "When I marry," but it was clear that education and career took precedence over settling down to a husband. Isabella was talking about studying commercial interior design, playing with the idea of going to New York City after she graduated. Spence and I felt it was far too early to make such a large decision, but we didn't dissuade her. She was such an independent girl, much more so than I had been, and if she wanted to continue her education in the States, we intended to support such a decision.

Chapter Thirteen

DECEMBER, 1949
MORE LOSS

In early December, 1949 Edwina succumbed to the cancer, which had spread throughout her body. We were not asked to attend any services for her. Eugene rang me, and told me she had passed away, and it was a sad occasion. Regardless of what had happened during our friendship, I couldn't help but remember the fun and laughter we had shared, and the times when I'd leaned on her for support. Still, it was difficult to see my name listed as her stepdaughter in her obituary in *The Times*. Shortly after her death, we received an enormously startling piece of news. Blake rang me and made the shocking revelation that Edwina had left everything to her brother, Eugene. There were not words to describe my feelings. Obviously, Papa had gifted our inheritance to her, and instead of leaving it to the Somervilles, she had left it to her family! I knew that this was not what Papa had intended. He and I had discussed it, and at the end, he had wanted to add the codicil to his will. But, it appeared that what she'd done was totally legal. Blake was not informed about the law, and said he intended to contact a barrister to learn what our options might be. I certainly wasn't opposed to his doing so, but I didn't have a lot of hope that anything could be turned around. I couldn't help but think of Mummy, and all of the lovely items she had so adored, which now belonged to the Phillipses. Primarily, it broke my heart that my beloved home would never be owned by the Somerville family again.

Blake *did* file a lawsuit. It was based upon the obvious influence that Eugene had with regard to Edwina. Edwina's brain was so filled with cancer, and I even had to wonder if she was in her right mind when she chose not to follow Papa's wishes. The barrister whom Blake retained had an exceptional reputation. However, he had very few details upon which to carry through on the case, since my brothers really knew very little about what had transpired. They had been in favor of the marriage, and had spent no time speaking with Papa or Edwina about anything pertaining to how financial matters would be dealt with, if one or the other, or both, should die. Naturally, they had been led to believe that I was terribly money motivated, which had caused all of the difficulty between us to begin with. They'd never realized that what I was so disgusted about was the illegality of what Edwina had proposed, and the unfairness connected to the possible loss of our home. I would rather have inherited the money legally, and paid the taxes owed upon it. Spence and I had a good life, and I was not concerned about our finances. I'd never seen that money brought happiness to either my parents or my brother Blake. Drew and Annie were comfortable and happy, certainly not devoted to material things, but they had been lied to so many times, in order to give the impression that I was totally consumed with having money. No matter. It was now time to deal with the after- effects of Papa's poor decisions. The lawsuit continued on and on. Months and months would go by, with no word at all from the barristers, and then we would receive a flurry of papers and forms to complete. Half of the time I put it aside, and just carried on with our lives. I tried several times to speak with Blake by telephone, but he always cut me short, making it clear that he didn't want to have an extended conversation. For that matter, neither did I. Nevertheless, I knew that unless he understood what the case was about, and there was no way on earth that he did, we hadn't a prayer of winning. I had been sending him copies of every letter, paper, diary entry, card, and legal document I had in my possession, in hopes that he'd educate himself. The barrister was costing a bloody fortune, and I had no intention of going into a courtroom and making a fool of myself, because my brother did not have his ducks in a row.

Susan wrote me at one point, with a lot of balderdash about how the best thing to say in court was 'I don't remember.' I replied that such an answer might work well if one was the defendant, but as the plaintiffs, we had better do more than say 'We don't remember anything.' At any rate, the thing dragged on. Apparently, Eugene Phillips was firmly established at *Willow Grove Abbey,* enjoying life as a country gentleman. Two of Edwina's sisters and their husbands were also there, so I imagined the staff was busy. The thought of Edwina's family making themselves at home in the place I had grown up and still loved with all of my heart did make me livid.

We had never planned on being on *St. James Road* for such a long time. But, so many things had happened in our lives, that it had been nearly impossible for us to put our minds to making any sort of change in our lives. Then, in March of 1952, I had solemn news. Within a matter of months, both the Duke and Duchess of Winnsborough had died. I was truly saddened, as they'd always been so good to me. They'd mentioned at that long ago birthday party for Isabella that they intended to leave *Winnsborough Hall* to me, but I didn't know if anything had ever been legally settled. To my astonishment, I had a letter from a solicitor telling me that they'd done just that. I had some thoughts regarding what Spence and I might do with the property, but needed to do a considerable amount of research before I spoke to Spence about my ideas. The Winnsboroughs had wanted me to arrange some sort of philanthropic use for the property, and I had put my mind to that task back when it had been mentioned to me. I did not tell Spence about my inheritance immediately, as I knew that he was working so terribly hard, and that he would probably not be pleased to be reminded of my marriage to Owen.

What I considered a horribly gruesome occurrence also took place that month. I received a letter from Eugene Phillips, Edwina's brother, telling me that he intended to euthanize my parent's beloved little terriers. I nearly hit the ground when I read the letter. The reason given was that one of them could not climb the stairs, and the other little one had developed a grass allergy. I was infuriated. There was absolutely no reason why a four-pound dog could not be carried up the staircase, and why any half way competent veterinarian could not treat a grass allergy. By the time I rang him, and spoke, they were already gone. I wept for days. I asked Eugene to have their little bodies cremated, and to send the ashes to me. He wrote me back, saying that as soon as he received a check from me, he would forward the ashes. Spence couldn't believe it, but I *did* send the money, as I knew he would not forward them otherwise. The next I knew, I received a brown grocery bag, filled with the ashes and tiny bone fragments from both of those beloved animals. It was pure, unadulterated cruelty. I was so heartbroken that Spence bought me two puppies, in an attempt to ease my devastation. His kindness and generosity did help to fill the void in my heart, but I have never forgotten those sweet dogs. . I named my new little girls Nikki and Poppy, and both Spence and I grew to adore them as though they were true babies.

1949 was not an easy year, in many ways. Several things of historical significance occurred. One positive was that the Russians ceded in the Berlin airlift. It had been highly successful. In May, the blockade was lifted and the Germans were embarrassed. However, the final upshot was that there was a creation of two German states. The Federal Republic of Germany (West Germany) and the German Democratic Republic (East Germany) split Berlin in two. Also in 1949, a spy plane that was equipped with a device that could track and identify radioactivity got a "hit", and the world learned that Russia had tested their first Atomic Bomb. I needn't say how much that sent shock waves round the world. It was hard to imagine that after just having gone through a frightening war, the Russians were placing themselves into the position of the new bully.

Still later in the same year, the communists led by Chairman Mao, overtook the loyalists led by Chaing Kai-chek in China. This resulted in the North Koreans equipping themselves with arms from the Chinese, North Korea attacked South Korea resulting in a war that lasted from 1950 to 1953. There were so many hotspots cropping up around the world, and sometimes when I stepped out of my insulated concerns about family, I realized that the Earth was becoming a dangerous place.

In spite of global concerns, our life went on and Spence began to talk about what he wanted to do with his future. It was past time for him to be leaving Maudsley. The question was "What to do now?" He had been at Maudsley four years. He definitely wanted to run his own clinic, but didn't want to be relegated to strictly administrative duties. Therefore, when the news came about *Winnsborough Hall* I already had a wonderful idea. When

Saturday came round, and we had the entire day together, meaning Spence wouldn't be rushing off to Maudsley, I knew it was the proper time to discuss my plans with him. We awakened, and I made a rather fancy breakfast, with Nan's help. We ate in the formal dining room, with fresh spring flowers on the table. As we sat down and helped ourselves to French toast, eggs, kippers, bangers, and fruit, we began to speak about Spence's plans for the future.

"So darling, what is it you think you're going to do, now that the time at Maudsley is drawing to a close?" I asked.

"I'd like to have my own Clinic. I have even thought about building one, but it would be too prohibitively expensive."

"Exactly what do you have in mind, darling?" I asked, munching on a piece of toast.

"Oh, if I could have whatever I wanted, it would be a big, old rambling country house, converted to a clinic/hospital. You know the sort I mean, with restful grounds and peaceful scenery. A place where patients could reconnect with nature and with their true selves. A place they wouldn't feel confined, where they'd be free to walk on paths through grounds and gardens, and smell the fresh air. However, I'd have to buy an old country house, and you know the price on something of that sort."

"Let's say you were able to procure an old manor house or estate. Would there be a lot of renovation involved in order to transform it into a clinic?"

"Not terribly much. Most of those old estates have countless bedrooms and wings, and have already been refurbished to include lavatories with each sleeping room. Since I'm not speaking of a proper hospital, where surgical facilities would be needed, there would actually require little renovation, depending, of course, upon the condition of the property. Anything that I could afford would probably require a great deal of renovation." He laughed. "This French toast is delicious," he added.

"Well, thank you darling. I actually made that myself. Spence, I think I have just the place, and it would require almost no renovation. It has thirty-two bedrooms, each with its own bath, and servant's quarters, as well as a massive dining hall and drawing room, each with fire bins. There is a library, a solarium, a large kitchen with all amenities, and 10 other receiving rooms, which could be used for office space. It sits on 500 acres of magnificent midland property, complete with a lake designed by Capability Brown, himself."

"Sophia, have you gone bonkers? Where is this fantasyland? Who owns it?"

"It's called *Winnsborough Hall*, and Owen owned it," I replied.

"So, what does that have to do with me? With us?" He was frowning.

"Now, Spence please let me finish before you say 'no'." I took a deep breath.

"The Duke and Duchess left me *Winnsborough Hall*! Some time ago, I told them that I hoped to create some sort of charitable institution in Owen's name. They liked the idea. It's to insure his immortality. Oh Spence, it's such an incredible opportunity. Can't we at least drive over there, and have a look? I'd use the money I got when Owen died, as well as proceeds from the sale of Sumner Street, to cover any costs incurred with the renovation and so forth. There is still a substantial lot of that money left. Plus, the Winnsboroughs not only left the property, but a large sum of money for its upkeep." Spence was silent for so long, I began to wonder if he wasn't going to answer me.

"Spence, did you hear what I said, darling?"

"Yes, Sophia, I did, and I'm overwhelmed. I don't know what to say. It would be hard for me to say 'no' to this. It sounds as though it's exactly what I have dreamed. Yet, you know my feeling about Winnsborough money."

"Spence, Listen to me. Yes, I do know your feelings about Winnsborough money, or anybody else's for that matter. You've proven your point. You paid back every penny I loaned you to buy this house. No one is going to think you're a 'fortune hunter.' Moreover, for that matter, I wouldn't give a damn if they did!"

Spence stood up and walked around to my end of the table. "Sophia, have I ever told you that you're the most remarkable woman I've ever known?" He said, with tears in his eyes. "How could I say no? It's everything I've dreamed. Shall we take a drive down there tomorrow and see what the new *Owen Winnsborough Mental Health Center* is going to look like?"

I hugged him with all of my strength, burying my face in his crisp, white shirt. "Oh Spence, we'll be starting a whole new adventure. I'm so excited. Of course, we'll go tomorrow. I have a key, so we can get in. Anyway, I'm sure there's still a staff on the premises to show us round."

The next day, by late afternoon we arrived at *Winnsborough Hall*, in the West Midlands. The nearest village of any import was Stroud. Constructed in 1710, in the reign of Queen Anne and designed by a pupil of the renowned Sir Christopher Wren, it was a building of special architectural interest. It was very grand and formal, but I remembered from days past that a warm country house welcome awaited us. As we pulled the large knocker on the door, *Morris,* our former butler, dressed in a black suit with white tie, answered the door. I was so happy to see that he was still there. He looked older, of course, but not significantly so. Primarily, his hair was greyer.

"Why, Milady! What a welcome surprise! We haven't seen you in a good while. What brings you to *Winnsborough Hall?*"

"I assume you have been notified of the Duke and Duchess's plans for the property, God rest their souls. Morris, this is my husband, Doctor Spencer Stanton. He would like to look at the property with me. We need to determine what proper use can be made of this lovely old mansion, fulfilling the wishes of the elder Winnsboroughs. They wish it to be converted to a charitable organization of some sort. Morris, is Mrs. Whittaker still the head housekeeper here? I was so fond of her."

"Of Course, Milady. It's good to make your acquaintance, Sir," he answered, shaking Spence's hand. He stepped back, and motioned for us to enter the house. It was near teatime and a wood fire burned gently. The high ceilinged drawing room held books and fresh flowers. One could imagine relaxing on the large, comfortable chairs and tufted sofas. A wide, thickly carpeted oak staircase led to the bedrooms, all of which had spectacular views. The library retained its fine old mahogany bookcases, and opened onto the adjacent terrace overlooking 500 acres of parkland, formal gardens, forested land and a putting green. All of the rooms contained handsome paintings and interesting oddments, such as a mahogany knife box converted to a depository for outgoing mail.

I turned and said "Oh Spence. Yesterday lingers here so gracefully. I'd forgotten how lovely it is."

"Yes, it's truly spectacular. Do you think it might be almost too luxurious for the sorts of patients who'd be here?"

"Darling, I don't think so. I think it's ideal. It's true that the drawing room is very formal, but the library looks 'lived in', and that would probably be the place most patients would gather. The bedrooms are divine, and each does have its own bath. The kitchen is obviously capable of taking on preparation of food for a large number of people. I'm just overjoyed at how perfect it would be."

"So am I Sophia. So am I. It's almost like a miracle, you know? Did you say that it's even to come completely furnished? I can't imagine that there aren't family heirlooms that someone might want to remove."

"There may be a few, but I strongly doubt it. I suspect that the Winnsboroughs took anything they wanted to their primary residence, *Snow Hill.*"

As we were about to take a walk-about through the entire mansion, Mrs. Whittaker came into the room, her face rather red from having been hurrying. "Oh, Milady. How grand to see you. It's been such a long time. We've never forgotten you here at *Winnsborough Hall.* You was always so good to us. Is this your new husband? You're looking mighty happy these days." I stepped over and hugged Mrs. Whittaker. "Yes, this is my husband, Doctor Spencer Stanton. He is the physician who will be heading up the transformation of *Winnsborough Hall* into the new medical clinic. We're very excited about the prospect, and I'm so happy to think that you may still be with us to help with all of the changes. That is, of course, if you wish to be. We would like to appoint you Head Housekeeper, with all maids, reporting to you. We shall have a nursing staff, and there will be a Chief Nurse, who will see to that part of duties, but I know how long you've been here, and how well you know the operation of *Winnsborough Hall.* Had you heard of the Duke and Duchess's plans for the Hall?

"Yes, Milady. Morris told us of them. We're all delighted to think that the house will be put to use again. All of them poor boys who returned from the war in such a sad state, can come here to be cared for and treated in a peaceful and loving atmosphere."

"That is exactly what we hope, Mrs. Whittaker."

"Shall you be living here too?" She asked.

"No, but there will be doctors on the premises. We haven't figured out all of the complexities yet, but you won't be left alone to cope with the patients."

"I wouldn't mind so much, Milady, except that I don't have the training called for."

Of course. We understand that. But, the house will need you more than ever for your wonderful skills and knowledge about running such a large home. What about the cook? Is she still here, as well?"

"No Milady. She married. We've gotten along without a head cook, just using the under cook, and kitchen maids."

Well, we shall need a very good cook, and that will undoubtedly be one of your first responsibilities; to find someone for us. I shall give you all of the details, and we can discuss a timeline later. This is going to take a bit of time to set up everything in a professional manner. But, when we're ready, I want your advice on many things."

Mrs. Whittaker looked pleased at the confidence that was being placed in her, and after several years of just keeping the house going, she sounded happy at the prospect of actually having a mission to pursue.

We walked through the entire house twice, paying particular attention to any needed improvements. We didn't find many. We discussed, at length, possibilities for refurbishing each bedroom suite. It was our goal to make certain that each of the bedroom suites be decorated to look as differently as possible from the usual hospital or rehabilitation facility. It was my thought that each room would be nothing more than a splendid guest's bedroom had always been at *Winnsborough Hall*. Tranquil colors, soft fabrics, fluffy towels, pale Edwardian prints. Each would play a part in making the whole a haven of calm. We took a stroll about the gardens, which were superb, even in March; peaceful and filled with all the flowers that the English love so dearly. I remembered how magnificent it was in the summer, and tried to paint a picture for Spence. Upon finishing our excursion, we were very much smitten with the idea that it would become a mental health center. On the way home, we discussed the question of where *we* would live.

"Darling, do you suppose we'd have to sell the house on *St. James Road*, if we do this?" Spence asked.

"Well, I don't know. Now that Isabella is off at school, it wouldn't be as traumatic for her, but I do so love our home. I love you more, however, and I want you to have your dream. Could we live at *Winnsborough Hall*, in one of the wings?"

"We could, I suppose, although I'm not terribly keen on that idea. Life in a mental health center can be harrowing, dearest. Even though we won't be treating severe mental illness I really prefer to keep our home life and my professional one completely separate."

"Won't there need to be a psychiatrist on the premises at all hours?"

"Yes, of course. The accommodations are lovely, so I don't think there'll be any problem with hiring a good staff. We can house them in one wing. They'll probably be young men, younger than I was when I began to study under Sir Aubrey, so they'll expect quarters."

"Spence, you aren't exactly ancient now," I laughed, punching him on the arm.

"I know, Sophia, but I *am* nearly 42. Most of the chaps I'll be looking to hire will be in their late twenties."

"And nurses?" I asked?"

"I'll start with surrounding villages. I suspect there are many who would jump at the chance to work closer to home. First, we need to find out if any of the staff there now wish to stay. I don't want to turn anyone out, as obviously it's been their home for a long while."

"They're a good staff, Spence. I remember them, and think that most are still there. I suspect they'd love to feel needed again. They have been living in that lovely home with no one to appreciate their hard work."

"Fine, then, let's look into that as soon as possible. Of course, there'll be paper work involved here, so it's going to take some time. I'll need to establish a non-profit organization, and select a board of directors. Do we still agree that the name will be *The Owen Winnsborough Mental Health Center?*"

"I think I prefer *The Owen Wood Winnsborough Clinic.*"

"Yes, that has a nice ring. I like that, Sophia. I think leaving out the words 'mental health' would be a positive change. There is most definitely still a stigma about mental health, and I assume I'll have to approach the Councils in surrounding villages to explain this scheme, so there isn't any uproar."

"Who are you going to recommend for your Board?"

"Well, Sophia, you, for one. This entire project would not become a reality if the Winnsborough's hadn't entrusted *Winnsborough Hall* into your care. As a Trustee, there is no question that you should sit on the Board, to oversee all transactions, and to make certain that money is being spent wisely and well."

"I hadn't thought of that. It's a big responsibility, Spence. I hope I'm up to it."

"You're up to it.. Then, of course, I think Sir Aubrey Lewis should be asked. I'd like to have his sound advice. I think he's filled with integrity and would make a fine board member. Also, what about Dr. Hausfater? His research would be very helpful, and he is another well-respected man in his field."

Oh Spence, I love that idea. He would be so honored."

"We are going to need to put someone on the Board who understands finance and business. Yet, that someone also needs an understanding of mental health, at least a need for a good, well-run institution of the sort we're contemplating."

"Someone like that may be a bit more difficult to come by," I answered. I'll have to think about someone who could fit the bill."

"I want a very interesting, and diverse Board. Next week I'm meeting with the village Council, to broach the idea to the town elders. I believe if it's presented in the proper manner, they'll see that it will only enhance their property values, and that they need not be frightened about having a mental health clinic near their lovely, little hamlet."

"I have no doubt that you'll come out of that meeting with lots of solid supporters.

Although it was to be a massive undertaking and would take nearly a year to become reality, the seeds were sown that day. Spence and I embarked on a wonderful new path together. After a tremendous amount of deliberation, we decided that we would remain in the house on *St. James Road*, unless the lawsuit ended in a positive fashion, and *Willow Grove Abbey* became a viable alternative, since it was quite close to the new *Winnsborough Center*. Spence could make the short drive back and forth, which was approximately twenty minutes. In the event that we remained on *St. James Road*, Spence would be able to commute by rail.

While he was busy with preparations for the new facility, I turned my attention to the upcoming deposition that Eugene's barrister had scheduled for me. Interrogatories had already been completed and returned to our barrister, and the deposition was the next step. I wasn't looking forward to it, but all I intended was to tell the truth. We requested a judicial trial, as opposed to one where a jury would decide the outcome, due to the complexity of the issues. That request was granted.

Chapter Fourteen

June, 1952

A Settlement

In June, I arrived at the office of Eugene's barrister in Bristol, where my deposition was to take place. I had hoped to meet with Blake beforehand, but he decidedly avoided any face-to-face discussion with me. It was such an odd situation. He and I could sit at a Board meeting and calmly discuss matters pertaining to the clinic, yet he showed absolutely no interest in having a personal relationship. He and Susan still lived in Scotland, but he had bought his own small airplane, which he piloted himself, and he made the trips to and from the Midlands easily. By the time of my deposition, Drew had also joined the case, as a Plaintiff, because our barrister felt that it would present a more united front if both of the brothers sued. I, on the other hand, dropped out of the suit as a Plaintiff, and decided that I would serve as only a witness. That action surely showed that I had no interest in any monetary gain. I didn't believe that either of my brothers had the slightest indication of what I would say, since they'd not cared to ask. As far as I was concerned, I had much to gain if the suit prevailed. Primarily, I would have the satisfaction of seeing that my family home and possessions did not end up in the hands of a fortune hunter, who had scarcely known our family, or our father. I readily admit to being nervous, but I kept reminding myself that all I had to do was be honest. I glanced at Eugene Phillips, who appeared arrogant and self-confident. His barrister began by asking me what my relationship to Countess Edwina Somerville had been.

"My relationship to Countess Somerville was quite lengthy and complex." I replied.

"How do you mean? Could you explain that?" He asked.

"I first met Edwina when we shared a room at the *Ashwick Park School*, in Kent from 1931 to 1935. She was my dearest friend in the world. That friendship lasted until 1939, when I discovered that she was involved in an extramarital affair with my father, the Earl Somerville, owner of *Willow Grove Abbey*. She married my father in January, 1949, after my mother passed away, and thus became my legal stepmother."

"Mrs. Stanton, please tell the Court why you believe that Eugene Philips, the defendant in this suit, was the primary confidante and financial advisor for Countess Somerville and guided her financial dealings."

"I believe it because Edwina told me that was the case. After my father died, she told me that she leaned heavily upon her brother for advice and that he was helping her with financial concerns."

"Mrs. Stanton, you have charged in your deposition that 'Edwina and Eugene' devised a scheme to convince Nigel Somerville that he could save estate taxes by giving assets to his wife, Edwina; and that she, in turn, would 'gift', within her annual exclusion from gift taxes during her lifetime and her unified credit against the estate taxes at death, to the children of Nigel. Also, that she would do so with the intent of defrauding Nigel Somerville and his family and directing assets to her family. Please tell us in your own words why you believe this to be so."

"Indeed. This scheme caused me to withdraw my reluctant support for my father's wish to marry Edwina. I went to my father's home in the fall of 1948, to pick up my mother's china and a few other items she had designated were to be mine. I sat in the kitchen with my father. His exact words were, 'Edwina has a splendid idea'. I asked to what he was referring. 'Edwina says that she wants to be an asset to me, not a liability', my father replied. Then, he went on to tell me that Edwina had suggested that he gift a substantial portion of his children's inheritance to her, which she in turn would gift back to the children after Papa died. This also included the family home, where my father and Edwina were living."

"What was your reaction to such a suggestion?"

"I was appalled. I argued vehemently that what he was suggesting was illegal; that a person cannot gift money with strings attached. That it was not only illegal, it was horrific to think that Papa would place that sort of trust in *anyone*. I reminded him that nothing could be put into writing. It would be one hundred percent based upon believing that once Edwina got the money, she would keep her promise to gift it back. I asked him why she would want to do such a thing. He replied that it showed how much she loved him."

The barrister smiled.

"Papa said that if he refused her offer, she would think that he didn't trust her. He said that Edwina had never had a mean bone in her body and that he trusted her implicitly."

"Did you believe that to be true?"

"I knew it wasn't true. I gave him several examples of times when she had exhibited mean, nasty behavior to him, to me and to my mother, particularly during their affair. Nothing I said made the slightest bit of difference. He was bound and determined not to disappoint Edwina."

"Did you speak to anyone about your concerns?"

"Yes, absolutely. I spoke to a Mr. Cooper Bennett, who is an expert in tax matters, and also to Mr. Porter Marquis, a barrister who has an advanced degree in economics. Both assured me that my assumptions were correct. They voiced concern that my father was making irrational decisions."

"What do you know about Edwina's family's attitude toward her marriage to your father?"

"When Papa and Edwina made the decision to marry, I specifically asked Edwina how her family felt about it. After all, Papa was near seventy-six years of age, and Edwina was thirty-two. Edwina told me that they were one hundred percent in favor of it. They were supportive throughout everything that occurred during the period of the affair. When they married, none of my father's blood family was present. They were married at the Phillips home in *Bury St. Edmunds*, with only her family present. Edwina also told me that her mother felt that every one of her children, except Grace, had married below themselves, and that it would be wonderfully refreshing to see at least two of her daughters married into the society they deserved to be a part of."

I continued with my testimony throughout the entire morning, bringing the barrister along with me on the path of deceit, pain, and heartache that my family had travelled. When midday arrived, I felt that

I had done the best job I was capable of. Nevertheless, the opposing counsel wasn't about to stop at that. After breaking for lunch, we settled back into our chairs.

The opposing counsel rose, shot his sleeves, and resumed his questioning. It was abundantly clear that he was irritated by my previous answers. I had noticed that he and Eugene had been deep in conversation before the deposition resumed. "Mrs. Stanton, you did not like Edwina Somerville, did you?" He asked.

"That would depend upon what time period you are referring to," I answered.

"Well, certainly you did not like her when you learned that your father was involved with her, before your mother's death?"

"I wasn't happy about the affair, no Sir. In addition, I was confused about my feelings for Edwina. She had been my dearest friend. The sister I'd never had. It was hard for me to reconcile her actions with the Edwina I'd always known. Therefore, whether I liked her or not would be difficult to say. I didn't like what she was doing."

"Yet, you agreed to allow her to spend a portion of the war years at *Willow Grove Abbey*, with your family, knowing that your father and she were having a relationship, and would be living under the same roof with your mother present?"

"Sir that was not a decision for me to make. It was my father's home."

"Still, you were on somewhat cordial terms with her at that time?"

"I was trying, until I saw Papa coming out of her room on Christmas Eve, kissing her at the door, at three o'clock in the morning."

"That made you change your mind about Edwina?"

"No Sir. What made me change my mind, for the last time, was the fact that the next morning she took her breakfast with my mother in the Master Bedroom wing. I couldn't imagine how she could look my mother in the eye."

He cleared his throat and looked through some papers. "All right, Mrs. Stanton, do you deny that your father loved Edwina very much, and that she, in turn loved him?"

"Actually, I do have to deny that. I never once heard my father say that he loved Edwina. In fact, what he said was that she was a 'wild woman in bed.'" There was a collective gasp from those gathered round the conference table. Even the court reporter, transcribing the proceeding, seemed shocked. Opposing counsel's face grew red. Eugene looked aghast.

"And what of Edwina's love for your father?"

"Edwina admitted to me that her love for my father included love of his money, title and *Willow Grove Abbey*, my ancestral home. She occasionally mentioned that she loved him, but that her love included all of the aforementioned. She *did* tell me that she had had her first orgasm with him." There was total bedlam. It took a substantial amount of time before everyone calmed down. Eugene's barrister had gone purple in the face, while Eugene looked as though he might be having heart pains, or gas. "In addition, I continued, "my father gave me this small scrap of paper when I last saw him. It is difficult to read it clearly, but I believe it says that he wished to add a codicil to his will. He'd asked me to have his solicitor come to him as soon as possible, just a moment before he passed me the scrap of paper, out of Edwina's sight."

"I wonder if we might have a brief recess." The barrister requested. I had no idea what the recess was meant to accomplish. I assumed Eugene's barrister wanted things to calm a bit. However, after disappearing for several minutes, everyone returned, and the opposing barristers were walking side-by-side. Then, our barrister approached my brothers, and gave them astounding news. Eugene had decided to yield. He wanted to settle the case. Apparently, what I had said disturbed him greatly and didn't bode well for a verdict on his behalf should we proceed to trial.

The opposing counsel cleared his throat, and said, "Mrs. Stanton, you may be excused. Counsels have agreed to settlement of this case. Thus, there will be no need for further testimony."

I was jubilant. When Court recessed for the day, our barrister said I had done an outstanding job. I'd hoped for such a finale. Now, the only remaining question was what the legal proceeding had actually accomplished, in the matter of settlement. I hoped that it would completely reverse what Eugene and Edwina had done. It turned out that we were not as fortunate as that. The settlement provided that any assets that should have been ear-marked for Nigel's children's inheritance should be returned to Nigel's children. All furnishings still at *Willow Grove Abbey*, could remain intact. The Abbey itself was to revert to the original heirs, the Somerville children. Each of us would own a third of the property, and any one of us, or all of us, could live there, as long as the others were in agreement. The difficulty was that a complete audit of Edwina's financial dealings would have to meticulously be prepared, as it was not easy to determine which money Papa wanted to go to us, and which he intended for her. That part became very complex, and since they had tried to cheat the Government out of their rightful share, there were enormous penalties and fines, Edwina's estate had to pay them, but of course, Edwina's estate was really *our* money. However, while we did not inherit nearly what we would have if Papa had never married Edwina, the important thing to me was that we *did* manage to win back lovely *Willow Grove Abbey*. Because barrister fees were so exorbitant, it cost a great deal of money just to pay for the law-suit. And, until everything had been audited, we would not be free to return to my ancestral home. One other detail was included in the settlement. A substantial sum of money was settled upon Kippy, to be kept in Trust by his Uncle, Eugene.

The last time I saw Eugene Phillips he was leaving the courtroom, with his head down, eyes glued to the floor. I assumed he was contemplating what life was going to be like living in reduced circumstances. Since I was not a party to the lawsuit, I had no idea what the verdict meant for me. Certainly, I hoped that Blake and Drew would do the honorable thing, and split whatever was left after solicitor's fees, but there was nothing to say they would. I was much more concerned about the ownership of *Willow Grove Abbey*. Blake walked over to me after the settlement and was actually quite nice. He said that they would have to wait and see what figure the Judge came up with in awarding the settlement, but that I could be assured that I would receive my one-third. He also wanted me to know that if Spence and I wished to move back to *Willow Grove Abbey*, it would be fine with him. Blake and Susan were permanently settled in Scotland, and at least for the moment, Drew and Annie were in *Wraxall*, a village not far from *Willow Grove*. There was conversation about the possibility that Drew would indeed take the position of vicar at the Winnsborough clinic. It appeared that Spence and I were the only ones who really had any interest in living there. Since we had been given *Winnsborough Hall,* free and clear, and it needed so little renovation, we knew that we would be fine, without having to beg for money from my family. I knew that my father had expected that Edwina would leave *Willow Grove Abbey* to his heirs upon her death. Now that was reality. Drew and Annie were so very nice about the outcome, and I felt that a definite page had turned with them.

Chapter Fifteen

1952-1964
A Coronation

On the way home from Bristol, Spence and I talked non-stop. The trial had served to solidify our plans. As soon as we returned to *St. James Road*, I went in search of Nan, as I knew that she'd be thrilled at our news. Of course, she was ecstatic at the prospect of moving back to *Willow Grove Abbey*.

"Oh Mum. Do you mean that we can be movin back to the *Abbey*, then? That it will be like it were when your folks was alive, before that 'orrible girl come along?"

"Yes Nan. We shall be moving back to the *Abbey*. But, it won't be like it was when Mummy and Papa were alive. My hope is that it will be vastly different. It will be the happy home it always should have been."

"I'm s'posin you're right about that, Milady. You and the doctor will make an 'appy 'ome wherever you are. And of course, your dear Isabella."

"Well, our little Isabella is growing up, you know. I imagine we'll only have her during summers from this point on, but there'll certainly be room for lots of parties for her friends.

"Oh Milady, I'm glad it's worked this way. You have such a lovely 'ome here on St. James Road, but *Willow Grove Abbey* is just like a part of you.

"Yes Nan, that's true. If I didn't love the *Abbey* so much, I wouldn't have fought so hard to keep it. We have made a major decision, too. Spence is opening his own mental health clinic in the old manor house where I lived when I was married to Owen Winnsborough."

"Well, fancy that," Nan smiled, as she wiped her hands on the freshly starched apron she wore. "Ain't it funny 'ow things work out?"

"Yes, Nan. Spence always has a word for these sorts of happenings. He calls them 'serendipitous'. It means they were meant to happen and weren't an accident."

"Well, I think I'd be agreeing with 'im," Nan chuckled.

Changing the subject, I asked if Nan knew of any way we could trace Joseph, the marvelous chauffeur the family had during my growing up years at *Willow Grove Abbey*. I intended to try everything in my arsenal to entice him to return to our employ. Not at St. James Road, but at *Willow Grove Abbey*. He could drive Spence back and forth to work, and would make an excellent person to pick patients up at the train, or even at the airport, as more and more people were starting to fly commercially.

"I'll get to thinking on it. Will yer still be goin on with yer work at yer clinic, then?"

"Quite. Nevertheless, I'm scheduled to finish soon. I think I'm going to be helping Spence in the new mental health facility when it's open."

"How grand, Milady. Won't that be nice, working side by side with your 'usband?"

"Yes, I think it will be Nan, but you mustn't refer to me as 'Milady" anymore. I stopped using that title when I married Spence. I'm simply Mrs. Stanton."

"But…but, you are still the daughter of an Earl, and Lord 'ave Mercy, even I know that you should 'ave a title Mum."

"I could keep the title of Lady Somerville, if I so wished, but I don't. I'm perfectly happy with Mrs. Stanton. I always have been. It's the only title I ever really wanted, Nan"

"It don't feel right some 'ow, calling you Mrs. Stanton."

"Well, Nan, for as long I can remember, you've always called me 'Miss Sophia'. Can't we just continue on in the same way?"

"Will it be proper, Mum?"

"Absolutely proper, Nan. You should know by now that we don't stand on ceremony. I've always wanted our guests to feel welcome, and to instantly know that it's a happy home, filled with love."

Therefore, by spring 1953, Nan had managed to help track down most of the old, loyal employees whom the Somervilles had counted on for years. Even Joseph returned, filled with wonderful tales of his days with the Royals, chauffeuring the Princess Margaret. He had loved the job, and said the Princess was quite charming, but also demanding. At any rate, he seemed glad to be 'home'…working for us, and he was quite happy with the housing accommodations at *Winnsborough Hall*. At the same time we made arrangements to move back to *Willow Grove Abbey*, I felt a lot of sorrow saying goodbye to *St. James Road*, as it had been our first home together. But, we went with wonderful memories, and were eager to at last be able to call *Willow Grove Abbey* ours. Both of my brothers had given their approval for us to live there, as well as the Court. We were to pay each of my brothers one third of the estate's value, or whatever the fair rate would be for leasing such a property. I wanted to buy it outright, and after putting pen to paper, we felt that we could afford to do so. That would be the end of my Winnsborough money, which was fine by me, and from then on, we would be dependent upon what Spence earned from our mental health clinic, and from my own employment there. Spence felt that his future looked very bright as far as earnings, so while we would always have the upkeep on *Willow Grove Abbey*, we felt we could meet those obligations.

When I made my first visit to my ancestral home, once we knew it was to be ours again, I was delighted, but also horrified. It was ghastly. Edwina had certainly done everything she could to make it hers, starting with the décor in the Drawing Room. She'd had the Chartreuse colored carpeting laid in that magnificent room, and hung matching draperies. The sofa was a bright yellow, in a Danish Modern style, with metal, peg legs, and a square back and sides. The paintings on the wall looked like Picasso's. One had the appearance of a woman with three breasts! Others were just total blobs of color, and one looked like it was a child's finger painting in oil. Gone were most of the precious antiques that had lined the walls, and it was obvious that she had gone for what was being called the 'minimalist 'look. Her coffee table book on chocolate was on the table, but otherwise, there was not a book in sight. Even in the library. All of the books had been stored, and she had strange looking pieces of pottery scattered about in the shelves, as well as African masks, and Japanese fans. She'd had a wall of bookshelves torn out, and replaced that area with a wet bar. The lovely, old leather furniture that had graced that room since my grandfather's days at *Willow Grove Abbey* was gone, and in its place was a chartreuse fabric sofa and loveseat. There was also a television set in the bookcases. I could go on and on, through each room of that grand, old mansion, but I suspect I've made myself clear. It was quickly apparent to me that we would have our work cut out for us, refurbishing the *Abbey*, and converting it back into the gracious home it had always been. Thank the good Lord I found out later that most things had been stored, so we hadn't lost those priceless family treasures. Nan and I set about searching for our old familiar items, and before too terribly long, the place began to look normal again. Of course, it was necessary that the vile carpeting be removed immediately, and then the Aubusson rugs could be cleaned and re-laid. There was more work that had to be done at *Willow Grove Abbey* than at *Winnsborough Hall,* and we were transforming the larger, grander estate into a hospital! We were finally able to move back in September of 1952. The house on *St. James Road* sold almost immediately to a lovely family, with two children, and I felt happy knowing there would be a nice family there to carry on the love we had for the house.

We set about the renovation work that needed doing at *Winnsborough Hall*. There wasn't a tremendous lot. We removed any priceless art objects and paintings, and simplified the surroundings, still keeping it warm and homey. All of the bathrooms were equipped with safety devices, such as bars in the tubs. Doors to every room were widened to accommodate wheelchairs. The kitchen was outfitted with the newest and latest in cooking apparatus. The Dining Room, Library and Drawing Room, were redone in soft, soothing colors, and the entire atmosphere of the home was one of relaxation and peace. We redid one of the smaller drawing rooms into a smart and comfortable office for Spence to have one-on-one conversations with patients, and another was transformed into a lovely office for me, where I could counsel, administer tests, and write reports. The facility opened its doors for patients in November. It immediately filled with referrals from Sir Aubrey Lewis at Maudsley. He came down one weekend, toured the facility, and jokingly told Spence that if he ever needed another psychiatrist, he was the man. Nothing would have pleased Spence more, but Sir Aubrey was terribly committed to Maudsley and was not planning to move anywhere. Spence was able to hire four of the very best young psychiatrists with whom he had worked at Maudsley. They were energetic, with fresh ideas and eager to implement the new programs Spence was putting into place. They all agreed upon the modern concept that mental illness could be helped by a combination of group and individual therapy, as well as the latest medications coming on the market.

As early as 1949, neuroscientists had begun to make discoveries of monumental importance in the field. Julius Axelrod, an American pharmacologist, was beginning his discoveries into the actions of neurotransmitters in the brain and their regulation of the metabolism of the nervous system. The pharmaceutical drug, *Milltown*, began to be widely used that year, and had some revolutionary effects upon hospitalized patients who hadn't responded well to other treatment. Spence was excited about the future and so was I. Mental illness would no longer be treated like something shameful, to be kept hidden. It was coming out into the sunshine, where it belonged, and those persons who'd studied the field couldn't have been happier. Dr. and Mrs. Hausfater also made the move to *The Winnsborough Center*, he as a researcher and she as an intake person. It was nice seeing them on a regular basis. Of course, he now served on the Board of Directors, as well. I threw myself into the new project, too. I administered a battery of psychological tests to incoming patients, and interpreted them so that the treating physician had a tool to help in the planning of a proper treatment regimen. It was wonderful, satisfying work, and I learned something new every day. We began to work with children who were suffering from traumatic stress from the war footing too, and that became my specialty. I adored children, and was able to establish a good rapport with them. I had good success with a large number of patients.

Our life was so splendid that very little worthy of true upset occurred during that time. Perhaps the most upsetting thing that happened in 1952, was when King George died, making his daughter Elizabeth the new Queen of England. Spence and I were not terribly social and we didn't choose to participate in many of the spectacular events surrounding the coronation, but there was no way to completely avoid the festivities, and I wanted Isabella to see the pomp and majesty that surrounded the crowing of a new Queen. We were invited to the Coronation itself at Westminster. The service took place on the second of June, 1953, and the young daughter of the deceased King George the Eighth was just a girl of twenty-five years. Norman Hartnell was commissioned by the Queen to design the outfits for all the members of the Royal Family and especially the dress Elizabeth would wear at the coronation; Hartnell's design for the latter evolved through nine proposals, the final reached by his own research as well as numerous personal meetings with the Queen. What resulted was a white silk dress embroidered with the floral emblems of the countries of the Commonwealth at the time: the Tudor Rose of England, the Scot's Thistle, the Welsh Leek, Irish Shamrock for Northern Ireland, the wattle of Australia, the maple leaf of Canada, the new Zealand Fern, South Africa's Protea, two lotus flowers for India and Ceylon, and Pakistan's Wheat, cotton and jute, unknown to the Queen at the time of the gown's delivery, though, was the unique four-leaf clover embroidered on the dress' left side, where Elizabeth's hand would touch throughout the day.

Elizabeth, meanwhile, rehearsed for the upcoming day with her maids of honor, a sheet used in place of the velvet train and an arrangement of chairs standing in for the carriage. So that she could become accustomed to its feel and weight, the Queen also wore the Imperial State Crown while she went about her daily business, sporting it at her desk, at tea, and while reading the newspaper. Elizabeth took part in two full rehearsals at Westminster Abbey, on 22 and 29 May, though other sources assert that the Queen attended either "several" rehearsals or one. Typically, the Duchess of Norfolk stood in for the Queen at rehearsals.

The Coronation ceremony of Elizabeth II followed a similar pattern to the coronations of the kings and queens before her, being held in Westminster Abbey, and involving the peerage and clergy. However, for the new Queen, several parts of the ceremony were markedly different. The coronation of the Queen was the first ever to be televised and was also the world's first major international event to be broadcast on television.

Along a route lined with sailors, soldiers, and airmen and women from across the Commonwealth, guests and officials passed in a procession before approximately three million spectators gathered in the streets of London, some having camped overnight in their spot to ensure a view of the monarch and others having access to specially built stands and scaffolding along the route. For those not present to witness the event, more than 200 microphones were stationed along the path and in Westminster Abbey with 750 commentators broadcasting descriptions in 39 languages more than twenty million viewers around the world watched the coverage. The procession included foreign royalty and heads of state riding to Westminster Abbey in various carriages; so many that volunteers ranging from wealthy businessmen to rural landowners were required to fill the insufficient ranks of regular footmen. The first royal coach left Buckingham Palace and moved down The Mall, which was filled with flag-waving and cheering crowds. It was followed by the Irish State Coach carrying Queen Elizabeth and The Queen Mother, who wore the circlet of her crown bearing the Koh-i-noor diamond. Queen Elizabeth II proceeded through London from Buckingham Palace, through Trafalgar Square, and towards the Abbey in the Gold State Coach. Attached to the shoulders of her dress, the Queen wore the Robe of State, a very long, hand woven silk velvet cloak lined with Canadian ermine that required the assistance of the Queen's maids of honor. The return procession followed a route that was five miles in length, to Buckingham Palace. 10,000 service personnel from across the Commonwealth and Empire marched in a procession that was two miles long and took 45 minutes to pass any given point. A further 15,800 lined the route. I chose to wear a smart crème colored cashmere day dress, with a matching wide-brimmed hat, and crème calfskin gloves. It was an incredible day, and one none of us would ever forget.

Chapter Sixteen

MARCH, 1954
ANOTHER DEBUT

Soon after that occasion, Isabella graduated from *Ashwick Park*. The next question that loomed was what she intended to do after her commencement? Of course, in my day, in 1935, when young ladies graduated, the next step was a debut, Presentation to the King, and the Season, where each girl did all she could to pursue a husband. Things had radically changed. There was still to be a debut and presentation, but in a much different manner. The girls were brought out in an en masse presentation, to which all eligible were asked. Of course, because of my family heritage, Isabella was included, I left it up to her as to whether she wished to be Presented, and she decided, since it was a sort-of dying tradition, she would.

It was the usual wild March weather, cold winds ruffling the girls' full-skirted silk dresses, we mothers in our furs and many mustached fathers wearing top hats as we lined up by the railings, gaped at by waiting crowds kept at a discreet distance as if in an Ealing comedy. The scene had been made poignant by the recent unexpected announcement from the Palace that these would be almost the last presentations. These lovely girls were a soon-to-be extinguished species, the last of the English debutantes.

How had we got there in the first place? What was the selection process for what Jessica Mitford, most reluctant of debs, described as "the specific, upper-class version of a puberty rite?" By and large it was family tradition. Most debutantes were presented by their mothers, who themselves had been presented. In the circles in which I grew up, curtseying to the Queen was not a matter for discussion, it was, quite simply, the 'done' thing.

The end was a symptom and a symbol of wide changes in Britain in the mid-Fifties. The debacle of Suez in 1956 led that parade. The Suez crisis was a diplomatic and military confrontation in late 1956, with Egypt on one side, and Britain, France and Israel on the other. It was a diplomatic and military confrontation in late 1956 between Egypt on one side, and Britain, France and Israel on the other, with the United States, the Soviet Union, and the United Nations playing major roles in forcing Britain, France and Israel to withdraw.

The attack followed the President of Egypt Gamel Abdel Nasser's decision of the 26 of July, to nationalize the Suez Canal, after the withdrawal of an offer by Britain and the United States to to fund the building of the Aswan dam. That came in response to Egypt's new ties with the Soviet Union and recognizing the People's Republic of China and recognizing the People's Republic of China during the height of tensions between China and Taiwan. The aims of the attack were primarily to regain Western control of the Suez Canal and to remove Nasser from power, and the attack highlighted the danger that Arab nationalism posed to Western access to Middle East oil.

Less than a day after Israel invaded Egypt, Britain and France issued a joint ultimatum to Egypt and Israel, and then began to bomb Cairo. Allegations began to emerge that the invasion of Egypt had been planned beforehand by the three powers. Naturally, those allegations were denied. The Anglo-French forces withdrew before the end of the year, but Israeli forces remained until March, 1957, prolonging the crisis. In April the canal was fully reopened.

The next change in Britain was the resignation of Anthony Eden which spelled the end of Britain's imperialist ambitions. Almost overnight Britain's strength had dwindled and it had an obvious effect on the morale of the people who considered themselves the ruling classes. The system itself was also becoming open to abuse, as well-born ladies charged large fees to bring out girls whose credentials were not always of the highest. The most notorious of these was Lady St John of Bletso, a Lady Bracknell figure who would launch several debutantes at once. By 1958 the exclusivity of the Season had eroded. In the immortal words of Princess Margaret, "We had to put a stop to it. Every tart in London was getting in. the way. Their curtseys must have given them away.

They were trained to make the curtsey, which was by no means a perfunctory bob but a low, sweeping curtsey. The left knee needed to be locked behind the right, allowing a graceful descent with head erect, hands by your side. They learned the technique from Madame Vacani, a dancing teacher who held a kind of royal warrant for the curtsey. A Vacani curtsey was part of the mystique. I couldn't help but remember my days of practicing for this same ritual back in 1935. Edwina and I had still been close friends then, and we had giggled and laughed through all of the practicing.

However hard the girls practiced, the experience was nerve-racking. Their hearts thumped as they assembled on little stiff gilt chairs in an antechamber, waiting to be called into the ballroom where the Queen and the Duke of Edinburgh sat on twin thrones under a crimson canopy adapted from the Imperial shamiana, redolent of the then relatively recent British rule in India. One curtsey to the Queen, then three sidesteps and another deep curtsey to Prince Philip. What if you wobbled? What if your heel caught in your petticoat and ripped it, the disaster that overtook a friend of Isabella's? How should you respond if a bored Prince Philip winked? Isabella wore an enchanting gown. It was a Pierre Balmain original, with a narrow waist and full skirt, exquisitely hand-embroidered in a custom inspired floral motif with meandering vines of silk threads on the taffeta dress, with pearls scattered over the skirt. It had a boned-fitted strapless bodice, and a draped sweetheart neckline. Multiple tulle crinolines and a custom hoop were worn with it. She looked poignantly beautiful. She wore her incredible hair with the curls piled softly atop her lovely crown, and graced the beautiful arrangement with a diamond tiara.

The ceremony, or something like it, had been going for 200 years. The curtsey ritual went back to the reign of George III, when daughters of the court circle who reached marriageable age were presented to Queen Charlotte by their mothers. This signified their entrance to the marriage market. Through the 19th and early 20th centuries the system grew and solidified. Presentation was followed by the London "Season" in which potential suitors could eye up the girls newly released into society. It was a means of meeting only the "right" people, a system of exclusion, link-ing like with like with the sovereign's blessing and an obvious means to unify wealth and influence. It was that sort of attitude which had created all of the furor and uproar when I wanted to marry Spence. Mummy had not considered him one of the 'right' people. While I had always been a traditionalist, and thus was pleased that Isabella wanted to participate in this age old ritual, I certainly wanted no part of the supercilious attitude that had once accompanied the pageantry. I made certain that Isabella clearly understood that Spence and I did not consider ourselves superior to any-one, and that she should base her choice of a future spouse upon her own values and not upon whether any man was considered worthy because his mother had bowed to the Queen.

After the Lord Chamberlain's announcement that curtseys would be ceasing after 1958, there was a record number of applications for the final presentations, like a wave of panic buying. One mother was said to have presented all four of her daughters. Under-age girls were brought out of boarding school to curtsey. Isabella's own presentation day was one of three that week, in which 1,400 girls in total curtseyed to their monarch in a ceremony whose semi-sacred overtones took me back to confirmation services at *Ashwick Park School*. After it was over, the debutantes assembled in the Green Dining Room to giggle, chatter and munch the celebrated chocolate cake provided by the Palace. They were still greedy teenagers in a country in which rationing had ended that very year.

Presentation was for many just the prelude to a non-stop sum-mer of lunch parties, cocktail parties, dances and country house week-ends. However, Isabella did not want to participate in that phase of the event. Instead, Spence and I discussed the three of us taking a splendid Mediterranean cruise, to let Isabella explore a bit of the world, before she might leave us for university. Of course, I was taken back to my own ball, which was the night I met Spence and my life changed in a million ways. I hoped and prayed that Isabella would one day find that same sort of happi-ness, without all of the heartbreak that I'd had to go through to achieve it. After the Ball, Isabella was pleased that she had participated, but she said it was all rather boring. Most of her friends felt the same way. She was much more excited about looking forward to our planned trip abroad.

We booked tickets to sail on the S.S. Stella Solaris from Istanbul to Barcelona, with a route that would take us through the Greek Isles, the Dalmatian Coast, Italy, Capri, Sicily, the French Riviera, and on to Barcelona, where we would disembark for a flight back to England. Our journey began with a flight to Paris, and a three-day stay in the City of Lights. Then on to Istanbul. I was nearly as excited as Isabella was. I had never been to any of the aforementioned countries, with the exception of France, where my memories were very mixed. It was Paris where I'd escaped with Edwina, before Isabella's birth; and it was also Paris, where my precious Isabella had been born. I remembered Paris with the young Edwina. I remembered sitting in a restaurant under chestnut boughs on the Champs-Elysees. I'd never actually seen all of the splendid landmarks one should see while there. And so, in April, we spent two days seeing all of the wonders of that incredible city. We dined at Maxim's, rode to the top of the Eiffel Tower, visited Versailles, toured the Louvre and the tomb of Napoleon, at Les Invalides Then we boarded a train which took us to La Havre, where our cruise began. There, we boarded the ship for our wonderful and memorable journey. It was a luxurious vessel, very large, and opulent. Isabella had her own cabin, right next to ours, so we didn't have to wander all over to find one another. The first night, we all dressed rather simply for dinner, and were placed at a table with some lovely people two other couples and an elderly lady realizing a lifetime's dream of taking a cruise. I loved meeting people like that. The other two couples were also English, and about our age. We bonded very quickly, and found ourselves laughing and enjoying ourselves immensely. From that point on, they were our tablemates. Our first two days were spent at sea, en route to Istanbul. They were peaceful and calm, and we enjoyed the solitude. Spence and I read a lot, and Isabella met the young people who were lounging about near the pool area. The meals were absolutely unforgettable, and I knew I would be going on a diet when we returned to England, for the first time in my life!

Finally we reached Istanbul, and spent two days there immersing ourselves in the history and culture. Then we were on to Ephesus, where Paul, Jesus's disciple had preached in the arena, which had been unearthed by years of archeological digging. The entire city was beyond one's imagination. From there it was on to several Greek islands; Rhodes, Crete, Patmos, and a final stop in Athens. We climbed to the Acropolis, and spent hours in the old Agora district. From there, we sailed on to Italy. Oh, Italy! There are not words to express my feelings for that lovely country and its people. We anchored offshore, in the Bay of Naples, which gave us the ability to explore Naples and the Amalfi Drive area, plus Capri. I fell in love with that land. More importantly, Isabella met her first summer romance there. A newcomer, he had boarded the ship back in Athens, but we had not met him yet. We all had thought that he was of Greek heritage, due to his black hair and handsome visage. But, it turned out that he was starting his trip from Athens, and that he would be aboard throughout its duration, until we reached Barcelona. He was not Greek, but Italian, and had, just like Isabella, recently completed his schooling. He had attended Oxford, and spoke excellent English, which was convenient, but I think Isabella preferred to hear his lovely Italian. Don't they call it the language of lovers? At any rate, his name was Lucca Rossi, and he was every young girl's dream. Tall, well built, dark-eyes and a gorgeous smile. Isabella had never shown any interest in romantic sorts of things. She'd had plenty of boyfriends through her school years, but none ever meant more than a good friend. But, I don't think that there is a young girl alive who hasn't at least once dreamed of a ship-board romance on a lovely summertime cruise, with a magnificent Italian man. I am exceptionally glad that Spence and I were there, for obvious reasons. While Isabella was a very good girl, and I had never worried about her in regard to men, she was still beautiful and eighteen years old! They met by the pool, and before the day was over, he had made arrangements for a car and driver to carry us through the Amalfi Drive, and also to Naples. Obviously, money did not seem to be an issue for young Mr. Rossi. It *was* thoughtful of him, however, to make certain that Spence and I were included. Actually, we would not have let Isabella go with him, if that were not the case. Both Isabella and I dressed in darling cotton sundresses, and brought sweaters along in case we needed them. We packed a big floppy bag full of sun lotion, comb, brush, cameras, and everything we could conceivably think we might want or need. The car and driver met us when the dinghy from the boat docked at the shoreline. Spence helped me to step ashore, and Lucca helped Isabella, and we settled ourselves in the large sedan. Our driver was Italian, but also spoke English, so we were comfortably off on a splendid afternoon. The drive was breath-taking. There is simply no other way to describe it. The road was a mass of hairpins turns, with literally only one lane, and to our right we could see a drop of several hundred, if not thousands, of feet, to the blue Bay of Naples, and across to mount Vesuvius. Lemon trees were thick along the roadside, and one could smell their fragrance in the air. We passed, first, through the popular and well-known town of Sorrento, and then on to smaller, quaint villages. To the road, overlooking the sea, were marvelous hotels. What stupendous views they had. We lunched at one of the prettiest restaurants I have ever seen. It sat on the terrace of the Santa Catherina Hotel. The hotel enjoyed a gorgeous coastal setting of incomparable beauty. It sat at the summit of an extensive property, which began along the Amalfi Drive and tumbled down the water in a series of landscaped terraces. Elevators and scenic paths transported guests past citrus groves and lush gardens to the seaside level, which included a sea-water swimming pool, sunbathing decks, gym, café/bar and open air restaurant. Lunch was served on a private beach terrace, just above the hotel's private beach platform. Traditional Italian dishes were served, and I even had to admit that the fish I ordered was excellent. I believe we all felt as though we could have spent days gazing out at the blue, blue waters of the Mediterranean, and dreaming dreams. But, our agenda was long, and our time much too short. We continued on to the town of Amalfi, which lies at the mouth of a deep ravine at the foot of Monte Cerrato, surrounded by dramatic cliffs and coastal scenery. Amalfi is the main town on that coast, and was first recorded in ancient manuscripts in the sixth century. It was well-known at that time for maritime activities, and they shipped goods to places such as Venice, which was still a fledgling city. There was an important Cathedral there, and ever so many other places of historical value. On our return trip, we detoured and visited the ancient city of Pompeii, which was destroyed in 79 A.D. when Mount Vesuvius erupted and killed nearly all of its residents, some 20,000. It was a place of great historical value, and archeological digs had been going on there for years. Eventually, I am certain that they will uncover the remains of the entire town. But, what we were able to see was like taking a walk down the streets of that ancient city. Entire homes were still complete, as they had been, as well as the cities central forum, shops, and even the imaginative water system, not so much different than ours today. We were all thoroughly enchanted. We really wished we could have had more time to spend there, but the day was growing late, and none of us wished to drive that twisting road after darkness fell. We arrived back on board ship just in time to change our clothing and enjoy an excellent experience dining at the Captain's Table. He was most charming.

The next day, we explored Naples. Of course, Naples still clearly showed the signs of being ravaged by war. Once magnificent palaces had been reduced to ruin, or their owners were now forced to take in boarders to pay for the necessary repairs. Still, while it seemed war torn and weary, it was also a quintessential Italian city, to me. Clotheslines stretched across the backyards, and one could hear the voices of housewives yelling to friends and neighbors. Many buildings had terrible damage from the war. We chose to spend a night in in old palace, at 29 Via Possilipo, in what had been an old palace, and was now converted in to individual flats. Spence and I had a window covered with Italian shudders, and when they were opened, we could look straight across to Vesuvius. The waves from the sea lapped at the shore beneath our balcony. While the accommodations themselves were not splendid, the ambiance more than made up for any comforts we lacked. One had to make their way down a very long walkway to arrive at the door to our flat. There were many twists and turns of the steps. The walkway began where the seawall surrounded the Bay of Naples. Horse drawn carriages took those who wished on carriage rides around the bay. Everything was enchanting, and if it was to me, you can imagine what it was to an eighteen year old. Lucca and Isabella spent a good amount of time in those horse drawn carriages! Lucca's father was the President for Air Italia Airlines and was stationed in Naples, so we were all able to meet him, and dine with him at his private club, high up in the hills, over-looking the city. I tried Calamari for the first time in my life, and loved it! We chatted with him at length about the war years, and how glad we were it was all over. He seemed pleased that his son had taken the time to introduce us.

On the way we sailed, up to the East Coast of Italy. Our next stop was Dubrovnik on the Dalmatian Coast. An ancient walled city was there, and since all of us adored history, we marveled at the ancient edifices. I remember back in 1935 the stories of Edward VIII and Wallis Simpson strolling seaside near Dubrovnik. From there, the ship turned back south, and we headed for the city of my dreams, the city of a million dreams before and after me, Venice. Considered the Jewel of the Adriatic, I left a part of my heart there. After doing a day of the requisite sightseeing, we settled into two more days of wandering the back lanes, and sitting in St. Marc's square, drinking Galliano on the Rocks, and watching people. One evening, two darling gentlemen came over to our table and presented both Isabella and I with a nosegay of lovely violets. It was such a sweet gesture. They were German, and we invited them to join us. In speaking with them, we learned even more about the horrific deprivations they had undergone during the war. Both had lost their parents to the Third Reich. There was certainly no evidence of any hatred or anger toward the Allies; only thankfulness that someone had stopped Hitler before they had also lost their lives. I was so pleased that my mother wasn't present. Of course if she had been, they never would have been asked to join our group to begin with.

Instead of staying on board the ship in Venice, we rented a suite in the old wing of the Danielli Hotel on the Grande Canal. Lucca stayed at a relative's home. The Danielli was absolutely the top in luxury, but also retained its historical ambiance. The walls in our room were covered in pale green Fortuny fabric, with matching bed clothing and draperies. There were shuddered doors onto a small balcony, from which we could view the Grande Canal, as well as the tables of visitors sitting outside in the front, at small, round table, sipping after dinner aperitifs. Isabella and Lucca spent their evenings in that spot, which was convenient for us, as we could sneak a peek at them through our shudders, without their ever knowing. They had reached the point where, when they were seated at a table, his hand was perpetually over hers, and there were many kisses exchanged from cheek to cheek. There was no question that she was smitten, as I too would have been at her age, and we did not want to spoil this new romance. But this was all new for our daughter, and we wanted to keep it within the proper bounds. One particular night, after we had retired in Venice, she knocked quietly at our door. I put on a dressing gown, and went out into the hallway to meet her. She was so thrilled, I could see that she wanted to bounce on her toes,

"What is it darling? You are positively glowing. Has something happened?" I asked.

"Well…yes…and no. Mummy you will never, ever guess. Lucca says that he is in love with me! Can you imagine? Me!"

"Yes, I can imagine, sweetheart. This is Italy. All Italians are perpetually in love. You mustn't take this terribly seriously. Enjoy it for what it is. Italians don't necessarily mean the same thing when they use the word 'love.' It doesn't necessarily carry the same connotation that it does in our culture. I would expect him to love you. Look at you. You are gorgeous, sweet, educated, and kind. Who wouldn't love you? Especially a young, Italian man. You are going to have a lot of men tell you that they love you."

"So, you don't think I should believe him"

"Certainly believe him. I'm sure he means it. Just as he will in a month when he meets another girl."

"But, Mummy, we're serious about this. Lucca wants me to go home and study Italian, and finish my schooling and then to return to Italy. He means for us to eventually marry. We both know that we're too young, now."

"Isabella. By all means, study Italian if you wish. Papa and I would want you to follow the plans you've originally made to study at The Rhode Island School of Design in America. You can also study Italian, as well. If your feelings for Lucca are as strong when you finish up there, as they are now, we can discuss your next move. If living in Italy is what you think you would like, we will see, Darling."

Isabella leaned over and kissed me on both cheeks. "Grazie Mama," she laughed. "I knew you would understand."

"Isabella, of course I understand. You are in the most romantic place on Earth, and you have met a very nice and handsome young man. The fact that he is Italian adds to his charm, don't you suppose? I only want you to promise me one thing."

"What is that, Mummy?" Isabella asked, suddenly looking more serious.

"Promise me that you won't let this become a full-fledged 'love affair' You have always spoken of keeping yourself for the man you marry. While

I understand that you believe that the man may be Lucca, wait and make certain of that, before making any rash decisions."

"Oh quite, Mummy. I agree completely with you. I've already told Lucca my feelings about pre-marital sex. Of course, Italian men think differently, but he has agreed to comply with my wishes."

"Then there should be nothing to worry about. After the cruise, the two of you can write letters, and perhaps even visit one another. There will be time to make certain you truly want to spend the rest of your lives together."

"I know, Mummy. I'm not ready to ring the ship's Captain and have him marry us, on board. I just wanted you to know all of this, because I suspect that Lucca will speak with Papa tomorrow. I didn't want you to be upset."

I kissed her again, and sent her on her way, as I returned to our stateroom. Crawling in bed next to Spence, I thought about the feelings I'd had when I'd made my trip to *Willow Grove* in 1935, to tell my parents how much Spence and I loved each other. What a different reaction I had been met with. This time, I'd tried to handle the situation deftly, always remembering not to negate Isabella's very real feelings, nor to treat the romance as something childish. It seemed to have worked out well.

The next day the ship pulled anchor, and we left Venice, sailing back around the boot of Italy, and on up the Western coastline to Cittiveccia, the port used for passengers to and from Rome. We dropped anchor there, and a car and driver carried us into the Eternal City. We had made reservations at the Excelsior Hotel on the Via Veneto, and our accommodations' were splendid. Spence had reserved a two-bedroom suite, and Lucca had a room right next door. That night, after unpacking and getting settled, we wandered the streets of Rome, and found a marvelous small café in which to eat dinner. It was owned by a husband and wife, and on the table was a large bottle of homemade Grappa, with a spigot. It was Spence, Isabella's and my first taste of that odd, very strong liqueur, and we were a bit tipsy as we strolled back toward the hotel. Lucca had taken Spence aside earlier in the day, and told him that he loved Isabella 'molto grande,' and that he wished permission to marry her. Spence and I had already discussed my conversation with Isabella, so Spence virtually repeated the things I had said. We did not agree to any plans for a marriage in the foresee-able future, but told them we would not be opposed if they felt the same way when all schooling was completed." The two lovebirds accepted that pronouncement.

The first full day in Rome, we had our driver take us to all of the renowned sights on our agenda. The Coliseum, the Forum, the Pantheon, the Circus Maximus, and the Trevi Fountain, of course. We had lunch at the hotel, and then set out for a half-day visit to Vatican City, and a private audience with the Pope. Even though Lucca was also Catholic, and had lived in Italy his entire life, he had never been through the experience of an audience with the Holy Father. Spence made arrangements for him to be included. We were incredibly fortunate to be even considered for such a privilege. Spence had connections in England, and it was all arranged before we left on the trip. We were led by a monsignor who had a close connection to Pope Paul XXVI. Each of us had to make a substantial contribution/donation that was presented to the Pope during our private audience. We were on call from the time we arrived in Rome on that Monday until we finally received word to meet with the Pope on Friday. It was understood at the onset of the trip that there was no guarantee we were going to actually have the private meeting based on the health and schedule of the Pope at that time. When we finally were granted the meet-ing it was a once in a lifetime, awe inspiring audience with Pope John Paul XXVI. We went up single file and greeted the Pope and spoke to him in English, Italian or Polish and then kissed his ring. He was quite elderly at the time but had a childlike aura about him. It is something none of us will ever forget. After that unforgettable moment, we toured the Sistine Chapel, and St. Peter's Basilica. Everyone marveled over Michelangelo's breathtaking murals on the celling of the chapel, and his sculpture of the *Pieta*. We were overwhelmed by the beauty we saw that day. I was happy that Isabella was seeing these magnificent relics and works of art early in her life, as I wish I had been afforded such an opportunity. It only helped to bring forth more understanding of the church's antiquity. Late that afternoon, while all of the shops were closed, we went back to the hotel and had a lie-down. Then, we dined in a great place to enjoy a romantic dinner, which I think meant the world to Isabella and Lucca. The name if the restaurant was Sapori del Lord Byron in the Hotel Lord Byron, a stunner of a place that also just happens to serve the best Italian cuisine in town. The decor was as romantic as the atmosphere with its all white lattice and bold Italian colors highlighted by masses of fresh flowers. The setting was in a hotel, an Art Deco villa set on a residential hilltop in Parioli, an area of embassies and exclusive town houses at the edge of the Villa Borghese. After our dinner, Isabella and Lucca left, and went to a dance spot near the Tiber River. Spence and I wanted to just relax, so we stayed put, and drank lovely Italian after-dinner aperitifs. By that time we knew we could trust Lucca. He had, indeed, spoken with Spence while we girls were shopping on the Via Condotti, the designer shopping street in Rome, and they were sipping Italian beer in a nearby café It seemed that Spence handled it all well, and the two youngsters felt we were on their side, if they continued to act in a sensible manner. Deep in my heart, I didn't think anything at all would come of that young, Italian summer romance, but the surest way I knew to make certain that didn't happen, was not to fight against it. I had been there before after all, if one could compare Venice and Rome to Twigbury, in the Cotswolds Hills, in our beloved British Isles. Young love, however, is young love. If I could have fallen madly in love with Spence in that tiny little Cotswold cottage, there certainly seemed nothing extraordinary about Isabella's believing she was in love in the country that was probably as famous as any in the world for its romantic settings.

From Rome we traveled to Florence by train. The city stole our hearts with its plethora of artworks. It was literally a walking museum. We all spent hours in the various galleries, studying the perfection of De Vinci's paintings, and Michelangelo's sculpture. We strolled to the Ponte Vechhio, the ancient covered bridge over the river Arno, which was laden with magnificent jewelry shops on both sides. There, Spence bought me a lovely gold bracelet, with a collection of old lockets hanging from the links. Lucca bought Isabella a sweet gold necklace, with the word 'Amore' engraved on a disc. I wondered how many years it would be before she took it off. That night, back in our stateroom, as I was preparing for bed, while showering, I noticed a very small lump in my left breast. I didn't think much of it. It did not hurt, and was very tiny, the size of a pencil eraser, if that. I mentioned it to Spence, who also didn't seem overly concerned, but wanted me to see our doctor upon returning to England. I put it out of my mind, as we had so many, many other things to think about at that time.

After those golden, summer days spent in that wonderful, romantic land, we re-boarded the ship and were on our way to the French Rivera. Our first stop was Monte Carlo, where we visited the Casino, and lunched at the Hotel de Paris, where I remembered that the famous movie star Grace Kelly had stayed with her bridesmaids before her wedding to His Highness Prince Rainer of Monaco. The views from Monte Carlo were spectacular. From there we continued on to the French Riviera, where we made stops at Nice, Cannes, Grasse, Marseille, and St. Tropez. While in Nice, we rented a car and drove to Cap d'Antibe, where the property that Papa and Edwina had purchased before their marriage was located. It had been left to the Somerville children when the court case was reversed. Neither Spence nor I had ever seen it, although my brothers had. It was a necessary duty on this trip, for our plans were to either sell it, or to lease it for various parts of the Season, and then keep it for family use in the interim. We finally found it, after many wrong turns, and reversing of our course. At long last there it was, a few meters from the port of La Salis Beach. It was a delightful period country house, which had 4000 square feet of living space. There were four bedrooms, four baths, a large living area and a lovely swimming pool.

Nestled in the heart of a stunning landscape planted with pines, cypress, fig, and olive. The house was filled with character and was one of the oldest houses in the Cap d'Antibes area. With its round roof tiles, stone walls, its laundry and well pulley, this property was witness to a by- gone era. It was easy to see why Edwina and my father had made such a quick decision to buy it. We wandered through the grounds, and then on to the main house, which was absolutely divine. The views were magnificent, and I could see ourselves settling in as a family in this lovely spot. Of course, the way things had been progressing among my own Somerville family, I saw very little chance that we would all be spending time together there. I would have liked to think that Spence and I, and Isabella and friends would enjoy long, leisurely summer days on the veranda. But, it was an enormous amount of money to spend for such short periods of entertainment. The question lay in whether or not the home could be rented on an almost continual basis when we were not using it? Yet, it *was* simply breathtaking. I really hated to see it leave the family.

Spence and I decided to give it a good deal of thought. We were very happy that we had gone out of our way to find the lovely villa, so at least we could picture now what we were discussing. I hoped that perhaps my brothers would agree to split the expenses three ways. Spence intended to attempt a conversation with Blake when we returned home. The Rivera itself was divine as well, and it brought back many memories to me of the time I had spent there with Owen. I would never have believed in January of 1936 that I would one day return to that enchanting part of the world with my dear Spence and our darling Isabella. Life really does have a way of knocking us on our noses!

When we arrived in Barcelona, all of our moods were a bit blue. Of course, Isabella and Lucca were the worst. It was hard to wring a smile out of either one of them. They huddled at the back of the top deck of the ship, where we were queued up awaiting our turn to disembark. I could see tears streaming from Isabella's eyes, but I did not try to intervene. This was her first experience with the heartbreak of love, if it was indeed that. Certainly she believed it was. They promised to write, and were already making arrangements for a visit to see one another during the first break from school. Isabella intended to find out if Rhode Island School of Design had a 'study abroad program', wherein she might be able to study in, perhaps Florence, and receive credit at her own school. I knew such programs were beginning to become popular at universities, but was not certain about a specialized school like that which she had selected. Neither Spence nor I was overtaken with joy at the idea of such an excursion. We both really believed that time and distance would serve to turn down the heat on their flaming romance. Finally, the porter took our luggage, and we slowly made our way down the gangway. Lucca was going straight to the airport, where a flight back to Italy awaited him. We were staying one night, and then boarding our flight to Heathrow. We all hugged goodbye, with tears, and made firm promises to keep in touch. Spence and I left them alone for one final passionate kiss goodbye. Then, Spence, Isabella and I got into a taxi and headed to the Grande Hotel Central, a lovely, old vintage hotel in the heart of the city. Isabella waved to Lucca in his taxi until he was out of sight. Then, she burst into a flood of tears.

"My life is over," she howled.

"Darling, your life is not only not over, it is just beginning," laughed Spence." I know you don't see it that way now, Isabella, but some day you will, I promise. Even if you and Lucca *do* end up together, then this time apart will be good for you. Both of you need to learn much more about life, and about the world. Would you give up your plans to study in the States to stay in Italy?"

There was a long pause, punctuated with sniffles. "Well...perhaps not. But, it is just so hard to say goodbye, when I don't know when I'll see him again."

"I know sweetheart," I answered. "Think about how your parents felt every time the train pulled out of the station at *Bedminster with Hartcliffe* during the war?'

"It had to be unbearable, Mummy. You didn't even know if he would be coming back alive."

"That's absolutely the truth, darling. So, you see, barring something terribly unforeseen, you and Lucca will indeed see one another again, probably before you know it, and then think of all of the marvelous things you will have to tell one another."

In the meantime, you will be so busy learning about your new environment, and studying hard, that you won't realize how swiftly the time passes," Spence added.

Isabella stopped sniffling, and pulled out a small compact. She touched up her nose and lipstick, and fingered the necklace he had given her. The worst was behind us. "Our next step is to get you all packed to start school. We really don't have long. You must make a list of any frocks or anything else you think you'll need. The school sent a list of clothing and other items. You need to look it over."

"Yes. I'll get on that as soon as we get home. I *am* excited about starting school. It's the first time I've ever been so far away from you and Papa. Do you think I'll get homesick?"

"Well, you didn't at *Ashwick Park,* although that was a short distance. We will always be as close as a telephone, you know. You can always ring us if you're feeling blue. I should imagine that they keep you so busy that you won't have much time be lonely."

"Oh, I do hope so," breathed Isabella.

Thus, I flew to New York, and on to Providence, Rhode Island with Isabella in August 1955, and together we explored the school. Founded in 1877, the school was one of the best colleges of art and design in the United States. It offered very rigorous art and design programs in art, architecture, art education and fine arts. We had a wonderful stay at *The Biltmore Hotel*, which was built and designed by the same persons who founded Grand Central Station in New York City. The hotel had opened to wide acclaim in 1922, and we adored the accommodations. We were very impressed with the student accommodations at the school, which consisted of suites with connecting baths, and were especially spacious. I made note of the various articles we would need to purchase to make Isabella's room fit her personality. Isabella had tears in her eyes, as I readied for my departure. I understood her feelings. She put her arms about me, and held me close, burying her head against my chest. "I'm not ready to let go, yet," she cried.

"Oh, my sweet Isabella, yes you are, but you won't know it until you've done it. Think of this as a wonderful adventure. You haven't been exiled. You can return to England, to Papa and me anytime you wish. We are as near as a pen and paper, or as the telephone. Your happiness means the world to us. This is your time, sweetheart. It's your time to grow, and to learn. Broaden your horizons, and dig down deep inside for all of the talent I know lies there. You are truly special, Isabella. Don't ever forget that. And you are a part of us. No matter whether you're here in Rhode Island, or in England, we are always connected." I hugged her tightly, and then let her go.

She gave me a watery smile, and wiped her eyes. "I'll be all right, Mummy. I so want to make you and Papa proud of me."

I shuddered. "Isabella, never do anything in your life because you want someone else to approve of you or be proud of you. We are immensely proud of you right now, and we always have been. You needn't do anything except exist to make us proud. Spread your wings and find out what more you are capable of. But, do it for yourself, darling. We love you so much. The world is changing, and I know you will change with it.

But, keep your sensible values, and most importantly, never stop thinking about the joy you have brought to your parents, and to the world. Special delights await you darling. I'm so anxious to see you get on with things here, and then for Papa and me to hear all about them when we see you, which won't be long."

By the time I finished with my motherly homily, Isabella no longer had tears in her eyes. She was ready for her new adventure. I left Rhode Island feeling that our daughter was well settled and safe. And then I cried most of the way home to England.

Chapter Seventeen

1962
KNIGHTHOOD

Spence was making an enormous success out of *The Winnsborough Clinic.* In addition to the chronic mental illness cases that he treated, he opened a new wing in 1959, focusing upon addictions. There was a great need for such a facility, due to the escalating use of illegal drugs, which seemed to have exploded overnight. No one clinic in England specialized in such treatment, so *The Winnsborough Clinic* was the first of its kind. Spence was fast making a name for himself in psychiatric circles. As well as his work at the clinic, he'd authored several books, which became accepted works in the mental health field. In the summer of 1962, to my great delight, and Spence's astonishment, he was knighted. Each year, around 2,600 people receive their awards personally from The Queen or a member of the Royal Family. We were extremely fortunate because it was Queen Elizabeth herself who presided over the ceremony where Spence received his knighthood. His investiture was held in Buckingham Palace. It was a glorious event. It had been eons since I'd had to dress for a formal occasion. First there was the knighting ceremony itself, which took place during the day, and then that night an exquisite dinner-dance, held at the Palace. For the daytime ceremony, I selected a Galanos shell pink silk-linen sweetheart dress, with accordion pleated skirt. It also had cap sleeves and triangle shaped seams so it was assured that it fitted perfectly. My short curls were arranged in a tousled cap. Isabella flew home for the ceremony, and was tremendously proud of her father. She looked like an angel. She wore a gorgeous daytime frock, created by the great designer Oleg Cassini, who had been Mrs. Kennedy's primary designer, as well as Grace Kelly's and Marilyn Monroe's. It was light pink silk with an overlay of pink lace. Isabella had a wonderful hourglass figure and the dress hugged and flattered her curves, but in just the proper way, not revealingly so. The frock had marvelous details, such as a pencil skirt and a sweet, dark green satin bow at the waistline. Spence looked so incredibly handsome in white tie and tails, and as I looked at his remarkably attractive features during the ceremony, I was overcome with the fact that I still adored him as much, or perhaps more, than I had in 1935, when we met.

Queen Elizabeth entered the ballroom of Buckingham Palace, attended by two Gurkha orderly officers, a tradition begun in 1876 by Queen Victoria. On duty on the dais were five members of the Queen's Body Guard of the Yeoman of the Guard, which was created in 1485 by Henry VII. They are the oldest military corps in the United Kingdom. Four gentlemen ushers were on duty to help look after the recipients and their guests. The Queen was escorted by the Lord Chamberlain. After the National Anthem was played, he stood to her right and announced the name of each recipient and the achievement for which they were being decorated. The Queen was provided with a brief background for each recipient by her equerry, as they approached to receive their award. Those who were to be knighted knelt on an investiture stool to receive the accolade, which was bestowed by the Queen using the sword utilized by her father, George VI as Duke of York, and Colonel of the Scots Guards. After the award ceremony, those honored were ushered out of the Ballroom into the Inner Quadrangle of Buckingham Palace, where the Royal Rota of photographers were stationed. There, recipients were photographed with their awards. As the wife of a Knighted Englishman, I once again could revert to use of the title 'Lady'. It mattered little to me whether I did or didn't use this honorific, but I couldn't help but think about how my parents had so scorned Spence because he wasn't titled. I would have given anything to have had them present on that magnificent occasion. That evening we attended the splendid dinner–dance, which surpassed anything I might ever have dreamed. It even made my debutante Ball seem rather passé and simple. I chose to wear a stunning, white silk floral ball gown, designed by Jacque Fath, a renowned French artist in fashion. Sometimes you come across a dress that causes the butterflies in your stomach to go all a flutter, and that dress was one of those. It was an amazing, white ball gown with stunningly vibrant florals splayed throughout. There was a heart-shaped bodice, featuring pleats and a Basque waist. The hips of the dress had small underlining to create an effect of the truly Royal duchesses reminiscent of the eighteenth century. Isabella chose to wear a Balenciaga gown, of white organdy, with a pale blue overlay. The collar was Victorian in style and reached high up onto her neck. The skirt of her dress fell in swishing folds, and was trimmed in Alencon lace. It had long, sheer sleeves, with large cuffs, which buttoned half way up her arm. The ballroom at the palace was the most amazingly incredible room I had ever encountered. At the west end of the ballroom, the two thrones used for the 1902 coronation of King Edward VII and Queen Alexandra stood on a red and gold carpet beneath a canopy of gold-embroidered crimson velvet. Facing the throne dais down the length of the ballroom was the musicians' gallery at the east end. The great organ's gilded pipes were set against a crimson background. The color scheme of the room was a magnificent crème and gold, with a ceiling to rival the Court at Versailles. Spence I danced the night away, just as if we were young again, and then went back to our splendid hotel room at The Grosvenor House, and made mad, passionate love. I was forty-five years old, and Spence was fifty-two, but we both felt like the eighteen and twenty-five we were when we fell in love. From then on, I teased him unmercifully about whether I would have to call him "Sir Spencer" in bed. When I think back upon that time, it is hard to believe that *anything* could have lain in wait to disturb our hard won happiness.

The next year went by in a whisper. Isabella was settled in New York City in 1964, and absolutely loved it. We occasionally still heard mention of Lucca. In fact, he had visited her in New York, shortly after she'd settled there. She said he was still divine, but it was clear that her feelings had cooled. He had accepted a position at the University of Naples, teaching about the ancient Etruscan civilization, and was still living with his father. One day, at lunch, I asked Isabella what her feelings were for Lucca now.

"Oh, Mummy, he's still the same Lucca; unbelievingly handsome, with that continental flair. I compare him with some of the young men I've met in New York, and there is a world of difference. Not necessarily better, or worse, but just so vastly different."

"How do you mean?" I asked.

"Well, Lucca is *Italian*. He wears a Gucci belt, Ferragamo shoes, and Brioni suits. He has a rather brooding look about him, rather like Marlon Brando or Jimmy Dean, the actors. He drives some ghastly expensive automobile; I think a Lamborghini. He likes to hang out in small, intimate cafes and drink wonderful old wines, smoking Turkish cigarettes and writing poetry. He's just so *different*. Not that I don't like him. I find him fascinating. But, I really cannot imagine spending my life with someone like Lucca. I don't think we would fit terribly well. What we had was a wonderful summer romance, the best. I will never forget him, and we have transitioned into very close friends. I really think of him as a brother now. I know Lucca would do anything in the world for me, and I would for him too. But, he's dating others, lots of others, I suspect, and we have both gotten on with our lives. So, it had turned out as Spence and I had suspected it would, and I can't say I wasn't glad about that. There was truth in my mother's old belief that it was difficult enough to make a go of marriage when both parties were of the same cultures and backgrounds, and adding someone who came from the opposite end of the spectrum did not bode well for lasting happiness.

Isabella had secured a position as Chief Design Specialist at *Tate Motifs*, a Company dedicated to the renovation of old buildings in Manhattan. She worked with the various members of the crew to ensure that each renovation was done to the standards of the era represented. She had a darling apartment on 85th Street and East End Avenue. It was on the first floor of a Victorian townhouse, of red brick. She walked down a wrought iron stairway to reach her doorway, which was a shiny black, with brass fittings. The flat was not large, but really quite perfect for one young lady. The woman who owned the entire building was a lovely person. Both Spence and I spent a week in New York while Isabella was getting settled there, and highly approved of her neighborhood and the landlady. Isabella said that she didn't intend to stay in the States forever, but that she wanted to gain experience there, and for the time being, was living a wonderful adventure. She had definitely fallen in love with New York City.

When spring came again to *Willow Grove Abbey,* Spence and I decided to take a picnic out to my favorite old knurled tree, in the burying ground. While this might sound a bit ghoulish to some, it had always been my very favorite place for a calm haven, and Spence had grown to see it through my eyes. Both of my parents were now buried there, laying next to one another, under a lovely copse of ash, willow and birch trees. Buried with them were the anger, pain and heartache I had gone through when they were alive. I had learned forgiveness, and it brought enormous peace to my world. I had planted masses of flowers around both of their graves, particularly yellow roses, which they both had adored. I still thrilled at the prospect of spending a golden afternoon with Spence. We spread a blanket under the ancient tree, and set about exploring what delights Nan had prepared for us. It wasn't quite as fancy as Fortnum and Mason, but still a delightful supper. Liver Pate, Blue Point Oysters, a freshly baked loaf of Nan's special bread, Cucumber and Chicken Sandwiches without the crusts, fresh fruit, lobster salad and Nan's homemade jam. And, of course, two marvelous bottles of white Chardonnay. It was a beautiful afternoon, and after all of the tasks we'd had to tend to of late, it was heavenly to just be able to relax and enjoy one another, as we did during that long ago summer when we met. It was hard to believe that it was now 1965. Thirty years had flown by. Spence was now 55 years of age, and I was 48. Neither of us felt that much older. Spence was the same gorgeous man I had met at my debutante Ball. He still had his full head of dark hair, mixed with a bit of grey, which only made him more attractive, and nothing could have taken away his lovely smile, and sapphire eyes. I'd purposely made him wear a white linen shirt, rolled at the elbows, and I had chosen to wear white, as well, in remembrance of our 1935 picnic. My dress had a

Victorian look. It was white voile trimmed with fine lace, and had a high collar, with long sleeves trimmed in lace again at the cuffs. Spence had given me a pair of lovely, old cameo earrings for our anniversary the year before, so I wore them. Everyone told me that I didn't look anywhere near my near fifty years of age. My hair was still short and tousled, and it was true that I had very few wrinkles, which was undoubtedly due to my Mediterranean coloring. Since I'd not had multiple children, I'd kept my figure, so while, of course, I didn't look like the young girl Spence had fallen in love with in 1935, I was still an attractive lady. At first we talked about all of the incredible things that had taken place in the last two years; how much our lives had changed. Spence had always told me that if the day ever came that I lost both of my parents, he believed I would totally blossom. He seemed to have been amazingly on the mark, because I had left behind the insecure, lacking in confidence young girl I had been, and replaced her with a much more mature, still sweet, but more confident woman. Spence continued to tell me that my eyes were my soul, and it still thrilled me to hear him say it. It was so healthy to not have to listen to biting sarcasm and constant bickering. There wasn't the slightest doubt in my mind that Spence and I had truly been meant for one another. I thanked God every night that we had both been wise enough not to let life take us down different pathways.

Of course, the one major topic of conversation between us was Isabella, since we had been In New York not very long before. I hoped and prayed that someday our Isabella would find the same sort of happiness that we had discovered with each other. We had raised her to believe that there was one person in the world whom God meant just for her, and that she needed to take her time before rushing headlong into any sort of romance. We promised her that she would know when she'd met that perfect person. Naturally, she'd thought that her lovely Italian man was the one. Isabella was very, very levelheaded, and very intelligent. She was not in any hurry to settle down to a married way of life. She absolutely adored her work, and apparently, her employer adored her, since she immediately began to advance with promotions, responsibilities, and increases in her salary level. When she first settled in New York, of course Spence and I helped her financially, as we quickly learned that apartments in good areas were amazingly high-priced. Yet, we wanted her to be situated in a good neigh-borhood, and didn't mind in the least supplementing her income. She was nearing the point now, though, where she really didn't *need* our help, but we still kept sending a check every month. After all, she was our only child and we wanted a good life for her. Isabella had never lost that sweet, gentle nature that had been hers since she was born. But, because we had allowed her to travel more, and experience life in a manner which wid-ened her knowledge of the Arts and of other cultures, she was much more sophisticated than I'd been at her age. She was also extremely spiritual in nature. We never had to remind her to attend Mass, or Confession. That was something I had missed growing up. No one had ever explained spiri-tuality to me, but Isabella had enormously strong values. She had already told both Spence and me that she had no intention of giving herself to any man before she married. We were thrilled at her Christian moral values, and wholeheartedly believed that she would keep such a promise. Thus, we never worried too terribly much about her choices, since she had such a good head on her shoulders, and neither Spence nor I thought she would find herself enamored with anyone who didn't have like values. As every-thing turned out later, her strong morals had an enormous amount to do with so much that came later in her life.

When we finished eating our sumptuous picnic lunch, we sat there in that splendid setting, sipping our chilled wine, and listening to the leaves rustle in the trees. Spence leaned his back against the old, knurled tree. "Would you ever have dreamed, Sophia that our life would turn out so peaceful and fulfilling?" He asked me.

I picked a wild flower growing next to where I was sitting, and tucked it into my hair. "I think I always knew that if I could spend my life with you, we would have a delightful existence. Nothing else really was impor-tant to me, except having you there in my life. All though the uproar with Edwina, and Mummy, and Papa, it was *you* who kept me strong. We really were made for one another, Spence. You were so right."

"No, I wasn't right. God was right," he smiled. "While you may think that you couldn't have been as strong as you were, if I hadn't been there, I believe you would have been. You're the most resilient woman I've ever known. You have had so much hurt, and yet, you amaze me the way you refuse to let it stop you in your tracks. You always see 'hope' around the next corner."

"Spence. You completed me. I can't imagine where I might have ended up without you by my side. I thank God every night that he gave me you. Of course, according to you, back in 1935, we had already been together through several lifetimes." I laughed.

"I still believe that, Sophia. I don't think that such a belief goes against anything in Christianity. It's just a different way of looking at life."

"You know, the older I grow, the more I look about me, and realize that if God meant for the trees and the flowers and the crops in the fields to have more than one chance at life, why not also human beings? I find nothing contrary to such a belief in the Bible, I concurred."

"Yes, we still live and die. And Jesus is still our Savior, and the deity whom we try to model ourselves after. But, why should we not have more than one chance to get it right? I think I'm beginning to believe that the better person you become, the closer you will come to emulating Jesus. That, after all, is everyone's goal. But, what if a person mucks it up completely, due to a horrific childhood, or lack of exposure to the Scriptures? That seems eminently unfair, doesn't it? I'd like to think that we are given more than one opportunity to be the best we can be. The better life we live, the closer we come to being God-like. We keep coming back until we get it right. That could take many lifetimes. Am I making any sense, Sophia?"

"Yes. I feel that way too. I'm not certain our church would agree with us.. I'm not certain any Christian church would.

"Oh, I feel quite certain that there are many that would and do. There are people who strongly believe that Christianity, in its earliest form, once included the belief in reincarnation. Then, after centuries passed, those teachings were excluded, because of the belief that if everybody followed such a creed, a lot of people would not even make an attempt to live a Christ-like life. Sophia, have you ever read anything about Edgar Casey?" he asked me.

"Yes. Wasn't he a Christian school-teacher who was from Kentucky in the United States, and was able to diagnosis patients while in a trance? Didn't he believe in Reincarnation?"

"Yes, that's him. He was a very simple man in many ways. He had no education beyond grade school. He was extremely religious and led a fascinating life. There are many, many books written about him and his life. A great university in the States has an entire department devoted to the study of his works. It's called the Edgar Cayce School of Paranormal Psychology at Duke University in North Carolina. He found no incongruity between the marvelous powers he was given by God, and Christianity.

"I think it's an interesting concept. I don't totally rule it out. While Jesus was certainly the Son of God, perhaps in order for him to understand the compete make-up of the human soul, it was necessary for him to actually live each and every emotion that man is capable of experiencing. That would take several lifetimes," I continued. Anyway, I already know that we were lovers in a former life. You were undoubtedly a, dashing polo player, and I was a simple farm girl.

"Oh, Lord. Let's not get into that again," he laughed. We were both remembering Charlotte Ross's comments long ago about how she thought that Spence looked like a professional Polo player'.

"I wonder what ever became of Charlotte." I mused. "I'm sure she married. Perhaps she found another RAF pilot."

"No, I heard she went to New York, and became quite a big star on the Stage. I believe she married a fellow actor."

"Well, I'm happy for her. She certainly wanted your heart terribly."

"As I told you that night at the Thames Room, there was only one heart I was interested in then, and there is still only one heart I'm interested in." Spence looked at me with a look I'd come to know as 'lustful'. He put his glass down, and reached for me. I found myself buried in his arms, feeling that I was right where I belonged. There were dappling's of sunlight visible through the leaves of the ancient tree, the sound of a brook in the grass, and the ripple of tree shadows on the old tombstones. Each time Spence and I made love, it was like the first time. I never tired of his warmth and his ability to make me feel like the most desired woman on Earth. He always treated me solicitously, and took his time, making certain that we were both ready for one another. There, in that old, burying ground, we rededicated our love to one another, and it seemed highly appropriate that we brought new life to a place where people we once loved lay peacefully at rest.

Chapter Eighteen

When we returned to *Willow Grove Abbey* we had a letter waiting for us. It was from Isabella, and was filled with all of the latest happenings in her life. The biggest news was that she had met someone she was very interested in. It was the first time Isabella had ever told us anything like that, since having met Lucca so long ago. She was twenty-eight, and had been in the states seven years, with four of those years in New York City. The man of interest had an MBA from Cornell University's School of Hotel Management, and had a very good position with Kaplan Hotels International, a well-known and prestigious firm. She had met him at a business dinner. We looked forward with eagerness to meeting the young man as we suspected he just might become our son-in-law. She didn't tell us a lot about him; just his career, and schooling. Our daughter was planning on bringing Chris to meet us for a two-week summer vacation. In all of that kerfuffle, I'd never had time to make an appointment with a physician to find out about the lump that I'd discovered clear back on our cruise. It still had not grown significantly larger, and it just seemed that something always took precedence. I knew that I needed to have it looked at, especially with my mother having had cancer, and I finally did ring for an appointment to go in and see about it.

I was dumbfounded when the doctor told me that he felt I needed to have the lump biopsied, which would mean a short stay in hospital. He did not seem overly concerned about it, so I didn't worry terribly much. I believe Spence was more concerned than I was, but then he was a doctor, and knew more about such things. I was told that they would do what is called a 'frozen section' while I was still under the anesthetic, and if the lump proved to be negative, they would do nothing, except remove it, but if it was positive for cancer, my breast would be removed! My self-esteem had never been centered on my body image, so I wasn't sent into a tailspin about the possibility of a mastectomy, but I *was* terribly concerned that if I had waited too long to see a physician, and it was indeed cancer, it could well have spread.

Spence was with me when I went into the hospital the morning of the procedure. Because he was a physician himself, he was allowed to scrub, and stay with me throughout the operation. He held my hand as I went under the anesthetic. When I awakened in the recovery room, he was seated by my side, still holding my hand. I had significant pain in my chest area, and cried out for something to relieve it. The nurse told me that I could have something as soon as all of the effects of the anesthetic had worn off. Spence had a terribly worried look on his face, and I already knew, before he spoke the words, what the outcome had been. Yes, it was cancer, and yes, the breast had been removed. The good part was that it did not seem to have metastasized to any other organs, including nearby lymph glands. Tears trickled down my face, and Spence leaned over and kissed them away.

"Darling, the important thing is that you are going to be all right. They are going to follow up with some radiation treatment, just to be sure, but they believe they got it all, and you will be as good as new."

"I'll never be as good as new again, Spence. You know that," I wept. "The thought of your having to see such a disgusting sight sickens me. It will look hideous."

"Sophia, don't you know by now that you mean more to me than a simple body part? You could lose an arm, a leg, anything. I'd love you as much as ever."

"I know that, Spence. But, I still hate it. Do they feel that the prognosis is good? Is there a chance that this could reoccur?"

"There's always a chance of that, Sophia, but your odds are significantly better than if it had spread. They really cannot give you a clean bill of health until you've been five years cancer-free, but we shall keep a very close eye on you. No more putting off examinations."

"How long will it take for me to recover from this?"

"Not terribly. You'll be given pain medication for a bit, and then you will start rehabilitation immediately. You'll need to build your muscles up. I'll do anything I can to help."

"Shall I tell Isabella of this? Here she is about to bring this young man, who may or to see us. I don't want her to be upset about my health."

"We still have several months before their planned visit, so don't make that a concern. If you want her to know, of course, tell her. But, I think that is entirely up to you."

"I think I'll wait until after the impending visit.

"Are you hurting like the devil, Sophia?"

"Yes, and I'm dry as the desert. May I have some water?"

"Not water, but let me see about ice chips." He located the nurse, who brought over a cup of ice chips, and also a hypodermic needle, which she injected into my bum. It was but a few minutes before the pain magically disappeared. However, it made me sleepier, and my words were not as clear. Spence kissed me again, and told me to rest, and I went back to sleep, until I awoke in my own hospital room. As I lay there, with my eyes still closed, I thought about the twists and turns my life had taken. Every life has a story. Mine wasn't so different than millions of others. Very painful in some ways, but filled with intense joy, as well. This was just the latest of the ups and downs which had brought us to the present time. I felt blessed to have Spence there by my side, loving me as he always had, and still looking forward to happier times.

My recuperation was not one of the more pleasant times in my life. I tried to keep reminding myself that I was so lucky that it hadn't been worse. I did not hear from either of my brothers, which did not terribly surprise me. Nothing did, anymore, when it came to my family. The one person I had reestablished contact with was Pippin, who was now grown and married. She was still the spectacularly beautiful girl she had been. She had married a handsome, successful man, with Polish ancestry, who had come to England after Dunkirk. His father had been a pilot during the war, and he had grown up in Cornwall. Pippin's brother, Blake Jr., had moved to Liverpool, and no one saw a lot of him, but he and Pippin were very close. Recuperating from something like what I had endured is something one cannot do communally. I mean by this that there are moments and happenings in life that only you yourself can dig down inside and find the courage to experience, alone. Of course having a husband who was there for me every moment meant the world to me, and certainly made the shock of what had taken place easier to bear. But, just like I could not re-live his experiences in the war for him, nor grieve the losses he had suffered, nor he could grieve my loss. For indeed, suffering the loss of a body part, especially a body part that society puts so much emphasis upon, in terms of femininity, could only be done alone. And the process *was* one of grief, just as real as if there had been a death. For in essence, there had been. Whether I should have or not, I viewed my illness and the surgery as the death of a way of life, the death of my youth, the death of a part of me. I carried on, not showing my feelings, and made slight alterations in my routine, such as always changing into my day or night clothing in the bath, and always bathing when I knew Spence would be occupied elsewhere. I knew that I was being avoidant toward him, and used the excuse of my surgery for much longer than necessary to avoid lovemaking. One night, after the lights had been turned out, and Spence and I were in bed, Spence reached for me in the darkness. I turned to him, and let him hold me, and then found myself engulfed in his arms and lost in a lovely, deep kiss, filled with longing. But, I then tensed up, as his hand began to caress my remaining breast, and I knew where our lovemaking was heading.

"No Spence. I'm not ready for that yet," I murmured, as I drew away from him.

"I'm not trying to rush you, Sophia. But, it *has* been three months. You've completely healed for some time. Tell me what you think you aren't ready for."

"I don't think I'll ever be ready for you to touch me there, or to look at me unclothed."

"Are you saying that you feel that our days of making love have ended?"

"Perhaps not ended, but changed. I no longer feel aroused when you come near that part of my body. I want to shrink from you. I know you say it makes no difference to you, but Spence I have looked at myself in the mirror, and there is no way that you could possibly not be affected by the change in my appearance. It is truly gruesome. Shocking. Repugnant."

"Darling, if I had surgery, and it left a scar, if when I returned from Germany I had been disfigured, would you have felt that way about me?" he asked, pulling me closer, but not straying toward my chest.

"Of course not, Spence, but, that's different. The world puts such emphasis upon breasts. From the time a girl is really quite young, that is one of the first body areas that boys make comments about. We grow up with a vision of ourselves as unfeminine without breasts, even the *right size* breasts. You have always made me feel so womanly, Spence. You were my first love. You made me celebrate being a female. Now, I don't feel so womanly anymore. I didn't even feel so unattractive when I had my hysterectomy. That was different. It affected me greatly. But only internally. I am so glad I'd had Isabella, or I would have felt like a failure. Oh, that horrid word 'barren'. I still dream sometimes that I'm miraculously pregnant, so obviously it affected me. But this is visible and that makes all of the difference. Feeling feminine is important to any woman and I'm no exception. No, I haven't ever wrapped myself up in my appearance, but then again, I've always known, deep down, that I was attractive. How can a woman feel attractive when she is some sort of freak? "

"Sophia, you are not one iota different than you were before. Your femininity wasn't wrapped up in your breasts. It is who you are. It is in the ladylike way you pick up a glass, and the girlish way you smile when you're very happy. It's in your kindness, and your wit; your empathy and warmth; it's in your forgiveness, and the beauty you carry inside of your heart."

Tears began to fall, even though I wanted terribly for them to stop. He held me close, and let me weep. Then, suddenly, he reached up and turned the bedside lamp on low. I tried to wrestle my way away from him, and to bring the sheet up to cover myself, but he wouldn't allow it. We each pulled on an end of the fabric, as I cried "no, no."

"Yes, Sophia. It's time," he murmured. We have to get by this, darling." Spence pulled the sheet down gently, leaned over, and kissed the area where now there was nothing but scar tissue. There was no sensation there. It felt numb. I felt numb. He raised his head up and looked straight at that ugly wounded area. He did not look shocked, nor did he appear to be repulsed. Then, he ran his hand across the same area. I kept my eyes tightly closed. "Open your eyes, Sophia. I love you dearest. As much as I ever have. You are beautiful. As beautiful as you've ever been. Perhaps more so, because now you are even more unique. This does not detract from your beauty, sweetheart. Just as each line on your face, every hair that turns grey, every imperfection that comes as we both age, this is just one more thing that shows you have the legacies that come from living. It is nothing to be ashamed of. It is another battle scar of your victory over life's blows."

"Oh Spence, how dearly I love you, I cried. "You always seem to know just when to say the proper thing."

"It's simply the truth, Sophia. It's the way I honestly feel. You cannot truly believe that this small imperfection could ever undo the overwhelming amount of love I have for you."

I knew it was true. Spence saw things so differently than so many others might have. I reached down and took his hand, and placed it where my breast had once been. Then I put my hand upon his. "Without your hand there, I feel numb…but with it there, I feel warm, and the numbness dissipates.'

He clasped me to him, and we made love just as we always had. I did not try to stop him when he wished to touch that raw reminder of my loss, and I was able to put it completely out of my mind, as we both reached a shattering climax, which spoke of the love we felt but could never fully articulate.

After that I began to move ahead with my life at a much faster pace, and in a much more positive frame of mind. I began to look ahead to Isabella's visit, and if I had any worries during that time, they were not for me, but for my lovely daughter. There was no reason for me to be concerned. He sounded like a splendid chap, and we had never expected Isabella to marry into the aristocracy. I suppose if I worried, it was because any mother is concerned when their daughter brings someone home for the first time. You pray and pray that the young man cares as deeply for her as she does for him. In our case, there was the added concern of wealth and prestige.

Not his wealth or prestige, but ours. Certainly, we were aware enough to know that certain people became enamored of others because of their family name. I didn't like to think such things, because it reminded me too much of my parents and their refusal to consider Spence as a spouse for me. Of course we wanted Isabella to marry a decent man with good future prospects, but wealth was not a consideration for us. I had a tendency to worry, as Spence had often told me, but I wished I could do away with a nagging feeling I carried around, waiting for my daughter's arrival.

But, I managed to maintain my usual optimism, and scurried about making certain everything was ready when they arrived. I didn't want to make a terrible fuss, but there was that natural desire to put our best foot forward. Before I blinked twice, the day of their arrival was upon us. Isabella rang us, and told us that she and Chris were at Kennedy Airport, and would be leaving shortly on a plane bound for Heathrow. As we were chatting, she dropped a bombshell on us.

"You aren't going to believe this, Mummy, but Chris and I have discovered that we are sort of related. You have actually met him before! His mother was Edwina Phillips, who married Grandpapa. Isn't that astounding? I won't go into all of the details now, about how we discovered all of this, but it's true. We think we probably played together as children. Papa will be so certain this is another one of his 'serendipitous' moments. I think he could be right."

I scarcely knew what to say. Was she telling me that she was bringing Kippy home? Kippy? They could be uncle and niece. I stammered about, and said that we would be anxious to hear everything when they arrived. Isabella ended the call, saying the plane was boarding. I turned to Spence, and put my head in my hands.

"Oh God, Spence, what next?"

Other Books by Mary Christian Payne

The Somerville Trilogy

Willow Grove Abbey: Book 1 of the Somerville Trilogy

St. James Road: Book 2 of the Somerville Trilogy

Serendipity: Book 3 of the Somerville Trilogy

The Claybourne Trilogy

The White Feather: Book 1 of the Claybourne Trilogy

The White Butterfly: Book 2 of the Claybourne Trilogy

White Cliffs of Dover: Book 3 of the Claybourne Trilogy

The Thornton Trilogy

No Regrets: Book 1 of The Thornton Trilogy

No Gentleman: Book 2 of the Thornton Trilogy

No Secrets: Book 3 of the Thornton Trilogy

About The Author

Mary Christian Payne was highly successful in several management positions in Fortune 500 Companies, in New York City, St. Louis, Missouri, Orlando Florida, and Tulsa, Oklahoma. Her work included Grant writing, and designing and writing Training Manuals for Executive Training Programs.

She left the corporate world, and became Director of Career Development at the Women' Resource Center at the University of Tulsa, where she designed a program that enabled hundreds of adult women to return to college and better their lives. She received the Mayor's Pinnacle Award in 1993 for this achievement. Mary left that position when the Center closed, and then opened her own Career Counseling Center. She retired in 2008.

Mary Christian Payne became a successful, best-selling author at the age of 71, with the help of her publisher, Tom Corson-Knowles. All of her life, she had wanted to write, and had received accolades for her unpublished work. She was encouraged in college, and writing was a significant part of the various jobs she held.

In 2013, she read Tom Corson-Knowles' book about publishing on Kindle. She wrote to him and he telephoned her. The rest is history. Since that time, she has published nine books, with more on the way.

Mary lost her husband in June, 2015, after 33 years of marriage. The grief process brought a lull to her writing, but she found that putting words on paper helped immensely. She is now in the process of writing her second novel since his death. She lives in Tulsa, Oklahoma, with her two beloved Maltese dogs.

One Last Thing...

If you enjoyed this book, I'd be very grateful if you'd post a short review. Your support really does make a difference and I read all the reviews personally.

Thanks again for your support!

Sign up for the newsletter to get news, updates and new release info from Mary Christian Payne: http://bit.ly/MaryChristianPayne